RAVES FOR GEORGE V. HIGGINS'
BRILLIANT NEW NOVEL
TRUST

"I didn't get around to reading [George V. Higgins], somehow, until now. After finishing *TRUST*—with its tight little plot that unfurls like a ball of satin and its tone-perfect dialogue—I became an instant fan. The general effect of Mr. Higgins writing is dazzling."—Hilma Wolitzer, *The New York Times Book Review*

"*TRUST* is a rich read—the kind of book best savored slowly, like good brandy."—*Seattle Times*

"Critics have compared George V. Higgins to the 19th-century Honoré de Balzac for creating a Boston as hungry, raucus, lusty and shady as Balzac's Paris. *TRUST* is a brilliantly elevated piece of sociology. One never doubts Higgins' authority is presenting this narrow, unctious world."—*Richmond Times-Dispatch*

"This year, I am happy to say, is a vintage year for Higgins fans. *TRUST* is full of hard-edged gab and it's also a hilarious comedy of errors set in the New England demi-monde."—*Wall Street Journal*

"Must reading."—*Wilmington News Journal*

"It was during the recent Oilers/Bengals game when I started *TRUST*. The next day I called in sick to finish it. Higgins has the ticket to the most amusing and hard-boiled dialogue being done today. It reads the way alcohol goes down."—*Houston Chronicle*

TRUST

GEORGE V. HIGGINS

ZEBRA BOOKS
KENSINGTON PUBLISHING CORP.

ZEBRA BOOKS

are published by

Kensington Publishing Corp.
475 Park Avenue South
New York, NY 10016

First Zebra Books printing: November, 1990

Printed in the United States of America

1

The third Saturday in July was the fourth day of a heat spell caused by a low-pressure warm front stalled over southern New England by a ridge of high pressure near the Canadian border. The temperature recorded at 3:00 P.M. at Theodore Francis Green Airport in Warwick, Rhode Island, was a record of 96 degrees.

Earl Beale had left Boston at 1:30 P.M. He had taken the afternoon off. His boss, Roy Fritchie, had not been pleased. "This," he had said, "this is not gonna make Waldo happy. When I tell him."

"So don't tell him," Earl had said. "Then he'll never know. He's out on his goddamned destroyer there, whatever he calls the damned thing. You ever know Waldo, stay away from the place, there was a snowball's chance in hell some dumb asshole'd come in and buy a car? No, you never did. Because if Waldo thought there was, he'd be in here himself, and he'd scoop the sale right out from under you, save himself commission. If Waldo ain't here, it's because Waldo knows nobody in his right mind'll come in."

"You should've told him yourself," Fritchie had

said. "You should've gone in and told him yourself, before he left last night."

"Well," Earl had said, "I didn't *know* about it last night. That I hadda. When I left here. The call, I didn't get the call until I got back the apartment. It was almost eleven, for Christ sake, time I had something to eat and got home. The hell could I tell him, then? Call him at home? You know how Waldo is. Bastard's in bed by nine. I'd've gotten him outta bed, he'd've come up my place, beaten the shit out of me."

"Yeah," Fritchie had said. "Well, I just wish to God I knew what the guy called you's got on you, make you jump like this. What's *he* paying you? More'n Waldo is?"

"*Every*body pays me more'n Waldo does," Earl had said. "Now just stop giving me a lotta crap, all right? I got, it's some personal business, I got to take care of. Just personal business, is all."

"Yeah," Fritchie had said. "I just didn't realize, is all, Broons're still playing hockey. Seems kind of warm for that now."

"The Bruins," Earl had said.

"Yeah, the Broons," Fritchie had said. "I assume they got to be, either Islanders or Rangers, and Penny's down New York again. And that's what your business is. Picking Penny up."

"Go fuck yourself," Earl had said. "I'll see you on Monday."

The air conditioner in Penny's black Dodge convertible needed a Freon recharge. He put the top down before he left her apartment in Somerville. He was late getting into Lafayette, Rhode Island, just after four o'clock, because he had been delayed. He had made

2

good time on Interstate 95 south, but he had begun to feel light-headed in the heat. Just south of the Providence-Cranston line he finally had to pull over onto the shoulder and put up the top. He had trouble with it.

There was a long plateau to the west, cut by a deep, grassy trench ditched down twenty feet about fifty yards west of the shoulder, the steep inclines mowed very short. On the other side there was a chain-link fence topped with three strands of barbed wire that extended as far as he could see down the road behind him, and as far as he could see along the road ahead. Off to the west, a quarter of a mile or more on the other side of the fence, several large buildings surrounded a tall smokestack. Semitrailers rolled by at illegal speeds on the interstate, their roaring close to his ears; their slipstreams raised strong eddies of sand and small, sharp stones around his shins.

Earl hated stopping for reasons of his own comfort when he had some distance to cover and a scheduled arrival time. He also disliked the particular reason that interrupted him this time. It was not just that he resented feeling dizzy. "I like the heat myself," he would say, when a brief late-January afternoon brought some sun and a southwesterly breeze, and in a linen sport coat he escorted an overcoated customer through the lot. "It's the winter, bothers me." It seemed to him that when you stopped and put up the top in the middle of a sunny summer weekend afternoon, you were just asking for it—more snow, more grief, no car sales, and heating bills.

"Also," Earl explained to the young state cop with the bodybuilder's muscles testing the strength of the buttons of his gray uniform shirt, "sooner or later, and I don't care who makes it, every single one of these things gets just a little bit out of line. It goes down all right, goes down like a charm. But when you go to put it up again," he said, hitting the front rail of the top with the heel of his right hand to align the locking pins with the holes on the top of the windshield frame, "you got to jigger it around and, *uh*, almost force it, you know?" The pins rested on the left edges of the chromium receivers, and he shoved at the side rail with his left hand until they skidded slightly to the right and dropped in. He braced his left arm on the top, holding it in place, and reached with his right hand inside the car, groping above the steering wheel until he located the locking lever and clamped it closed. "Ahh," he said. He stepped away from the car.

The cop cleared his throat. He was about six two, an inch or so shorter than Earl, and the set of the expression of his mouth showed he did not like that. His eyes were invisible behind his aviator Ray Bans; Earl imagined them blue, and cold and mean. The cop's head was covered by his charcoal gray, nylon-mesh cavalry hat, but his brown hair was cut short around his ears and temples, and Earl knew it was military short under the hat. "I'm still going to have to see your license and registration, sir," he said, at parade rest.

Earl nodded, as though the request had been made a long time ago, and he had meant to comply with it but had been distracted by some other, inconvenient chore. He reached into the back pocket of his gray chino pants, took out his wallet, and without taking his attention from the car, handed the wallet still folded to the cop.

4

The cop shook his head. "Not the whole wallet, sir," he said. "Just the license and registration."

Earl shifted his gaze to the cop. "Oh," he said, "yeah. I forgot." He opened the wallet and extracted the plasticized card with his mug shot and the tiny print wrapping up his whole life in a small, unalterable package. He handed the license to the cop.

"And the registration, too, please," the cop said.

"Yeah," Earl said. "Well, I got to get that from the glove compartment, okay? See, this's Penny's car. My girlfriend's car. And that's where she keeps it, I think. I just borrowed it for the day. I *hope* that's where she keeps it, at least. That okay, I do that?"

"Do what?" the cop said.

"Go around the other side there, and get it from the glove box," Earl said.

"Fine," the cop said. Earl stepped away from the car and walked around the rear. He heard the cop unsnap the safety strap on his holster, and the sound of his booted feet as he shifted position on the gravel of the shoulder. Earl opened the passenger door and leaned into the car. He could see the cop's torso from the third shirt button down, the Sam Browne belt linked to the black holster belt, the cop's right thumb casually resting on the top of the belt, the fingertips just brushing the checkered walnut grip of the stainless steel Magnum. Earl unlatched the glove box and reached into it, rummaging blindly among a small box of Tampax tampons, a small cellophane package of Kleenex, two partial, crushed packages of Newport hundred-millimeter cigarettes, and a dog-eared Mobil map of New England. "There should be a flashlight in here someplace," he said apologetically. "She's supposed to keep a flashlight in here. I dunno how many times I told her that. 'S'pose you're out onna road at night. Something goes wrong. Whaddaya do, you don't have a light? The hell're you gonna do?' " The cop did not say anything. Earl found the chrome flashlight. "Ah, here it is," he said. He worked the switch. The bulb did not light. *"Shit,"* he said. "Battery's dead. The hell good is that, when you need a light, the goddamned battery's dead?"

He put the flashlight on the seat and used both hands to take everything else from the box. He piled it on the seat. He sorted through it until he found first the owner's manual and then a small manila envelope addressed to Mary P. Slate, Apt. 4E, 117 Maynard St., Brighton, MA 02135. He put the manual down and backed out of the car. He opened the envelope and removed a thick insurance policy and the small, pale blue stub of a punch card describing the car and stating its plate number. "Ah," Earl said, "here it is." He walked around the car again, watching the cop relax slightly, and diffidently handed the card to him.

The cop studied the registration. "Mary P. Slate," he said. "This is your girlfriend's car?"

"Well, yeah," Earl said.

"I thought you called her 'Penny,' " the cop said.

"Well," Earl said. "I did. Penny's what she goes by. Her middle name's Pauline, and I dunno, I guess her brothers or somebody got 'Penny' out of that. It was when she was a kid."

The cop nodded. "And this is the right address," he said. "The current one, I mean. She lives in Brighton, does she?"

"Ah, no," Earl said. "That one's her old one. She,

ah, moved a while ago. Moved to Somerville. But the registration's still good. Way I understand it. Isn't it, I mean?"

The cop frowned. "It's supposed to have the new one written on the back," he said. "She inform the registry? The registry up there?"

"Jeez," Earl said, "I really don't know. She just moved a while ago."

"I see," the cop said. "Well, this'll just take a minute." He started back to his cruiser, pausing to compare the 195–861 on the plate above the rear bumper with the 195–861 on the card. He got into the cruiser and made various movements partly obscured from Earl by the reflected glare on the windshield. Earl sighed. He stooped over again and picked up the stuff on the seat and shoved it back into the compartment. Then he took the two packs of Newports out again, pressed one of them between his fingers, felt the dry tobacco crumble, and dropped both of them on the floor mat. He slid into the passenger seat and forced the right locking lever closed on the top.

The cop came up behind the car and stood next to the door. He had the license and registration in his left hand. "Everything's in order, sir," he said, offering the documents to Earl.

Earl got out of the car. He took his wallet out again and put the license in it, holding the registration in his teeth. He started to put the registration in the glove box, then hesitated. "You know," he said to the cop, "I don't think I'm gonna put this back in that mess of shit right now. I might need it again, 'fore I'm through, and I doubt I can find the thing twice." He put it in his wallet and shut the passenger door. He

7

grinned uncertainly at the cop. "Okay if I leave now?" he said. "I'm running a little bit late."

The cop put his hand on the top of the door and peered down into the foot well. "That stuff on the floor—cigarettes?" he said.

"Yeah, *old* cigarettes," Earl said. "She always does that. Leaves them around the house alla time, too. Lets 'em get real good and stale, 'fore she thinks about throwing them out. You light one of them bastards, boy, it's been in that hot box all summer? Man, I wanna tell you, you're gonna think you had a railroad flare in your mouth. I was gonna throw them out. But then I figure: 'Hey. You found the registration here, and everything. You don't want a ticket for littering.' "

The cop did not smile. "I'm sorry for the inconvenience, sir," he said. "Just routine, I assure you. Any time we see someone pulled over, this stretch, well, we automatically check everything out. You mind if I look at those cigarettes, now? Now that I've seen them, I mean."

Earl stared at him. "Mind?" he said. "No, I don't mind. Don't mind a damned bit. Not at all." He opened the passenger door, picked up the Newports, and handed them to the cop. "You can have them, you want," he said. "I wish you'd take them. 'Long with all of that other crap, too."

The cop removed two bent cigarettes from one pack and held them under his nose. He put them back. He worked his forefinger deep into the second pack and selected a third cigarette. He smelled it. He put it back in the pack and handed the packs back to Earl. Earl tossed them back into the foot well. "That it?" he said.

The cop studied him. "For now, it is," he said.

"Miss Slate shows up, her arraignment on that marijuana charge, she won't have any trouble either."

"She'll show up," Earl said. "You don't have to worry, 'bout her. She was set up on that thing. Penny don't smoke. Not the funny stuff, at least. No worries at all, about her."

"I'm not," the cop said. "I'm worried about you." He nodded toward the cruiser. "The guy with the Teletype up at headquarters tells me that if you weren't born this morning, you've led one charmed life. Because I keep looking at you, and I know I've seen you before. Know who you are, at least. And there's nothing in the box." Earl said nothing. "I don't know all that many people," the cop said. "There's very few people around that I met, or I didn't meet but I know, that I couldn't place in my mind. Even without the damned box. And I know I know you, and that damned box doesn't, and somehow, that bothers me."

Earl remained silent. The cop shrugged. "You picked a bad place to stop," he said. He gestured over his right shoulder toward the west with his thumb. "You know what that is over there?"

"I can guess," Earl said. "I don't know, but I can guess."

"Yeah," the cop said. "ACI Cranston. So you can understand, I'm sure, anybody stops along here, they're almost always going to meet up with us. Identify themselves and state their business. I'm sure you understand why."

"Not really," Earl said. "All I was tryin', do, was put the goddamned top up."

"Yeah," the cop said. His face below the glasses

9

creased into a small smile. "You played *basket*ball," he said. "You played basketball."

Earl shrugged. "Didn't everybody?" he said. "I thought everybody did."

2

The center of Lafayette is eight miles east of the Connecticut border, six miles east of 95 on R.I. 189. On the eastern side of the road, the water of Rhode Island Sound shines blue and choppy white on sunny days; sailboats shimmer in the wind, and the waves roll in on small patches of tawny sand between big, black rocks. The westerly side of the road, bulldozed during the late fifties into a flat about two hundred yards deep and three-quarters of a mile long, is crowded by small shopping plazas and a small supermarket, all surrounded by asphalt parking lots and made of cinder block with brick fronts and flat, tarred roofs decorated with ventilator shafts and massive, faded green air-conditioning condensers.

Earl turned in at the third parking entrance and parked very close to a pair of white posts supporting a white sign made of hollow glass, very far from the yellow line marking the limit of his space and the vacant one next to it. The sign had been damaged by a thrown rock that had broken a jagged hole in the glass, exposing three fluorescent tubes inside and breaking a fourth in its trajectory. The remaining glass was block-lettered in red paint: "CHUCKIE'S DIS NT LIQUORS." Earl put up the windows of the Dodge, got out of the car, and locked it. He surveyed it from the rear and satisfied himself that he had left as much space as possible on the right side. He made his way through three double rows of angle-parked cars to the liquor store, its windows plastered with posters—red paint on white butcher paper—advertising "UNBELIEVABLE" savings on wines, "PRICEBUSTER SPECIALS ON BEERS FOR YOUR BUSTS," and "EVERYDAY PRICE-SLASHING BONANZAS."

There were three aisles of shelved stock inside and a wall-to-wall glass-doored refrigerator across the back. Three middle-aged men in faded plaid shirts peered myopically at the labels of imported wines and stocked their shopping carriages with half-gallons of Ballantine's scotch, Gilbey's gin, Jim Beam bourbon, and cases of Löwenbräu. An elderly woman with flying white hair and puffiness around the eyes made quick movements, selecting openly a bottle of domestic sherry, using it and a bag of unsalted potato chips to conceal partially the bottle of blackberry brandy she had furtively picked up first and placed at the bottom of her plastic basket. Her lips moved rapidly in silent speech as she went to the registers at the front.

Three large young men—gray sweatshirts, the sleeves ripped off at the armholes, Hawaiian-print surfing jams, and sneakers with no socks—carried three cases of Budweiser each from the cold room behind the refrigerator. The one in the lead stopped next to the gin. "I'm telling you, shithead, it's true," the first said over his shoulder to the one last in line. "You can

12

ask Joanie, don't believe me, that's exactly what Patti did. Right after you left, we went down to the cove, and Patti is so fuckin' drunk she's got no *idea* where she is. And Tony says: 'It's too cold to go swimming. Too cold for that. Patti, show us your tits.' And she says: 'All right then, I will.' And she did. Took off her sweater and did it. And then Philip says: 'I don't believe it. Too dark to see if they're real.' And she says: 'Oh yeah?' and goes over to him, and says: 'Give 'em a squeeze, and you'll see.' So he does, and says: 'Fuck, what do I know? They sure feel like real tits to me.' And she says: 'For punishment, suck 'em,' and sticks them way out. And, he's lying down. He says: 'How?' And she kneels down, you know, and then sits on his crotch, and sticks them right in his face, and he's sucking away, and she's grinding, and then she stands up, rips down his pants there, and of course he's as hard as a rock. And she jerked him off. He's lying there, moaning, 'Blow me, blow me,' and she's pulling away at his dick, and then he comes, all over his stomach, and she puts her hand in it and rubs it into his mouth."

"What'd he do?" the second one said.

"Tried to spit it out," the first one said. "Making all of these kinds of faces, and Patti puts her top back on and says: 'Well, I don't like sluck either. Not in my mouth, at least.' And she went home." He shifted the cargo of beer in his hands and resumed the march toward the front. The last one in line said, "Shee-it, those Texans're tough. She prolly blows horses at home. Should send *her* to Vietnam. Few broads like her got over there, war'd end tomorrow. Chinks'd drop their guns."

Earl went up the aisle between the second and third

13

rows of shelves and found a quart bottle of Cossack vodka on sale for $4.99. He retraced his steps toward the back and went up the last aisle between the fourth row of shelving and the cases of beer and soft drinks stacked high against the wall. He took two six-packs of canned Coca-Cola and headed toward the registers at the front. A tall woman—five nine or so, around thirty-five—in a dark leopard-pattern leotard top, very tight faded jeans, and camel-colored shoes with stubby high heels was in the act of bending over the lower basket of a two-tiered display of liqueurs. She had platinum hair, and she was deeply tanned. The neckline of the leotard plunged to the middle of her cleavage; she had a large costume jewelry brooch of fake diamonds pinned to it there. She had very long legs. Earl stopped and pretended to be interested in various brands of rum. She straightened up without taking anything from the basket when a blocky man in a blue windbreaker, sleeves pushed up, yellowed white polo shirt, and shorts came up behind her with two cases of Miller beer. He was running to paunch, and losing his blondish hair. "You want any, that shit for diabetics?" he said. She shook her head, and preceded him into the checkout lane. Earl followed them toward the register. When he reached the place where she had stood, he could smell a lingering aroma of perfume. It grew stronger as he came up behind the man, who was presenting a twenty-dollar bill. "Don't worry," the man said. "It's not one of those."

The cashier was a woman just shy of forty. She wore a short black wig with ringlets that framed her face, and a pink smock with "Chuckie's Discount" embroidered in red over her left breast. She accepted the money and snorted, ringing up the sale. "It's fifties now," she said, tapping a notice taped to the glass partition on the other side of the register. "I guess they're movin' up inna world." She glanced sidelong at the woman in the leotard. "Like lots of us'd like, and some already did." The woman did not say anything. She stared into the middle distance, and licked her bottom lip once.

The man chuckled and accepted his change. "Good thing for you, I guess," he said, "they didn't start two months ago." He picked up his beer, and the woman went ahead of him toward the exit, her buttocks swaying smoothly under the denim. She used her right hand to brush the hair from her right temple, tossing her head back as she did so. She gave the blocky man half a smile, her eyelids lowered, as he followed her out through the door.

"You, ah," the cashier said to Earl, "you want me to ring that stuff up, sir?"

Earl took a deep breath and put the bottle and the two six-packs on the counter. He shook his head as he pulled out his wallet. "Fine lookin' woman," he said.

"Best advertisement Revlon ever had," the cashier said, running her forefinger down a flip-card list of prices. She rang up the price of the vodka, and added $3.29 for the Coke. "Eight twenny-eight," she said.

"Revlon?" he said.

She nodded. "The perfume," she said. "She douses herself. Must pour it on over her head."

"I kind of liked it," he said. "I thought it smelled nice. Sort of spicy." He separated one bill from a respectable wad in his wallet and handed it to the cashier.

15

"Hell," she said, "I used to like it myself. Wore the stuff all of the time. But that was before she started coming in here every week, absolutely reeking of it. Now I wouldn't wear the damned poison. I dumped all of mine down the toilet. Right after the rest of my life." She rested the bill on edge on the buttons of the top row of the register. "Course the fact that the guy she comes *in* here with now, happens to be my ex-husband—well, that might have something to do with it." She peered at the bill. "Hey," she said.

"Your ex-husband?" he said.

"You deaf or something, mister?" she said, offering the bill back to him. "I can't take this."

"You used to be married, that guy?"

She sighed. "I swear," she said, "you got wax in your ears. You oughta go to the doctor. Yeah, I used to be married, that guy. We got what they call 'divorce' in this state. 'Providence, and these Plantations.' You come from some other planet or something, you never heard of divorce? You should live in Italy. But what I'm talking about now, though, is this." She waved the fifty under his nose. "This's what I'm talking about, all right? I can't take this, for your stuff. You got something smaller, that's fine. Or something bigger, a hundred—also fine. But no fifties no way now, in Chuckie's—we eighty-sixed them 'fore Memorial Day. Hell, we didn't even take twennies, till almost the Fourth of July. Counterfeit, you know? Like 'No good'? Like 'Dunno where you got this, ma'am'—you take it to the bank—'but the Treasury didn't print it and we sure don't want it here.' And you say: 'Do I do?' And they look at you, and they just sort of shrug, and they tell

16

you that that's your decision. Paper your spare room, if you got enough, or use them for toilet paper."

"Well, now it's fifties they're passing," she said. "So it's fifties now, we're not taking. And bad's I got burned, the first part of May, at least I'm glad it was twennies. Cost me, I hadda give Chuckie a hundred and eighty, taken right out of my pay. And Al and Lucy, and Chuckie himself, they all got nailed pretty bad too. Those bastards got into us a good thousand bucks, before the bank tipped us off. So, you got something smaller, if you wanna buy this stuff?"

"Oh," he said, fumbling for his wallet again. "I didn't know. Lemme see here. My boss always pays me, he pays me in cash. He just paid me that one last night. But maybe I got here . . ." He pulled out a number of one-dollar bills that had been wadded up and then smoothed out. He began to count them out. "Nine," he finished. He pushed them toward her. "That oughta do it," he said.

She picked up the soiled bills and raised her eyebrows. "How long you had these items?" she said. "Your mother at your confirmation?"

He grinned and tried to look sheepish. "I'm not very good about money," he said. "I buy something, I always use the biggest bill I got, 'cause it's easier'n counting out singles. Then I get the change, and I stick it in my pocket till I get home and change my pants and I just put it in my wallet."

She rang the drawer open and gave him his change. "You, ah," he said. "I'm looking, the Beachmont Motel?"

"It's downah road," she said, jerking her head to indicate the direction. "You should've followed those

17

three lugs with the beer—that's where they were going. Goddamned kids. Hiding out in college so they maybe miss the draft. Which they seem to think gives them the right, just roll right over everybody. Call a cop on those kids, they start whining right away: 'I'm gonna be in 'Nam next year.' Bull*shit* is what I say. They'll figure out another wrinkle. Wish my kid was like that." She paused. "Or," she said, "four-five years ago, you could've followed your showgirl. She used to spend *lots* of time there. Most of it on her back. But now that she's married, the owner, lady of leisure and all, she never goes near the damned place."

"That guy with her, he's the owner?" Earl said.

"Yup," the cashier said, extending her left hand to receive the purchases of one of the middle-aged men who had finished his deliberations. "Good old Jimmy Battles. Looks as soft as a bowl fulla custard, but mean-er'n snakes when he's pissed. And the closest thing to a jackhammer I ever saw in bed." She glanced back at Earl. "You're thinking of staying, staying at Jimmy's, I'd change my mind, I was you. I know that joint on the inside and out. There's not a bed in it, 'll fit you." She snickered. "'Less he cuts you down to size, like he does everybody else. Or has his beefboys do it."

"I can take care of myself all right," Earl said, picking up his goods.

"*Oh,*" she said. "Well, that's too bad. Jimmy don't like guys like you. Takes care of them himself."

18

3

The Beachmont Motel was a two-story cinder-block building shaped like a splayed V and set on a narrow, paved lot carved out of a small hillside (it was destroyed by fire two weeks after Labor Day in 1986; the fire chief in Lafayette told reporters the fire was one of "suspicious origin," with "clear evidence of the use of accelerants," and the office of the attorney general conducted an investigation; no charges were brought). It was painted sea green. It had a flat roof that overhung the cement balcony walkway giving access to the rooms on the upper floor. The roof was supported by wrought-iron grillwork, and the walkway was enclosed by waist-high wrought-iron fencing. All of the ironwork was painted white. The doors of the rooms and the frames of the picture windows fronting on the parking lot were painted pale turquoise. At the northeasterly corner there was a dark blue Dempster Dumpster. There were two brown and chromium ice machines, one at the crook of the V on each floor. The sign at the edge of the road was mounted on an orange trailer and fringed with light bulbs; black movable letters advertised "34

AIR-COND RMS, SOME W/DINETTES. TV. FREE COFFEE. VACANCY. $10.00s. $14 DBL." Off to the southeast of the V was a square green cinder-block building with a sign on the door that said "OFFICE." It had a small porch under the roof overhand on the front. There were two green metal lawn chairs on the porch, and a spindly white metal table with a glass top between them. There was a can of Miller beer on the table next to the chair nearest the door.

Earl parked the Dodge alongside a charcoal gray Lincoln Continental in front of the office. There were six other vehicles in the lot: a carmine Firebird Trans Am, a black Camaro, a neon green Dodge Charger, a black Plymouth Road Runner with oversized tires, a GMC four-wheel-drive truck with oversized, off-the-road cleated tires that gave it two feet of ground clearance, and a silver Honda motorcycle. The door to the fourth room to his left on the first floor was open; a four-wheeled cart equipped with a brown laundry bag on the front, festooned with large plastic bottles of spray cleaners, stood beside it. He could hear a man and a woman arguing inside the room.

"Well," the man said, "it's very fuckin' simple. It's not hard to understand. It's almost five o'fuckin' clock, and you're not fuckin' done. You're supposed to get in here, and get the fuckin' work done by *three* o'fuckin' clock, and you didn't fuckin' do it. As fuckin' usual. Now I don't have to fuckin' tell you, why this's important. The best we got in this place is a short season, all right? And this is the fuckin' season, which so far sucks, and we got to have stuff ready. We got to scratch for bucks. And the way we fuckin' scratch for bucks is we do our fuckin' work. Now I look at it this way, and you don't? Well, fuck me, then—and you can fuckin' quit. I bet I can find someone that'll take your fuckin' job, and be fuckin' *grate*ful to get two-five-oh an hour, in this godforsaken hole."

The woman's voice was half plaintive and half angry. The volume increased and the pitch rose as she spoke. "Mister Battaglia," she said. "I don't *rent* these rooms, these goddamned . . . *animals*. I don't bring the beer in here, and throw empties all around. I don't throw up in the bathrooms, onna walls and onna floors. I don't shit in the bathtubs. I don't pull the curtains down and break the goddamned springs, so they won't go up again and you have to take them down and roll them up. Isn't me, that falls asleep, eating pizza, I'm in bed. And then rolls around in it and stains the goddamned sheets. You know why there's no chairs in Twelve? Because the bastards broke them. I guess they threw them out the windows—they're out the back, back parking lot. You know why there's no blankets, in the laundry room? Because last night they ruined four, least they looked like that to me. You wanna let these cannibals in? Fine. Go and take their money. But don't expect me, make it like, they never were in here. I can't do it. Nobody can. They tear the place apart."

The man in the white polo shirt and shorts emerged from the room. He paused at the door and pointed his right forefinger back into the room. "All *right,* "he said, "all right. You made your fuckin' point. Now I will make my point, again, and what you should do is listen. It's a short season here, and it isn't being that *good* a season, and when it's over, it's gonna be over. So, as a result of which, I'm gonna keep this place running, we all got to dig in, *and work*. You got me? Because

21

if we don't do that, you, or me, or anybody else, pretty soon I'm gonna have to *close* the fuckin' place, and you're gonna be up shit's creek without a paddle, down the McDonald's in Westerly, up to your hogans in grease. All right? And that means I oughta have most of these rooms, *all* these rooms, ready to rent by two. And the rest of them by three. Because that's when people come around and start renting the rooms. Okay? Early afternoon. They get where they're going, they wanna stop, rent a room, change their clothes and go the beach, bake their asses off. Not at four. Not at five. Two. Two in the afternoon. And I don't care, you think of their morals, or what they do makes you sick. They pay me the money, they get the damned room. Maybe looks like a pigpen when they get out, but when they go in, it is clean. Okay?"

Earl walked over to the office porch and sat down in the chair farthest from the can of beer. He clasped his hands over his belt buckle. The blocky man hit the cleaning cart with the heel of his right hand and stomped his way to the porch. He collapsed into the vacant chair and picked up the beer can in his left hand. He drank deeply and wiped his mouth with the back of his right hand. He put the beer can down. He clasped his hands at his waist. He stared at Earl. "Yeah," he said, "the Vermont guy."

Earl extended his hand. "Earl Beale," he said.

The blocky man ignored the hand. "Yeah," he said, "so you're finally here. I finally get to meet you. I thought it was you when I saw you. You put on some weight, right? Since you quit playing ball? Put on a few pounds, you got out of the can? And also: you're late."

"Saw me," Earl said.

22

"Saw you scoping Maria, the packie," the man said. "Thinking: 'Jeez, what a nice ass she's got.'"

"Oh," Earl said. He put his hands on the arms of the chair and crossed his legs at the knees. "Yeah, that was me. And she does."

"Better'n that," the man said with satisfaction. "That, my friend, is a *perfect* ass. When that broad come down the assembly line, God's going through the parts bin there, and He fishes into it and comes up with it, and says: 'Jeez, a perfect ass. Don't see many of these things, these days. Well, easy come.' And slapped it on her."

"Yeah," Earl said.

"So," the man said, "I'm Battles. You're Beale. And you're late. You gonna give me, the courtesy an explanation? Or're you like everybody else these days, I practically got to kiss their ass for them before they'll get to work."

"I got hassled by a cop, the way down," Earl said.

"Son of a bitch," Battles said. " 'Hassled by a cop.' What was he, a basketball fan? Hadda a yard or two on Saint Stephen's, some night you went inna tank?"

Earl shifted in the chair. "You know," he said, "this's my afternoon off. Wednesday and Thursday nights, I'm gonna have to work late to make up. My brother maybe calls me up, tells me to get down here. But that don't make up for the commissions that I might've got today, and if I don't get commissions, boy, my draw goes down the sewer. Plus which, I drive about a hundred sixty miles, you know, see this guy that I don't know, and my *brother* doesn't know, because my brother called me? Because his friend asked him to? And for this I'm taking shit? Because you're a

23

friend in need, a guy I don't even *know?* Who is it needs the favor here? Isn't me, I know."

"Yes it is," the blocky man said. He grinned. "You got in the shit once. And *you* needed a favor. And you got it from the guy that knows your brother, all right? Now, the guy that called your brother, he owes *me* a favor. Because I did him a favor when a friend of *his* got dirty. So that is why you're down here, pal—because *you* need a favor. You got to pay things back."

"I don't have any trouble with that," Earl said. "Paying things back, I mean. I just don't like gettin' a lot of shit for my trouble, all right? You wanna piss on someone, fine. Go ahead and do it. But don't bring me down here, all this way from Boston, so you can do it on me."

"Well," Battles said, "I see they didn't break your spirit, any fuckin' thing like that. You got a fresh mouth on you, pal. Anybody tell you that?"

Earl shrugged. "I did my time," he said. "I owe nobody nothing."

"Yeah," Battles said, "but you didn't do as *much* time, as everybody thought."

"Hey," Earl said, "prisons're overcrowded. Everybody knows that. I didn't make any trouble. Kept my mouth shut, did my chores. So they let me out early. I'm supposed to complain? It wasn't as bad as I thought it'd be, but I wasn't about to complain. 'Get outta here,' they say, and I got."

"Kept your mouth shut, huh?" Battles said. "That's interesting to hear. There was some talk around, you weren't doing that. And that's how you got out so fast."

"There's always talk around," Earl said. "Look at the

papers they sell in the markets. 'I Got Knocked Up by an Alien.' 'Rabbit-faced Baby with Ten-Inch Ears Born to Buck-toothed Mother, Loves Carrots.' 'Fifty-seven T-Birds, for sale for fifty dollars, 'cause the owners died in them and rotted in the seats.''

"Then there was," Battles said, "you got out, but for a while you're not around. Nobody ever saw you. Guys inna can behind you saw you walk the fuckin' door, but nobody on the outside sees you, must've been a year."

"I was finding myself," Earl said. "That's what my daughter's doing—she's finding herself this year. You know where she's looking? Greek islands. I get a couple under my belt, I'm out after work one night. I always get sentimental, I drink—just a regular slob. So I call up the former bride, just to see how things're going. How's her new guy treating her? Has he got a ten-inch dick? All that happy horseshit. And she tells me Sarah's scrubbed the college, which I already paid about three hundred for the goddamned applications and the fuckin' goddamned tests, and the down payment, deposit, all of which I hadda *earn*. And I say: 'What the fuck is going on? She had her room already. I give her the TV set and I sent in the money. She's not going out to U. Mass. Amherst, Boston isn't good enough?' And I get told, well, it's my fault. 'She never had a father.' 'Fuck you, she didn't have a father,' 'cause by now I'm getting mad. 'She didn't have a father, then how come I got all those goddamned canceled checks?' 'It's not the same thing. Not like you were around.' Well, that's what I was doing, all right? Except I was older, and nobody sent me money. I got out the can and I dropped out, a while. And then I run out of the money, and I didn't see nobody standing by to buy me meals and keep me warm, so I went and got a job."

"Or our uncle got one for you," Battles said.

"Forget it," Earl said. "I must've heard that from a couple dozen guys. That I was in the program. If I was in the program, if they're protecting me, then how come you and those guys never heard a word about me? Did I ever testify? Did someone see me in court? Is there one single person who can say I ever did? Not a soul on this whole earth. Did they offer me? Of course. They offer everybody, if they think he's got something. Give you a week, try out the food, see if you're scared to death. And then they come around and see you and say: 'Wanna work for us?' Which some guys do, and some guys don't, and I was in the last group. Didn't do no work for them."

Battles stared at him. He drank more beer. He put the beer can down and nodded. "Okay," he said, "all right. I can't picture my friend, dealing me a ringer. He knows I would kill him, and that don't appeal to him."

"I think," Earl said, "I think maybe your friend don't give a shit what you think. He's the kind of guy that does what he wants to do. He called my brother because he trusts him, and my brother sent me down. So you trust him, he trusts my brother, my brother must trust me. That is what I think."

"You know something?" Battles said. "You are an asshole, all right? I don't understand it. You guys, all you guys the same age, doesn't matter what you see, doesn't matter what any fool'd know it meant: 'You do this and you'll get hurt.' My own kid's the same way, and you're the same way too. Only difference is, he

26

went in the fuckin' army—'I won't get *my* ass blown off,' and he won't listen when I tell him: 'Yes you will, it's Vietnam, and you're not goin' there'—and you went inna tank when you were playn' ball, *after* someone had've told you: 'You will go to jail.' I don't trust one son of a bitch under thirty, and that includes you, pal, and that includes him, too. And I don't trust no bastard *over* thirty, neither. Your type's problem is that you all think you're too lucky, so you won't get hammered. Their type's problem is that they all think they're too smart, so they won't get hammered."

"Well, they all do, of course, because lemme tell you something: Smart or lucky doesn't matter. Matters is not fucking up. I would think you'd know that after you been in the can. And if you sounded like you did, then I might listen to you. But you don't. So, I don't give a *fuck* what you think. You fucked up before, all right? You fucked fucking up, that's what you did, you fuck. I asked about you. I asked the guy I know. I said: 'Kind of bird is this? Name, it sounds familiar.' And he tells me, why it is. And so, and then I know. And I say: 'Fine. But is he gonna fuck me up? Because this not a thing, you know, that's very complicated. If I knew a donkey good, I would get the donkey.' And he says: 'No, he's all right. Lemme make a call.' And that is why you're here. So you better not fuck up."

"Jeez," Earl said, "you must be, you know, very powerful. Just be able, call a guy up, get a guy you need. What'd you do for this guy, huh? And who is this guy?"

"I never met the guy," Battles said. "I know him because he called me, asked me to do something that was up high on his list. Didn't know me from Shinola, but he called and asked me. And I did it, like he wanted, *without fucking up*. So now I get to call *him* up, when there's something that I want. And he does it for me, all right? Without fucking up. And that is why you're here. Maybe you learn something."

Earl sighed. "You should've been on the parole board," he said. "Either that or a priest. Whyncha just can all this baloney, tell me what you want?"

"That's better," Battles said. "I got a small problem. It's a car, is what it is. Mercedes fucking Benz. It's got to disappear. Can you make it do that?"

Earl grinned. "What's the matter?" he said. "You been missing payments?"

"It's not my fucking car," he said. "Belongs a frequent guest. He's the one that wants it gone. I want to help him out."

"What's the guy's name?" Earl said. "Not the guy that owns it—the guy that's in the trunk."

"There's no guy inna trunk," Battles said. "Don't be a wise guy, all right? It's just a simple matter. The car belongs his wife, all right? It's just a matter, going out, steal the fucking car. And then: lose it."

"The water?" Beale said.

"Not the goddamned ocean, no," Battles said. "Someone'd bring it up. This one goes the crusher."

"And there's nothing in the trunk," Earl said.

"Look," Battles said, "there is nothing in the car except the lug wrench and the jack. And prolly some cigar butts and some used-up matchbooks, that stuff. But otherwise there's nothing in it. No Luigi, nothing. It is absolutely clean."

"And when do you want all this done?" Earl said.

"Tonight," Battles said.

"Tonight?" Earl said. "I got to go to New York tonight. Got to pick up my girl in the morning. Besides, no crusher's working weekends. Scrapyards're all closed. What'm I gonna do with it? Go out and get arrested?"

Battles sighed. "Jesus Christ, it never fails. I ask a guy for something, get a fucking argument. It's in a barn, all right? I'll show you where it is today. When you coming back?"

"Tomorrow night," Earl said. "I'll be back tomorrow night."

4

Earl in the twilight entered the short-term parking lot at the international terminal at JFK Airport in Queens and found a suitable space six rows back from the Pan American terminal entrance: it faced a shiny, new red Buick hardtop. He released the inside hood latch of the Dodge, got out and removed his jacket, went to the front of the car and released the safety catch. He opened the hood and rested the palms of his hands on the top of the grille. He peered into the engine compartment for a moment. He went around to the back of the car and opened the rear deck. He removed an army blanket, a small tool kit wrapped in a plastic pouch, and a heavy-duty rubber-cased flashlight. He left the trunk open and returned to the front of the car. He draped the blanket on the window ledge of the driver's side door. He opened the tool kit and spread it on the left front fender. He used the flashlight with his left hand and illuminated the area at the front of the engine. Then he returned to the driver's side door and got in.

After about twelve minutes, a tow truck with a flashing yellow light on its roof pulled up behind him. Earl got out of the Dodge as the driver climbed down from the cab. He was a young black man in a blue coverall, and he had two steel claws fitted to plastic cuffs at the ends of his forearms. "Problem, sir?" he said.

"Ahh, minor, I think," Earl said. He went to the back of the Dodge and stood in front of the registration plate. He yawned and stretched, trying not to stare at the claws. "She was running a little hot coming down here. Probably a loose hose clamp or something. I'm just waiting, it gets cool enough, I can reach in there." He hooked his left heel on the rear bumper and lounged back against the trunk ledge.

"Yeah," the man said, raising his prostheses and grinning, "don't want to get yourself a pair of these. Right?"

Earl smiled. "You want the truth," he said, "I was sort of thinking . . ."

". . . if you *did* have these," the man said, "then maybe you could do it. Now, I mean, 'stead of waiting. 'Cept for one thing, which you only got to learn once and then remember it forever: there's very few cars, aren't brand-new, don't have at least one live wire floating around in there where it's not s'posed to be. And if you don't feel it when you brush it on the way to something else, and don't know it—these things aren't great for touch—you get yourself a mighty big surprise when you ground it in the dark."

"What happened to you, anyway?" Beale said.

The man leaned his buttocks on the left front fender of the tow truck, the yellow light turning lazily in the gathering darkness, the roar of jet turbines faraway but never out of hearing, and used his right claw to fish a pack of Luckies from his left breast pocket. "I could use a break," he said. He shook a cigarette out and captured it with his left claw, replacing the pack in his pocket and tapping the cigarette three times on his right cuff. He put it in his mouth. He reached into his right breast pocket and extracted one long wooden match, striking it on the inner edge of the wheel well. It flared and he lighted the cigarette, dropping the match on the pavement. "Oh," he said, "teenage accident. You know how kids are."

"Used to be one myself," Earl said.

"Right," the man said. "Full of the courage, you know? Scared of nothing, man. I was on a trip with my uncle. Always been very good to me, my uncle has. Asking me to go on trips. Taking me places, showing me things, I never would've thought of going. Real *interesting* places, I never would've seen. *Lots* of things to do. Night hikes? Plenty going on. And they had these woods, see? This forest? And, I forgot all the stuff, all the good advice they gave me, they told me about always being careful, watch where I was going, take it slow and easy, and all of a sudden one night, I got like, scared, you know? Spooked. Thought I heard something. It was dark. So I started running, and I tripped on this big root, this tree root there I didn't see, and I dropped all the stuff I was carrying, and I started to fall down, and I had my hands out in front of me, see?" He extended his arms before him like a swimmer preparing to dive. "And I fell. And that's how."

"You tripped in the woods and it cost you your *hands*," Earl said. "What hell'd you fall on? An alligator?"

The man grinned again. He exhaled a large cloud of smoke. "No, man," he said, "a Claymore mine. Those woods're in Vietnam. That's where my uncle took me. Hadn't been for that big tree, I would've lost my *head.*"

"Oh," Earl said.

"Uncle didn't ask you to go?" the man said. "Look about my age. Thought he asked all the kids. 'Course you are a different color. Maybe that was it. Uncle's prejudice."

Earl chuckled. "Well," he said, "no. Actually. He did want me to go, but I told him, you know, 'least let me finish school.' But I really wanted to. Sounded real exciting."

"I bet," the man said, smiling. "I met lots of guys like that, tell me how disappointed it made them, had to miss the trip 'cause they were still in school. But, you could've gone *after*, right? When you finished? And you still didn't get to go?"

"Nope," Earl said. "See, I didn't really finish. Didn't graduate. I was playing basketball all the time, see? And I didn't study enough. So I was short a few credits at the end of my last year, and then when I could've gone back in the fall, finished up, well, I was doing something else that he said I hadda do first. Which I didn't really want to, you know? But I didn't have a choice. And by the time I finish that, my uncle says I'm too old. Doesn't want me anymore. And besides, he doesn't like what I just finish doing, that he said I hadda do."

"Shee-it," the black man said. "First you play some ball, and he lets you finish that? I used to play some ball. Didn't cut no ice with him. What he must've had

33

you doing sounds real interesting. Wish I'd had that option."

"I don't think so," Earl said. "It was five-to-seven, Leavenworth."

"Ohhh," the man said, dropping the butt on the ground. "No, I think you're right. I think you're right on that." He nodded toward the Dodge. "You gonna be all right on that? Won't need any help?"

Earl nodded. "I'll be all right," he said.

The man opened the door of the cab and climbed back into the truck. "Well," he said, "you're not, don't do what I did, start running around inna dark. Just stay put, stay with the car. Leave the hood and trunk up. I come around about every forty minutes or so. You're still here, I'll take a look."

"Thanks," Earl said. "Nice talking to you."

The tow truck moved slowly forward down the row. Earl stood at the rear of the Dodge until he saw the yellow light had stopped about twelve hundred yards away. He went around to the front of the Dodge and moved the blanket from the top of the door to the top of the radiator. He took a blade screwdriver and a Phillips screwdriver from the tool pouch. He went to the center of the grille with the flashlight in his right hand and the two screwdrivers in his left. He bent over the engine and slowly dropped into a crouch facing the grille. Then he pivoted on the balls of his feet so that he faced the front of the Buick. He aimed the flashlight on the registration plate of the Buick: 7J7–N54, New Jersey. He used the Phillips screwdriver to unscrew the four bolts attaching the plate and chrome frame from the bumper of the Buick. He pivoted back to face the Dodge again, standing up slowly and folding the plate and the frame in the blanket. He replaced the tools in the pouch and picked it up. He held it and the folded blanket away from the car with his left hand and slammed the hood shut with his right. He went to the back of the car and put the tools and the blanket in the trunk. He got into the car, started it, and backed out of the space, turning in the direction opposite to the tow truck's route and leaving the parking lot.

On the third Sunday in July, Earl got out of bed carefully in the room he had rented at the Howard Johnson Motel at JFK, leaving the blond-haired woman sleeping, and padded nude into the bathroom, closing the door silently. When he emerged about twenty minutes later, his hair was wet and he was cleanly shaven. He wore the same shirt and pants he had worn the day before. He carried a Dopp Kit of toilet gear, which he put on the small, white, circular table in front of the window. He went to the low dresser-desk combination and picked up the white plastic ice bucket. He returned to the bathroom and poured the water down the flush. He took the room key from the desk and left the room almost silently, returning with fresh ice. The woman stirred. He put the bucket on the desk and picked up the water glass that was not lipsticked. He poured about half of the four remaining ounces of vodka into the glass, added ice, and opened a fresh can of Coke, which he mixed with the vodka, using his right forefinger. The ice clinked and the woman stirred again, moaning once.

He drank from the glass and went to the window. He opened the drapes and stared out into the gray glare of an overcast day. The woman groaned and rolled over, pulling the pillow over her head. He sipped reflectively. She sat up in bed, blinking, clasping the sheet around her. "Do you have to do that?" she said.

"Uh huh," he said. "Getting late. My boss expects me to be waiting, that thing hits the ground. I got to get over there. Be there, they come in."

She fluffed her hair. "What time is it, anyway?"

"Little before eleven," he said.

"Well, you said last night it was noon. Noon they were coming in," she said. "Not going to take you an hour to get there. Cripes, you can *see* it from here. Fifteen minutes, you'll be there."

"Look," he said, "inna first place, all right? You told me you hadda be there, you're now going out at one-thirty and you gotta be there at least an hour. Hour before that, you said. So that rolls us back to twelve-thirty. Except it's not the same terminals, is it? You're going a different one. So, I got to drop you off, and then there's the traffic, and then comes the damned place to park. So, I'm sorry. But get moving, all right? This's my job we're talking here. I'm not taking any chances, losing it because I'm late."

She got out of bed. She had small breasts and fairly broad hips and very good, long legs. "I want some breakfast," she said. "You could at least order breakfast."

"No," he said. "No time for breakfast."

"Some coffee, at least?" she said. She walked over to him and put her hands on his shoulders, shaking her hair and smiling.

"Not in the room," he said. "We haven't got time." He put the glass down and squeezed her breasts. "You

36

should have that operation," he said. "That implant thing they got."

She pulled away from him and flicked him on the crotch. "You do, I will," she said. She disappeared into the bathroom.

He let her off at the Butler Aviation charter terminal. "You're amazing," he said. "I really don't know how you broads do it. Forty minutes ago you look like you spent the night fighting with dogs."

"Well, only one," she said.

"And now you look like you got the full eight, up with the sun, did the push-ups and stuff, had your oatmeal and Mom did your hair. All ready for school. In your nice red dress. It's amazing."

"Sam," she said, "am I really going to see you again? Are you really going to call me?"

"Next time I'm in New York," Earl said. "What I said, and what I'll do. I fell in love last night."

"Oh, Sam," she said, putting her arms around his neck and kissing him. "I'm such a lucky girl. After all these years, I'm such a lucky girl." She pulled back, smiling at him. "Is your name really Sam?"

"Kathie, Kathie," he said, "how can you say that?"

"Well," she said, "a girl can't be too careful these days. All these bad men around."

"Did you have a good time, Kathie?" he said.

"I had a very nice time, Sam," she said. She got out of the Dodge. He pulled the seatback of the Dodge down, and she removed her wheeled flight bag from the backseat. She set it on the sidewalk and fluttered her fingers at him. "Bye, Sam," she said. "Call me soon."

"Bye, Kathie," he said. "Very soon." She shut the

door and watched wistfully as the Dodge pulled away, reaching absently into her shoulder bag. A jade green Chevrolet hardtop pulled into the vacated space. The passenger door opened, and a brown-haired woman dressed in an identical red uniform emerged, yanking her flight bag from the backseat and slamming the door. "You son of a bitch," she said to the driver. "It's not my fault about your lousy golf game. That you hadda miss your game. It's not up to me when they postpone these things, if something goes wrong with the plane." The man in the car said something. "Yeah," the woman said, "but you don't object to the money, though. The money's fine with you." The Chevy jumped away from the curb, nearly colliding with a taxi.

"Nice holdover, Ruthie?" the first woman said. The second woman stared at her. "Fuck you, Snider," she said. She eyed the first woman up and down. "You're outta uniform, Snider. You wanna go out and get laid, times like these, go ahead, do what you want. But you're on my crew, you show up the next morning, all fulla beans and dressed up. I may report you for this."

Snider opened her eyes wide and then opened her right hand toward Ruthie. In it was a pair of gilded wings imprinted Mavis. "I was just putting them on when you got here, Ruth," she said. She smiled. "I'm sorry you had a bad time."

Earl found a space in the fifth row of short-term parking at the domestic airlines terminal building. He locked the doors and unlocked the trunk. He reached deep into it to pull out a woman's small train case, light blue vinyl. He opened the case and removed a tan windbreaker, a red scarf, and a pair of sneakers. He uncovered a Mamiya/Sekor 35-mm single-lens-reflex camera with a 135-mm telephoto lens attached, a 28-mm wide-angle lens, and a 50-mm normal lens. There were three unopened boxes of Kodak Tri-X 24-exposure film. He opened one of them and took out the canister. He took the film cartridge out of the canister and loaded it into the camera. He inspected the lens. He put the camera down on the floor of the trunk and took out his wallet. He removed a worn dollar bill and used it as a lens tissue. He inspected the lens again. He put the dollar bill in his left pants pocket and draped the camera around his neck on the strap. He shut the trunk and locked it and headed for the terminal.

He found a place to stand on the second floor—Departures—near a post behind a long line of passengers checking baggage and themselves onto a Northwest Orient Airlines flight bound for Seattle. The majority of them seemed to be of Oriental ancestry, and carried woven wicker bags. He was vaguely puzzled about that, but put the matter out of his mind and made sure of his sight lines and surroundings. The public-address system carried a steady stream of orders and announcements that were hard to hear in the commotion of welcoming shouts and tearful farewells, crying children and shouting parents, but he had learned selective deafness playing basketball. In prison he had been able to listen in his cell to the kind of radio music he liked, the din of other prisoners, shouting guards, and crashing doors occurring somewhere else. "Ahh," he had told the prison counselor, "the usual stuff, you know? The Stones. The Beatles. And I still like the old stuff.

The Platters. The Four Tops. The Coasters. The Cadillacs. They often call me 'Speedoo.' That's what the guys on the team called me—'Speedoo'—'cause my real name was Mister Earl. Those guys. Heck, I even still like Chubby Checker, and Fats. Remind me the good days I had. You just tune out, when you're playing, all the hollering and yelling, people jumping up and down, and waving things. Just block it out, you know? You didn't learn to do that, you'd never make a foul shot. You play your first game in the Garden? If you didn't learn by then, well, you know it from then on."

He stood against the post and focused his camera on the corridor entrance between the American Airlines and Northwest gates, using the sign precisely above it as his reference point. He checked the light meter, set the lens at f/5.6 and the shutter speed at 1/100, and waited.

At 12:12 P.M., the P.A. system announced the arrival of American flight 641 from Nassau. Earl held the camera ready. At 12:18 incoming passengers began to come up the ramp. Sixth and seventh in line were a man about fifty years old and woman about twenty-eight. He had silver at the temples of his black hair and a dark tan. He wore a double-breasted blue blazer, white linen shirt open at the neck, and white pants. She wore a white sweater that contrasted nicely with her tan and her reddish hair, and tight white pants and high heels. Earl brought the camera up and started taking pictures, using the thumb lever to advance the film without removing the viewfinder from his eye. When they reached the sign she wobbled slightly, and the man grabbed her arm to steady her. He said something.

She put her hand on his right shoulder, held on, and bent her right leg. Earl continued to take pictures. She removed her shoe, still clutching the man, while the other passengers eddied around them, scowling, and the man glared protectively over her shoulder. Then she replaced the shoe, released the man, and smiled. She patted him on the neck. He kissed her on the cheek. They joined the flow of the other passengers turning right onto the escalator leading down to Baggage Claim.

Earl went out of the terminal on the departure level and took the sidewalk ramp down to the arrival parking lot. He went to the car, hurrying and perspiring in the heavy heat, opened the trunk of the Dodge, put the camera in the train case, replaced the clothing on top of it, closed the case, and shoved it forward, up behind the rear seat. He closed the trunk, unlocked the driver's door, got in, and drove quickly to the exit doors on the arrival level outside the American Airlines baggage carousels. He found a place large enough to accommodate the Dodge among all the other unattended cars parked next to the curb with the signs that prohibited parking or standing. He parked the car, locked it, and went inside the terminal.

He spotted the same man and the woman standing outside the velvet rope excluding nonpassengers from the baggage-claim area. Inside, many people competed for places closest to the incoming cargo doors. Porters in blue uniforms stood aloof from the travelers, waiting with aluminum carts and glancing repeatedly at tags clipped to ticket folders. The carousel began to revolve. Earl saw four bags come down before Penny's three-piece set of Gucci luggage appeared. He went quickly

41

back outside and opened the trunk of the Dodge. As soon as Penny and the man escorted the porter outside the door, he waved his right arm. The man waved back and directed the porter toward the Dodge.

"Mister Simmons," Earl said, bending from the waist and extending his right hand as though to assist the porter loading the luggage into the trunk, but touching nothing, "nice trip?" Earl straightened up. The porter put the last of the three pieces into the Dodge and stood back, expectantly.

"Very nice, thank you, Earl," Simmons said, putting on sunglasses. "Oh," he said, as though just noticing the porter. He reached into his right front pocket, fished out a roll of bills, and peeled off a twenty. "Thanks very much," he said to the porter. "Thank you, sir," the porter said. "Never last long enough, though," Simmons said, clutching Penny around the waist. "Never last long enough, do they?"

"Oh, Allen," she said, pushing him away. "Now come on now, all right?"

"Well, they don't," he said. He leaned toward her to kiss her, but she pulled away.

"All right," she said. "Tell you what we'll do. Earl'll just take my luggage home, and I'll get on your connection to Boston with you. And that way it won't be over. Least for another hour. You could tell her I'm just someone you happened to meet on the plane. But she might not believe you. And a lot of things might start."

He stepped back. He smiled. "Thank you very much, Penny," he said. "I guess I asked for that."

"Thank you for a lovely week, Allen," she said. She pecked him on the cheek and stood back.

42

He nodded. "Got to catch my plane," he said. He went back into the terminal.

Earl and Penny stood by the car until Simmons was back inside and they saw him go up the escalator. She put her arms around Earl and kissed him full on the lips. "Ummm," she said, standing back, "glad to see you again. Always nice to come home."

"Hard week?" he said.

She shrugged, releasing him and heading for the passenger door. "Not especially," she said. "I'm an ornament, mostly." She opened the door and got in. He slid in on the driver's side. "Get dressed up at night, get the bikini on, the daytime—'Oh, that's Allen's girl.' Well, he wants to pay me ten grand a week to hang on his arm and show to his friends, who'm I to complain?"

"Oh, cut it out," Earl said.

"Don't get shitty with me, chum," she said. "You knew the deal when we started. You gonna tell me, when we get home, you won't touch the cash? You won't live the apartment, and you won't drive the damned car? It's Allen that's paying for it. And now I got two whole weeks off. Three, if I like. He's going the Vineyard, his wife. But Allen is generous, say that for the guy. We fly first-class, and we stay first-class, and he gives me a lot of money. So lay off of him, all right? Allen's a generous man."

"Look," Earl said, putting the Dodge in gear and pulling out of the illegal space, "all I'm asking you is this: When we gonna do it? I got about sixteen more pictures just now, and if they turn out like I think, which they will, they're fuckin' beautiful."

"That worked all right, then," she said. "The part with 'I twisted my heel'?"

"Oh," he said, "it was beautiful. But when we gonna *use* them, all right? When'm I finally gonna get to call this guy and say: 'Uh, Mister Simmons, sir, this is Earl? And I wonder you'd be interested, a family photo album? Memento of your trips? Because we got about eighty pictures now. Or how about your lovely wife that's in the newspaper all the time? The museums and stuff? Think she might like to buy it and then show it? You know me, Mister Simmons. I'm a very humble guy. But I got my obligations, ex-wife, kid in school, all that shit, and I could use—well, me and Penny— say about a million bucks. It's a fuckin' bargain, Mister Simmons. What I'm offering you. You know I'm a friend of yours. Got your best interests, heart. Think what it'd cost you if your wife got hold these things. What, five, six million dollars? This's cheap, is what it is.' "

Penny leaned back against the seat and shut her eyes. "I don't wanna talk about it now," she said.

"Well, I do," he said.

She opened her eyes. "Tough shit, mister," she said. "I said I don't wanna talk about it now. I didn't have no breakfast, 'cept what they serve the plane. And I don't eat any damned thing that an airline says is food. Now you find a place where I can get some food. You oughta know a lot of them, somewhere around this city. Spent a lot of time here, I hear, 'fore you went to jail. And you take me there. And then I eat. And then you take me home, and I will take a goddamned bath. You got that?"

"You got to take yourself home," Earl said. "Part-

44

way I can take you, and I know a restaurant. But the rest you go yourself. I got some work to do."

"What's this crap?" she said. "I got to drive myself home?"

"Hey," he said, "we all got obligations."

5

Earl took the access road leading to the Lord Squire Motor Hotel off Route I-95 in New Rochelle. The hood of the Dodge shimmered heat. Penny raised her head and opened her eyes. "Hey," she said, "what you doing?"

"You said you wanted to eat," he said. The motel was two stories of varicolored brick situated between a convenience store and an Esso station.

"*Here?*" she said. "You think I'm gonna eat, *here?* Like what? Canned soup and burgers? An hour ago, I wanted to eat. Now what I want's some sleep."

"You're gonna eat," Earl said. "The sign says they got a brunch." He took a parking place near the green canopy extending from the main entrance. "Sundays, eleven to three."

"Yeah," she said. " 'All you can eat for two ninety-five.' Jesus, you really are cheap. I can imagine what the eggs'll look like. Should've eaten that shit on the plane. Christ, I'm hot."

"Three ninety-five, actually," he said. "Plus a complimentary Bloody Mary or screwdriver. You left Mon-

46

eybags at the airport, remember?" He shut off the engine. "And you're hot," he said, "because I been telling you since Easter to bring this goddamned thing the shop. Get the seals checked and the Freon reloaded. And you haven't done it. You haven't had time. You sleep all day and you bitch all night, and then you go outta town. Supposedly because we're setting up this rich guy, and it's the only way we can do it. But we're not. What we're doing is, I'm running in place, and you're kiting around on vacation, one week every month."

"Ten thousand a week is pretty good pay," she said. "More'n you ever made. You sure you want to risk it?"

"It's not ten a week," he said. "It's ten a month, six months a year. Plus the extras, when you get 'em, so we won't count those. Which is, twelve, twelve fifty a week, gross. You think it's ten grand a week, when you work once a month, half the year? Then I used to get a lot more'n that—a thousand for forty minutes. You wanna figure out what that comes to, a week? That's twenty-five dollars a minute. Plus what I made myself, my own bets."

"Yeah," she said, "but you got caught. What'd they pay you in prison? How much a minute was that?"

"Look," he said, "Penny, I don't want a fight. You don't understand what I'm telling you. Allen is paying you very good money, but Allen is good for much more. But just for a little while, he is good for it. We just got to explain this to him, before the time runs out. Because this, well, *job*, you got with him, it isn't permanent. You know what happened to Nancy."

"I don't want to hear about the bitch," she said.

"Allen ditched Nancy because of the drugs. Allen was right to do that."

"Allen may've *said* he ditched Nancy for that," he said, "but we both know that wasn't it. Allen ditched Nancy because she made a mistake. The mistake was letting you move in, and letting him see you. Nancy was branching out. Thought she had an assistant, handle some of her business. Nancy was moving up, and you were the first one she picked. Bad choice. She didn't count on you scooping her best customer. Didn't think about how she'd begun to sag a little bit, he might like a newer model."

"Bullshit," she said. She put her head back and shut her eyes again.

" 'Bullshit,' nothing," he said. "You're in a business, lady. It's purely a matter of business, and your attitude about it bothers me. You don't *want* to think about it, so you *don't* think about it, and that means it isn't a business. Well, it is, just the same. I used to be in a business just like it. They were using my ass like a bastard, getting rich off me, paying me chickenshit, I think I'm big time, while they're the ones getting rich. Buying me drinks, and getting me laid, and then who goes to the slammer? *I* go to the slammer. And where did *they* go? I dunno. Vegas, most likely. Never heard from the bastards again. Hell, I never knew most of their names.

"I'm trying to tell you, okay? Experience counts, all right? It counts against you. The longer you been at it, the less interested the customers are. I used up my eligibility? 'So long, baby—Ciao.' Just like Allen will do to you, some fine day. It goes with your line of work.

"And then what?" he said. "You wanna be an old

whore someday? Because you're *gonna* be old. You don't have a choice about that part. And the hooker part you won't, either. Old whores don't make much money. Old ladies with money don't hook, and old ladies with money don't care. You wanna be an old lady, with her own money? Or an old whore who can't make a dime? It's the same thing with me. *I'm* gonna get old. I don't wanna be an old ex-con. Nobody hires them for nothing. I wanna be a nice, *secure*, old man. Spending the winters in Florida. Playing the golf and stuff. Clipping my coupons and washing my false teeth. Driving my own Cadillac.

"That's what you don't understand," he said. "Or pretend you don't understand, 'cause you know what I'm saying is right. That's what I'm telling you, all right? There's only so many chances. You're lucky, you get one. I had my one, and I blew it. My brother had his one—he took it. He was smart, and I was stupid. I admit it. Tough shit for me. Now you never had one, but this comes along, and I'm telling you: this is your one. Now listen to what I am saying. I got myself in the shit once, and I climbed out of the shit. Which very few guys ever do. You haven't been in the shit yet, and believe me, you don't want to *go* in. Listen a guy who knows how it is, and we both stay out of the shit. Don't throw your one away. Just listen to what old Earl says."

"Shut up," she said. "Too hot to talk. Just drive and let me sleep."

He grabbed her by her upper left arm. "Listen to me," he said in a low voice. "I didn't know *you* till I met you, but I knew a lot of ladies in the same damned line of work. I met them, got introduced, by guys like

Allen, there. They *gave* those ladies to me. 'Here's a freebie on the house. Don't beat Temple by nine. Eight'll be fine, but not nine.' At the time I thought: 'Geez, this dame is old. Looks good, but she is old. Ah, what hell. Long as she sucks the cock.' I was nineteen, twenty, all right? These old broads *were* old. Some of them almost twenty-five. But to me, they were old.

"Okay," he said, "this was New York. A little higher speed. Boston? Maybe ten years later, but no more'n that. You don't believe me, just ask Nancy. Nasty, but the facts.

"Now," he said, "the next time Allen has a birthday with a zero in it, the first digit's gonna be six. All right?"

"Allen's in good shape," she said lazily, her eyes still shut. "His stomach's flat as a rock. He doesn't drink like you do, and he treats me very nice. You should look as good as he does, you get to be his age. You should look as good as he does, *now*. Let go my arm." She shrugged it.

Earl let go of her arm and turned in his seat. Her breasts rose and fell under the white sweater. She had a small smile. "He treats you like a toy," he said. "An expensive toy, but a toy. The next birthday you see with a zero in it's gonna have a three in it, too. He's going to the island now, be with his lovely wife. His *third* lovely wife. How old is she? Probably close to forty. Twelve years or so older'n you are. You think that when you're thirty-five, Allen's still gonna be interested? Fat fuckin' chance he will, thirty-five-year-old honey. I know you give great blow jobs, and that's what Allen likes. But sucking cocks is not a job you need much training for. Couple outings, any broad can do it. I hear some guys can do it, too. There was talk like that in prison. What matters to guys like Allen is that the broad is *young*, and her tits're high, and she looks like a fresh young tender piece of ass that only a rich man can buy. And then later on, replace. You got two years at the maximum before he goes and dumps you. You either get the bundle before he does that, or you go fuckin' without. Try to find some other pigeon, when you're thirty-three. You'll be hanging around lounges. Looking out for plainclothes guys, and hoping for a trick. That'll at least pay the room, so you got a place to sleep."

She opened her eyes. "Got lucky last night, huh?" she said.

"I got laid," he said, "if that's lucky. Doesn't take a lot of talent."

"Thanks a lot," she said. "I'm coming home, you're picking me up, but while you're waiting, you screw."

"Well," he said, "at least I didn't have Allen's dick in my mouth. Like some people that I could name."

She slapped him. "Earl," she said, "I did it for you. You were the one, thought of it. It was all your idea, I start sweet-talking him. 'Hey, this looks like love to me, Allen. How 'bout if I stop taking calls, stop going out to hotels?' And he went for it. Well, it was a good idea. So far, at least, it has been. But if it turns sour, that's not my fault. Wasn't me that thought it all up. Wasn't Allen, either. The whole thing was all your damned idea."

"Well," he said, "and it was a good one. So long's you remember the whole thing. The first thing's a good thing, but it's temporary. Guy doesn't hurt you. Pays you in cash. Doesn't need you around all that often, and the cops don't care about that shit. Very good thing all around."

He slapped her. "But then comes the second part," he said. "The big reason for this whole idea. You pick up some dingbat in some bar someplace, and you go his room with him, haul his ashes. And he's a nice guy. He's grateful. He does not beat you up. He gives you a big hundred bucks. Well, that's great, but it's like buying neckties wholesale for a buck, and selling them for fifty cents: You can't make a profit on volume. And you can't retire on what you make, turning tricks night after night, when Allen spots a new model.

"You also," he said, as she rubbed her left jaw, "you also can't do it on Allen. *Unless* you make Allen give you the bundle, and put the cash into the bank. If we shake him down, like we said we would do, and he pays us a million damned dollars, we got five grand a month for the rest of our lives, and the million still left at the end. And that, dear, is serious money."

She sat up straight in the seat. She yawned. "Why is it you're stealing this car?"

"Because I got to," he said. "I don't know what's going on. My brother called me, and he said: 'Go see this guy.' And I said: 'Who the fuck is he?' And Donald said: 'Look, you don't wanna know. And if I did, I wouldn't tell you. He's a guy that a friend of mine knows, that he owes a damned favor to. So go down and see him, find out what he wants, and then do what he tells you, all right?' And I go: 'Well, how's this involve me? Maybe he wants a guy killed.' And Don goes: 'Oh it's nothing as heavy as that. This's just kind of shady, and he needs it done, but not by a guy from down there. So, if you can do it, without fucking it up, just do it without fucking up. And if you can't, call me back, and I'll make some more calls. Inna meantime, just go and see him.' And I say: 'I'm not gonna do this. I don't know what I'm doing. I don't know who I'm doing it for. You can't get me into this thing.' And Donald says: 'Look, have you got a record?' I say: 'Well, I did time.' And Donald says: 'Yeah, but you ain't got a record. Keep in mind how come that is.' "

"It's that politician up there," she said.

"I assume so," he said. "It must be. But I still don't know why I'm doing this thing. I figure Ed Cobb's behind it. My brother'n him're like Siamese twins—but why Ed Cobb wants it done, I don't know. All I do know's that this guy Battles has got something on Ed Cobb, and Ed Cobb called my brother, and my brother called me. So Battles did something for one of them, once, or somebody that they like, and now he's calling his marker. And it must've been something damned big, Battles did, if the bastard can get this much service."

"*Jesus,*" she said, "and you talk about *me?* Taking chances, I mean, and all that? I could get batted around by the wrong guy? *You* could go back to jail. And you're doing what this fat shit tells you? Taking the car and just crushing it? You must be out of your mind. How much're you getting for this?"

"Peace and quiet," he said. "And some money, too. I'm not gonna crush the damned car."

"You're not," she said.

"I'm not," he said. "I have seen it. This is a prime Mercedes two-seater, worth about five or six K. One of those roadsters, robin's-egg blue, and the seats've hardly been sat on. I'm gonna drive it up to Donald's, have him put it on the lot, and some rich asshole'll buy it."

"And you think Donald'll *do* this?" she said. "Thought you said he thinks you're a crook."

"I *know* he'll do it," Earl said. "That's *why* he'll do it. Donald's very religious. Because he likes money, and there's nothing that goes better together'n money and religion, except gin and vermouth. And I got a story he'll go for right off. It's close enough to robbing a bank so that, coming from me, he'll believe it. I heard it from a lawyer that was on the bus with me. Going in for an estate thing that he sold some stuff himself, only the stuff went to friends that didn't pay much money. 'Less you counted all the cash they gave to him and didn't mention. I'm gonna tell him I'm getting the bill of sale sent. And as soon's I get back to old Waldo's joint there, and grab a clean one from him, you fill it out and I send it to Donald, and he sells the car free and easy."

"Me?" she said. "Why me?"

"Because you're a woman," he said, "and I'm telling Donald that I got this car from a hooker that's been shipped out by her old man. Which he will go for like a trout goes for mayflies. Just dirty enough to sound good, but in this case, as legal as hell. And then it's half for Donald and half for me, since I'm getting the damned thing for nothing. 'Cept for my trouble, I mean. And that's exactly why I'm pushing you now. Let's sell Allen the pictures. For the money. We do that and we both retire. Free, from sin, and free, from all temptation."

She lifted the handle and unlatched the door. "Come on," she said, "some wet eggs. And some sau-

54

sages soaked in the steam table too, cold toast and a watery drink."

"You're hard to please," he said, opening his door.

"I've had a hard life," she said.

"Have we got a deal?" he said.

"We've got a start," she said.

6

Earl took Route 189 off Interstate 95 and headed east toward Lafayette. "This's pretty down around here," Penny said as the car passed between tall maples that overhung the road. "Sort of like a long green tunnel. Only without walls. Nice big house, riding horses, smell the ocean, too. Very nice down here."

"I guess so," Earl said. "I didn't come down for the scenery."

"I don't see a bar, though," Penny said. "Nice friendly inn with a bar, sit on the porch with a drink."

"You don't need another drink," he said. "You had your drinks back at lunch. You got to get this thing home in one piece, and the cops in this state're vicious."

"I could still use another drink," Penny said. "Those ones I had, that dog-assed motel, all those crappy things were was water. Since I'm not gonna see you tonight after all. Could at least buy me, real drink. What the hell made you pick that place, anyway? You said you knew a place, and that's where we end up?"

"Old times' sake," he said. "Used to meet Joey in

here. That's where we had our meetings, in the coffee shop."

"All that way out of the city?" she said. "There's no coffee shops in Manhattan? You came all the way out of the city, meet with a guy, and then it turns out, he's working the FBI? That was smart. No wonder you got caught."

He sighed. "Penny," he said, "there's another thing you worry about, you're doing something like that. Besides the FBI. Sure, you don't want *them* to see you. Liable make them wonder: 'What's a nice college guy, plays for Saint Stephen's, what's he doing having coffee with this large layoff man?' But you also, you also don't want the high rollers, don't want them seeing you, either. They might start thinking, 'long same lines: 'Hey, how come Joey's having coffee with the guy that runs the plays?' Might cut down on the action, cut down the action a lot. So you stay out of their hangouts, too. And anyway, Joey wasn't working the Bureau, the first year. Or most of the second one, either. It was only the last four or five times, they had him. After his brother came coco. That's when they got him wired up. Joey never wanted, you know, set me up. Just they had him in the bucket when his brother spilled his guts, and he didn't have a choice. It was either he did what they told him, or else he did twenty-five years. I could see what a box he was in."

"Earl," she said, "Joey was the guy that set you up. Joey was the guy that picked you to do the dirty work with the team. Which means that Joey was the guy that arranged for you to go to jail."

"Well," Earl said, "but he didn't have no choice about that, either. I would've done the same thing myself."

" 'No choice,' " she said. "Whaddaya mean: 'No choice'? He had a choice. He could've left you alone. He could've picked some other guy. He could've bribed the whole team. Why did he pick just you? Why were you the fall guy?"

"Penny, for Christ sake," Earl said, "when you're fixing games, all right? You don't pay off the whole team. For one thing, it'd be too dangerous. The more people know, the more people can tell. For another thing, it'd cost too much, and some of the guys, it'd stand to reason, they wouldn't be cute enough to make it look good. No, Joey did what I would've done, if I'd've been Joey, you know? I was the guy that they needed. I was the guy with the ball. I was the play-maker. Joey just got my name out the papers. Coach said I was the best point guard he ever saw in college ball. He said maybe I was the best college point guard ever. I was the natural choice."

"Do I believe that?" she said. "Or is that like the ex-wife you call when you're drunk, and the daughter that dropped out of U Mass? Something you just tell people you meet, something that just never happened."

"You could go and look it up," he said. "I lost the clips myself, but it was all in the papers."

She shook her head. "Well, I don't believe you," she said.

"Well, that doesn't matter, you do," he said. "That's still the way it happened."

"I don't mean," she said, "I don't mean I don't believe what you just said. I just don't believe a guy like you can walk around like you do, on his way to steal a car—some guy's *expensive* car, which means he is at least rich, and probably he's mean, and will come after ou himself, if he doesn't like the cops—and tell me o take a chance on either Allen dumps me, or *Allen* calls the cops. So we *both* go to jail. And *then*, in the practically very next breath, you sit there and tell me, a perfectly straight face, this Joey that sank you was just a nice guy that just hadda get out of a jam. What's the *matter* with you? You get dropped on your head, you're a kid? You must've had some time yourself, when you were in the can. Didn't you ever start to think: 'How did I get here?' I mean, I *assume* you didn't like it. I don't know too many guys that actually did time, but my brother and the couple or so ones I did meet, said they didn't like it at all. So why're you so damned determined, do things like this, probably get yourself more? We're doing okay, just the way that we're going. Everything's not hunky-dory, but I had some worse times, my life, and I never even got busted. I figure that'd be worse, worse'n the worst day I had." She shook her head again. "There's no part of this that I see that I like. No part I see that I like."

"Look," he said, "inna first place, all right? You like these houses? You like the fields and the ponies? The stone walls and big trees and all of that shit? Wait'll we get little closer to town, you see all the boats onna bay. They'll make you cry, they're so pretty. But, this's the shit that you like? This is shit that you want? Well, you want to get it, it won't be from blowing Allen, and it won't come the job I got now. It's like when they teach you to swim, you know? When they teach the young kids to swim. First they get in the water, and then they teach 'em to tread it. So they can stay afloat. But they don't tell them: 'You keep doing that, you'll make it the end of the pool.' Get to the deep end, you got to do more. Got to use both your hands and your feet. And that's exactly where we are, where we are right now: treading the fucking damned water. We ever expect, get this kind of stuff, we got to start kicking and grabbing. And that's why we're doing these things."

She slumped down in the seat. "Maybe if I close my eyes," she said, "maybe if I go to sleep. Maybe then when I wake up, this all will be over, and I won't be meeting a matron."

Earl drove the Dodge through the village and up a long hill where big houses overlooked wide lawns and the ocean on the left, and old farmhouses guarded walled pastures on the right. He took the third road on the right after leaving the village. It was dirt, rutted with shallow washouts; the tops of boulders protruded. "Are you sure," he had said to Battles after following him to the faded red barn behind the white colonial house, "are you sure I'm gonna be able to get this fucking thing out of this place? 'Thout leaving the oil pan behind?" Battles had smirked at him, pulling the dust-cover off the blue roadster. "Well," he'd said, "I got it in here. And the guy that owned it's been getting it into places like this for years. Taking it out again, too. I didn't have any trouble, bringing it in here when I did. So, he did it, I did it, figure you can."

"Yeah," Earl had said, "but he knows the car. And you both know the roads. All the holes are, which rocks're too big to go over. I don't know any those things." Battles had bent over the cockpit and extracted the ignition key from the lock. It was fobbed on black leather that carried a Mercedes badge. Battles had held it up by the tip of the key, dangling the fob. "Come to Papa," he had said.

"And," Earl had said, "while he's been doing those

60

hings all these years, his neighbors and the other people that know him, they've been watching him do it.
udge must know a lot of people, he got to be a judge.
They see me in it, they're not gonna think: 'Geez, the
udge sure got tall. And younger.' They're gonna think:
Hey, that's not the judge. How come he's got the
udge's car? Somebody call up the sheriff, get a posse
started here.' Maybe that cop I met on the way down,
maybe tomorrow he's this side the road. I already told
you, he recognized me, and he knows what my license
says. It doesn't say 'judge' on it, not that I saw, and
what if he knows the judge? Maybe testified in his
court. Cops do that, you know. They do it a lot. They
know what judges look like. They know what they
don't look like, too."

"Look," Battles had said, "I know it's a sports car.
I know there's not many. But this here's still not the
only one the Germans made, you know? You put a different set of plates on this, something out of state, and
you just drive her up the road there and no one'll
bother you. Sunday traffic from the beaches, cops'll
have their hands full. Assholes running into each other,
assholes overheating their radiator, assholes running
out of gas? Assholes driving drunk? Assholes'll be everywhere, whole fucking *world* of assholes. All driving the
fucking cops nuts. Cops won't have the time to wonder
if some particular buggy's hot. Long's it keeps running,
don't clog up the road, that'll be all that they care."

"Yeah," Earl had said, "but that's you saying that.
You in a barn in a field. I'm gonna be the guy out on
the road. What if this fucking thing breaks? I don't
know these little sleds. 'Cept they can be delicate.
Maybe it doesn't like heat—that could be. Judge only
drove it cool nights. What if it decides throw a hose

61

on me? What if I'm one the guys that the cops stor to help? What the hell do I tell the cops then? 'Wel Mister Battles there, he said it'd be all right I just drov this puddle jumper up to Boston for the night. Sai you guys wouldn't mind.' Think that'll satisfy them do you? Think they'll say: 'Oh, that's fine.'? I got a close a look at that jail yesterday as I really want to ge I don't know if it's better, or worse, 'n the ones tha I've stayed in so far—and I don't want to find out, al right? The food's better in Cranston, it was out in Kan sas, well then, good, the inmates are lucky. But I don' want any more of that luck, no more of that kind o luck." He had turned to go out of the barn. "I'm no messing with this thing," he had said. "Get yoursel another boy."

Battles had grabbed him by the right forearm an spun him around. His face had hardened. "Now yo listen me, fucking punk. You got that? You just lister to me. You're here because you really owe somebod something, and that somebody owes me. You know what I did for a guy one time? I got him out of a fuck ing big jam he was in, because a fucking girl just fuck ing *died*. Because of me, it was a fucking *accident*, an that's *all* it fucking was, and it *stayed* that fucking way Not a fucking *murder* charge. Not some big fuckin thing that the papers would've gone and had a fuckin field day with. Just a fucking *accident*.

"Now," Battles had said, clenching his grip on Earl' arm, "I know how to *do* things, all right? I got a ki that doesn't know his ass from third base, and he want to go to Vietnam. Which means he gets it blown *off* and *I* end up supporting his kid and his fuckin' frog faced wife. You think I want to do that? I do not. S I called a guy I know and I said: 'Keep my fucking ki n Georgia.' And he called somebody in Washington, *and the kid is staying in Georgia.* So I know how to do things.

"Now," Battles had said, "the reason you are here is because the guy that owns this car's got a big fucking problem, and I got a connected problem. And I consequently called the same guy I called about my fuckin' kid, all right? It's not a problem like somebody fucking *dying* is a problem, but it's still a fucking problem. You can stand there and tell me: 'The judge must be stupid.' And I won't argue with you. The judge was fucking stupid, get himself into this, and I told him when he started that was what he fucking was, and he wasn't thinking straight. A lot of guys don't think straight, they get pussy on the brain. And you can tell me: *'You* were stupid.' I won't argue with that either. Maybe what I did was worse. Because *I* knew it was stupid, and I *was* thinking straight, and I still went along with it.

"But none of that fucking matters," Battles had said. "The judge asks me to help him? I hadda help the judge. He wants to come to my place on the Wednesday afternoons, use a room a couple hours? Well, I run a public place, and I rent rooms to people, and some of them get laid in them, or do some other things, and some of them aren't married, and some are but not to them, and some if you know what I mean can't get married anyway, 'cause guys can't marry guys, and gash can't marry gash.

"Well," Battles had said, "I told him, and I told him: 'This fucking town is small. People see what's going on, and they talk about it. They don't know who's doing it, they don't talk very much, but if they fucking *notice* you, they just won't shut fucking up. So

63

for Christ's sakes, all right? Do me a fucking favor. I know you done me a few favors, and I will do this for you. But: just be fucking careful.' And he said that he would." Battles had paused and laughed shortly. "I fuckin' near fuckin' died the first time I see this fuckin' car outside the room on a Wednesday afternoon. I mean: I fuckin' *died.* I call up the room extension, and I hear him breathing hard, and I said: 'Hey judge, all right? Sorry for the interruption. But parking that fucking car out there, with that fucking license plate, I mean, you call this "fucking careful"? You call this "being careful"? Like I thought we both agreed we'd fucking better be?' And you know what he says to me? 'My other car broke down.' He's a fucking wonder, he is, a fucking goddamned wonder."

Earl had looked down at the registration plate. Between the "Ocean State" and "Rhode Island" lettering were five capital letters reading "HONOR."

"Well," Battles had said, "I did, I guess, I scared the guy. I brought him back, his right mind. He didn't pull that fucking stunt again, about two years. And he stopped coming Wednesdays—Mondays he came in, about ten different cars. I think he must've been borrowing them, lawyers that he knew. There's a lot of lawyers I know, wouldn't bother them at all if you caught them fucking whores. Everybody knows they do it, so who cares if they get seen? And I figure, couple months go by, nothing seems to happen, must've got away with it. Which was where *I* was stupid. Should've known that one time was enough to do the damage. Might as well've put an ad in the fucking *Journal*— once they saw this fucking car, everybody knew. After that they all were watching. Pretty soon they tipped the cops. And the cops don't like this judge, or at least the top cop don't. Thinks the judge's been a little easy on bad guys. So, I don't think they were sitting out there, camped out watching us, but I do think they told some people, who it was that tipped them off: 'If another day comes when you're sure he's in there, drop a dime and let us know. We'll handle it from there.'

"I look at my watch. What good does that do me? I don't know how long he's been in there. He comes in at various times. The point is I don't know if he just got there, and maybe he's lucky, and nobody noticed it yet, or if he's been fucking his brains out for hours, and fifty guys noticed the car. I think: The fuck difference does it make? One guy saw it, or fifty? All it takes is the one—one's all it takes. I better go back in the office. Because, see, I can't just go down to the pay phone at Chuckie's, call him from there and scream at him. For one thing, the phones in the rooms only ring or go out after they go through the switchboard. For another thing, the pay phone at Chuckie's is inside of Chuckie's damned store. Right next to the cash registers. Where my fucking ex-wife works, and she don't fuckin' like me, and'd only jap me if she could. And she's got ears on her like a fuckin' radar dish. I'm surprised the navy didn't grab her up and take her down the boatyard there, install her on one of the subs. I talk to him and she can hear me, might as well call Walter Cronkite.

"I put the Lincoln back. I go back in the office. I call up his room. He answers the phone. Sounds like he's running the Preakness. I say to him: 'Judge, I know you're my pal. How come I can't go for some beer?' And he says: 'What?' I say: 'It's a very hot day, and I see I run out of beer. So I think: "Well in that case, I'll have to go out, pick up a six-pack of beer." But then

I go out, and I see that car, and therefore I'm back in my office. Because I got to ask you, you out of your mind? Have you lost all your fuckin' *grip?* Because that's what it looks like to me, you bring that car here again.'

"He says: 'Jeez, Jimmy, I hadda. I'm on vacation. I been on vacation all month. Which is why I haven't been in. My own car's the beach house, the Cape. My wife's sister's with her and my youngest's at home. So I hadda leave them my usual car, and then I come over, the bus, and there's traffic. I didn't have time, make arrangements, the city, borrow somebody else's today. But a month is too long, go without seeing Lauren. I *hadda* see Lauren, 'fore August. A month's too long a time. It's only one time. Why get so upset? Nothing happened, I did it before, you got so upset. Not a goddamned thing ever happened.'

"I say: 'Judgie, my pal, something happened. Believe me. What happened's the very same reason, you shouldn't't've done it again. Now take my advice for a change, will you, please? Get dressed. Get dressed as fast as you can. Come out alone, and get in your car, and get your ass out of this place. Maybe so far, just *maybe* so far, nobody's had time to get down here. I don't think the chances of that're too good, but maybe your fuckin' luck holds. So I'm going out for some beer now, all right? It's your own good, you know, I am telling you this. Be a good pal and take my advice.'

"I hang up. I go through the drill with the sign and the door. I act like everything's normal. I get into my car and I drive up to Chuckie's, exchange a few digs with my ex, like I'm not in a hurry and everything's peachy, nothing to worry about. I get back the motel and I pull in the lot, and the first thing I see is the car.

'The fucking asshole's still *here.*' I pretend it means nothing, nothing, just one of my guests, and I park in my usual place. I walk slow to the office and open it up, put my beer in the refrigerator. I am wondering if I get in more trouble if I do what I want, which is kill him. I decide that I probably will. I take one of the beers and go out on the porch. I sit down in the chair and I sip it. All I am doing is having a beer, wait for the night clerk to come. *I'm* not watching the parking lot and the road like a fucking eagle looking for a fucking fish. No sir, not me. I'm just sitting on my own porch, having a nice cold beer. I never even saw that unmarked cruiser with the two suits in it come rolling down the road like it's going to a fire, then slow down fast and pull into my lot, nice and quiet. I never even saw the two suits inside it, or the guy that wasn't driving start rolling down the window with this camera in his hand. It was just, I just happened to decide, you know, I hadda go inside for something that I all of a sudden remembered I hadda do in there. Could've been they pulled around, like I hear, so the guy with the camera could just sit there shooting picture after picture. I certainly didn't see it. I was onna phone.

"I said: 'Judge, there is a problem. There's a problem with two guys out there in a car, and one of them has got a camera, which my guess is he is using. I bet he's got film in it too. Now I don't know if you still got some lead left in your pencil, and I don't know how long these guys've got to sit around in my yard taking pictures, but I think what you and your roomie should do there is see if she can get another rise out of you, you know what I mean. Or if that doesn't work, get the Bible out the bureau there and read some prayers to each other. Because if what's going on that I think's

67

going on, you're gonna need all the help you can get anyway so you might as well start applying. And anything's better'n you running out there right now, which you should've done the first time I called you, and getting your picture took, too.'

"He sounded like he swallowed something that he didn't finish chewing. 'You think they're cops?' he says.

" 'Well, I don't know that for sure,' I say. 'They might be from one of those outfits that makes the picture postcards, and they picked my lot for the view. Or maybe they're from Duncan Hines, right? And I'm getting recommended, his next guide. Or it could be the Beatles checked in last night, and the night clerk forgot to mention it, and these guys out there're from *Time*. Does it matter? You just stay fuckin' put, and they're still here, it gets dark, *don't* turn the fuckin' lights on. Don't make any noise, even if you *don't* hear anything outside the door. Don't run the TV. Those guys're as quiet as cats. Don't open it, somebody knocks. If they pull that routine, talking loud: "I know he's in there, goddamnit—let's just kick the thing down," don't fall for it, all right? They need a warrant for that. Don't flush the fucking toilet. Gotta pee? Fine, then so piss down the side of the bowl. Don't let it splash. Don't run the fucking sink. Don't go in the fucking shower and start playing games in there. Those guys are likely to come in here, ask me, see my register. And I got to show it to them. That's the law. And don't be surprised if that happens. I'm not fucking around with you here. If these guys're cops, like my guess is, they are, they get their asses made by U.S. Steel, the very best grade. Rust's the only thing bothers them—they can sit on those asses forever. And if they do decide it's time, go and get a bite to eat, two more'll probably show up to replace them. So I'm not telling you, this's guaranteed to do it, get you out of this. But at least it won't make it worse'n it already is, and it might at least save something. Leave you one of your balls, at least.'

" 'I got to go home,' he says. 'My wife's expecting me.'

" 'You go out there,' I say, 'and she'll be divorcing you. Which she'll probably be doing anyway, those car pictures hit the *Journal*. Just don't make it worse, 's what I say.'

" 'I'll have to call her,' he says. 'Call her and tell her something. Get me an outside line.'

" 'The fuck I will,' I say. 'That's a long-distance call, your house over the Cape. It'll show up on the toll sheets the cops'll then get, probably already ordered them up, and if they don't get your actual picture, well that's almost as good. Who the hell else'd be calling your wife from my joint the same day her car's here? You wanna explain that, the papers? Now, stay put. Only one of us's thinking right here, and he's not the one in the room with the broad.'

" 'I can't stay trapped in here, Jimmy,' he says. 'I got to get out of this room.'

" 'No, you got it backwards,' I say. 'You're the one that wouldn't leave it when you could've. Now you can't, so stay. And keep something else in mind. I'm stuck in this office, too, and you're the one that did it. 'Less of course I want to pose for them too. Which I don't. Cops got enough pictures of me. Don't answer the phone again if it rings. Those cops do come in here, ask see my register, well, Room Four's vacant on it. The phone rings after this time, it's them. You answer it, not in the book, this fact could get me in trouble.

69

If they ask me to show the room, as they also can do, I'll tell them fucking lock's jammed. I'm waiting for the guy to come fix it.'

" 'The window in the back,' he says.

" 'Bullshit,' I say, " 'the window in the back.'' You don't think they figure that out? Oh, that'd make a great shot, you and Sister Mary Agnes climbing out the window. What do I say: "Well, they eloped?" No, just sit tight and try to think of what we're gonna do, you finally can go out, get you out of this—if there's any way. I see them leave finally, I will come out, start making a routine inspection. You'll hear me knock on Three, and say who I am, and either someone answers or I go in myself. Then I'll go to Five, 'cause we know Four's door is busted, and go through the same thing again. And then it's safe to come out. Unless, of course, they want to join me, in which case you'll hear us talking. Then, well, don't come out.'

"Well," Battles had said, "this's what we come up with, all right? He's not only got a lot of things, he's got to explain his wife, but it's also, he's gonna have to give up the car. The cops finally leave, it's after eleven, and I sneak him around to the back to where my wife's in her car, and the broad meantime takes off in her own. My wife drives him down to fuckin' La Guardia, and he takes a plane to the Cape. Rents a car at the airport, he says he got Providence, goes home and tells her hers's been stolen, he's out on a long lunch, the boys, having a few after that, and then they all took in a show. All this's going on, I call my lawyer, Providence, tell him the name the judge gave me, his best friend in the world. Who's supposed to call the cops there, tell him he's the judge and the Mercedes's been stolen. And that he's on his way back the Cape,

70

they can call him in the morning, tell him if they got it back or he makes a full report. I drive his car up this place, belongs a friend of mine that isn't even home, and lock it up in here. Then I walk four miles home.

"Now I am telling you," Battles had said, "I know this isn't taking candy, babies, anything, but something that's got to be done. It's almost two weeks since they filled out the hot sheet, and most cops see sixty a day. So hundreds of other cars made the list since then, and they're not just lookin' for this one. The tank's full—I checked that. You won't have to stop. Get a new plate, stick it on, and drive careful. Take it the crusher. Destroy it. Tell the guy that you owed that you're even."

In the deepening twilight, Earl stopped the Dodge at the edge of the pavement where it intersected with the dirt road that led to the barn. He backed it about forty feet up the dirt road and shut off the lights. Penny stirred in the passenger seat. He put the transmission in Park and set the hand brake. He shut off the engine. He went to the trunk with the keys and opened the lid. He removed the tool kit and the flashlight, and unwrapped New Jersey 7J7-N54 from the blanket. He took the Dopp Kit out. He shut the trunk and returned to the driver's seat and restarted the engine. He shook Penny awake.

"Huh?" she said.

"You're going," he said. "Wake up and drive."

She frowned. "Where am I going? Where am I?"

"You're inna fuckin' woods in Lafayette, Rhode Island," he said. "Home is where you're going. Now get out and swap seats with me."

"I can slide over," she said.

"No," he said, "I want to see you walk, even just a little bit."

"I'm not drunk," she said.

"Look," he said, "I'm not saying that. But you might be a little asleep, and I don't want you, falling back into it, soon's you get out on the road."

She said "Shit" and opened the door. She got out and slammed it, walking uncertainly on the edge of the dirt road, her left hand brushing the fender, the hood, and the fender until she reached the driver's door.

"Very good," he said.

"Shit," she said. "This's gotta be the most insane thing you've made me do yet. I don't even know where I am."

"I told you where you are," he said.

"I don't know how to get out of here," she said, peering at the dashboard.

"Put it in Drive," he said. "Take the brake off. Roll down to the end, pavement here and turn left. That's Route One-eighty-nine. Don't take any turns. Just stay on it. Route One-eighty-nine—you got that? Takes you to I-Ninety-five. Going north. That's it. Clear on that?"

She nodded. "I could still use that drink," she said. "You should've bought me a drink."

"Have your drink, you get home," he said. "Least you're going home. I got to go to Vermont. I don't step on a fuckin' snake first."

"Wasn't my idea, champ," she said, grabbing the gearshift lever. "This whole party's your great idea." The Dodge rolled down to the road. Earl with the plate and the tools and the flashlight started up the dirt road toward the barn in the hot dusk. Some night birds cried in the air.

7

On the last Tuesday in July, Ed Cobb drove his maroon Chrysler 300F to Donald Beale's Chrysler-Plymouth dealership in South Burlington, Vermont, trying to avoid puddles left by severe early morning thunderstorms and cursing his decision to spend the previous Saturday waxing the car. Beale was in his office on the second floor, talking on the telephone, his feet on the sill of the picture window that looked down on the showroom. He waved to Cobb to come up. Cobb acknowledged the invitation, but did not act on it until he had swapped views about the surprisingly tenacious Red Sox with Dennis McCallum, the sales manager, and Paul Oakes, one of the salesmen.

"It's *partly* this Conigliaro kid," McCallum said. "Jee-*zuss*, but he can hit. But it's mostly Yastrzemski, I think, that's keeping them in the thing."

Oakes disagreed. "I think it's the manager," he said. "They had both those two guys last year, and look where they ended up. Was it all Herman's fault? Yeah, I think it was. He'd've took the credit if they'd've won. So they lose? He takes the blame. This Dick Williams, boy, he is something else. Took us long enough, but we finally found ourselves a Williams who thinks more about winning the game'n he does about his own glory. Manager this year's the difference. Don't care what line of work you're in, and I've been in this one a long time, manager's always the difference."

McCallum laughed. "Ain't he something?" he said to Cobb. "Every time he's on the Saturday card, and he really wants it off, he starts in the first of the week, shinin' up to me like I'm a seventeen-year-old blonde with big tits, telling me how he respects me, because my brilliant mind."

"I didn't even see the card," Oakes said. "I didn't even see it."

"Oakesie," McCallum said, "in the first place, I never keep a salesman unless I'm sure he can count. Neither did Don's father. You were here when I was born, so I know you can do it. I also know you do. It's been three weeks since your last weekend tour, so you know you're next in the order. In the second place, I was out in the back with the boss. You come in here this morning, and I see you through the window in my office. You go in, peek at the card. And I say to Don: 'You wanna bet a cold one Oakesie's in my shirt all day?' And Don says: 'Why? You got him down for Saturday?' And Don wouldn't take the bet. He knows you, Oakesie, just like I do. So when it don't work with me, whatever story you cooked up, and it won't, forget about going to Donald crying. 'Cause it ain't gonna work with him, neither."

"You should run for the House, Paul," Cobb said. "You'd fit right in, in Montpelier."

"I'm not qualified to be a politician," Oakes said.

74

"I never stole a thing in my whole life, and I never tell a lie. What I need's one of those state jobs you're always giving your friends. Where you don't have to get anybody to vote for you, and because of that they give you money for not working. That's what I should have."

"You'd be great at it," McCallum said. "Look at all the experience you got."

"Jesus, Dennis," Cobb said, "how the hell can this guy make a living in this business? He's been here since Noah, and he doesn't lie or steal? Whaddaya keep him around for? Lead the Bible readings?"

"Same reason NBC hired Carson when Jack Paar retired,' McCallum said. "Everybody puts in a hard day, they like some comedy. Course Oakesie doesn't always mean to be funny, but that's when we get the most laughs—when he doesn't mean to."

"What the hell were you doing, Dennis?" Oakes said. "Out in the back of the shop? Thought you're the one says it's dirty out there, guys with all grease on their hands, cars all apart on the floor. Some customer dame with a short skirt on out there, bending over the trunk? I've been here over thirty-six years. You've been here now at least ten. Never knew you before to go out back in the shop."

"Don's got a new toy," McCallum said to Cobb. "Make him show it to you, 'fore you leave."

"Another one?" Cobb said. "What is it this time, a lake steamboat?"

"Make him show it to you," McCallum said. "It's a nifty little thing."

"Where's he *put* all this stuff?" Oakes said. "His father's ghost must be spinning. Between the motorcy-

75

cles and the T-bird and the old 'Vette and Healey, and the MG and the Jag—where's he put it all? He's gonna have to have a garage at home bigger'n the one he's got here. Which is bigger'n he needs."

"He bought this one to sell, Oakesie," McCallum said. "I asked him that, and he said he's gonna sell it, right person comes along. Said: 'I got to show some of the front-room guys that it really can be done. Actually sell a car. I don't wanna sell one from stock, 'cause they'll say I'm stealing from them. So I buy this one and sell it, and then I tell, say, Oakesie: "Hey, how come I can sell a nine-year-old German car, for big bucks, and you can't sell a brand-new Chrysler? For almost the same money. What's the matter with you?" It's a training thing.' "

Cobb laughed. "I'm gonna go up and see him," he said. "Nice talking to you guys again."

"Yeah," Oakes said, "but I'm still voting Republican."

"Course you are, Oakesie," Cobb said. "We never count on you guys. We know you do the best you can—reading's hard for you. But we're philosophical, 'cause you're a dying breed. And we're getting the young folks."

"You're getting them, all right," Oakes said. "You're getting them killed in Vietnam. And with the other war you got, the one on poverty, you're killing them, with kindness, at home. Give the guy with the scar on his belly, holding the dogs by their ears, give him long enough in the White House, all you're gonna have in this country's longhairs and Republicans. The Republicans won't vote for you, and the longhairs won't vote at all—they're stoned out of their minds all the time. So who's gonna keep your jobs for you, huh? You'll all be on welfare yourselves. Which is probably why you're so hot for it. Making sure you can survive."

"Don't envy you, Dennis," Cobb said. "Hope Don pays you a lot if this's what you've got to put up with."

Donald Beale had framed pictures of his father and his grandfather, and the two of them with him, crowding the top of the credenza behind his desk. The chronology went from his right to left, starting with the sepia photo of his grandfather standing stiffly beside the gas pump outside the first Beale dealership; the sign in the background advertised Beale Pierce-Arrow Motorcars, Winooski, Vt. In the middle there was a black-and-white picture of his grandfather, his father, himself, and his brother, the men standing behind the boys with their hands on the children's shoulders. There was a banner behind them that read "SEE THE NEW CHRYSLER AIRFLOW." Next to the end on the left there was a color picture of Donald Beale and his father in front of a hexagonal white bandstand with a banner that read "CONCERTS EVERY SUNDAY NIGHT. COURTESY BEALE CHRYSLER PLYMOUTH, S. BURLINGTON." The last picture was in color and showed Donald Beale standing in front of the brick colonial showroom, holding an oil portrait of his father and an enlargement of the sepia photograph of his grandfather. The banner on the front of the building read "BEALE CHRYSLER PLYMOUTH—40 YEARS OF INTEGRITY." On the wall above the credenza were numerous plaques for dealer achievements. On the wall to his right were Beale's diplomas from Dartmouth College and the Boston University Law School.

"Been lollygaggin' downstairs with the no-goods

that work for me, Ed?" Beale said. He was signing a stack of printed forms. "Hard enough to get those guys to work, 'thout having you distract 'em." He signed the last of the papers and threw the stack into the Out box. He stood up and grinned, and they shook hands. "Good to see you, old pal," he said. "Have a seat." He sat down.

"That Oakesie is a piece of work," Cobb said. "I suppose if you can't find a couple of hungry rats to put in your jockstrap, the next best thing'd be to have that bastard in your hair every day."

"Isn't he something?" Beale said. "Been around forever, and you know if my grandfather hired him, and my father kept him on, he must have something on the ball. But you look at him, you talk to him, you say to yourself: 'He's a *sales*man? This guy's about as smooth as a barbed wire on your ass.' But let me tell you something: Oakesie sells those cars. Oakesie knows his trade. He's got a bunch of skinflints that think every eight years or so's about the right time to trade in. They bring in these jalopies all clapped out and rusted through, tires're bald and brakes're gone—'Now, no point repairin' her this summer, Edith; gonna trade her two summers from now'—haven't had any real service 'cept what they got in the barn from the people who own the things; it's a wonder they don't feed them hay, but they take better care of their cows—and the first guy they ask for is Oakesie. Never even occurs to these people that maybe Oakesie's moved on since the last time they're in, back 'fore the Spanish-American War, should be up in heaven by now. 'Nope, bought this car from Oakesie. Seems to've worked pretty good. Need a new one now, though, so I come to see Oakesie.' And so Oakesie's the man that they see."

"Well, cripes," Cobb said, "but you can't make much money, the resale on junkers. Who the hell can you sell those wrecks to?"

"You can if you don't pay much for 'em," Beale said. "And Oakesie doesn't pay very much. That guy knows down to the *penny* what the margin is on a car. Look, I run the business, right? I own the goddamned thing. And I know what the damned margins are, plus or minus a ten-dollar bill. You let us load one up on you, well, we make about twenty-six percent on the air conditioning, the fancy radio, the power windows and the seats, the whitewalls and the fake wire wheels. And if you want the bucket seats—'My God, you'll pay for *leather?*'—we've got ourselves a nice fat cushion, and you'll get a trade-in offer that'll make you think we're crazy. On the base car, stripped, we gross somewhere between thirteen and eighteen percent, depending on which base car you happen to decide on. So you add the two things together, how much we make on the stripper, how much we make on the goodies, and subtract that from the price of the car, and that's what our gross profit is. *Gross,* I said. We still gotta pay the heat and the light, and the real-estate taxes, the mechanics and all of our people. But if you order a car that costs four grand, and add two more grand in equipment, we stand to make eleven hundred bucks. If this was a charity, we'd sell you that car for forty-nine hundred dollars. But it's not. It's a business.

"That's what people don't understand," Beale said. "It's the same thing as the things that you do. We can only work with what we've got to work with. You bring

79

in an El Ratto we can sell for two hundred, it's gonna cost us a half a buck to clean it up before we get even that. So we're gonna offer you one fifty for the thing. And you're gonna tell us the guy down the street offered you twice as much. Which means you want us to give you a buck and a half out of our eleven hundred. Maybe a buck seventy-five, if we've got to better his offer. Our profit is now not eleven no more: it's nine fifty, or maybe it's nine and a quarter. Are we gonna do that? Sure. I'd rather make nine twenty-five any day, 'n go home on empty at night. But, are we gonna give you half our profit? When we're making no money on your car? Are we gonna give you eight hundred bucks, something in that ballpark there? Hate to tell you this, friend, but we're not.

"The beauty of Oakesie is they believe this. He will not let them steal cars. On the other hand, they also know, he won't steal their cars from them. And since Oakesie knows, to the penny, how much margin he has got, the deals don't take long, and stick. Nobody ever backs out. His customers go for the strippers—he's got people don't even buy *heat*, for God's sake, let alone a damned radio—and they run them into the ground. But they keep coming back, to see Oakesie. And that's why my father kept him around, and why I do the same."

"Yeah, but every eight years?" Cobb said. "How can you make any money selling cheap cars to people that keep them eight years, and only bring them back in when they're ruined?"

"You got a lot of them, you can," Beale said. "And he's got a lot of them. He's also got, I think one of his daughters married a Canuck or something, but he's got

80

some kind of great reputation with the migrant workers, you know? Comes the apple-picking season, all of a sudden we got all these guys named André in here, looking for cheap cars. And Oakesie's the man they want to see. They heard he's got cheap cars. Well, they heard right. Last fall there was one day when Oakesie set a record. Sold sixteen clunkers off the back lot, some of which were sitting there since around Easter, I think. We added it up. We owned the bunch of them for somewhere in the neighborhood of twenty-seven hundred bucks, and he sold them one by one that day, for fifty-three hundred bucks. Cash. That is twenty-six hundred gross profit, to get which on a good day with the wind behind you, you'd have to sell about three brand-new yachts. To people with nothing to trade. Know how many people've done that? I don't know any, myself."

"Yeah," Cobb said, "but the cars can't last. Don't the Andrés come back here and bitch?"

"Nope," Beale said, "they expect them to die. They don't expect much, cheap cars. It gets them home, they can keep it going through the winter, it staggers back down here in the fall and they sell it the next poorer guy. Then they come back and see Oakesie. You know what his secret is? Every one of those clunkers's got a brand-new battery. Tires're smooth, suspension's shot, steering's pretty slack. But that sick old bastard starts in the morning, and that's what brings them back." He paused. "Those that don't get killed, of course, sliding off the road."

"You guys're asking for trouble, you know," Cobb said. "That Nader thing's just the beginning. He can wallop Corvair out of business, all by his virtual self, lots of big heroes like me in the government, we tend to pay some attention. Maybe we can do something like that, get ourselves idolized. And also, perhaps, re-elected. Or move on to some bigger job."

"Ahh," Beale said, "you're not gonna do anything, and you're not gonna tell people, either. I know what you want, and you know what I want, and we've both known those two things since college. I'm gonna help you get what you want, you're gonna help me get mine. We've been doing things this way about twenty years, and so far things've been fine. We had fun in the practice, and we weren't going broke, but we were not gonna get rich. So we did something else, and we're still having fun, and we're still helping each other."

"One of us is getting rich," Cobb said. "The other one isn't."

"Sure you are," Beale said. "You're just as rich as I am. Difference is, I'm rich in terms of money. You're rich in terms of power. That's what I mean, the deal is. We trust each other, okay? I do you favors with money? You do me favors with power. Today, since you come to see me, I figure it's money you need."

Cobb frowned. "I will," he said, "I probably will. If I can do what it seems like I have to. But right now, today, I'm not asking for money. What I'm asking for's honest advice."

"Uh huh," Beale said, "that's what I thought: today you come here for money."

"Jesus, Don, pay attention," Cobb said. "I said I want some advice. I've got to think things out, which means I've got to tell someone I trust, with some brains, to help me think my way through this thing."

"Son of a bitch," Beale said. "I guess you don't want money."

"I'm getting rumblings," Cobb said. "Rumblings I don't like. There's nomination papers getting circulated in the Second District. For a long-haired kid named Greenberg. He wants our nomination. I never heard of him."

Beale laughed. "So he can run against Bob Wainwright? Leave him do it. Bob'll cream him. That district's been Republican since Hector was a pup. Why's the kid think Bob's still there? Because no Democrat can beat him, and so no one wants to try. After he gets through with that, he can try kamikaze school. Get a plane for his next trip."

"Don," Cobb said, "goddamnit, you've really got to listen. This kid gets the papers in, no one else even files. Even when he loses he will be the power there. That's what these kids're doing now. They've finally smartened up. Some of them, at least. After this kid takes his beating, he will still have something. He will have something I don't want him to have: a fucking organization, in the Second District, and a bunch of committed little rich fuckers, with nothing to do but make trouble. For me. They all think he's running against Lyndon Baines Johnson, and this goddamned war that they hate. Not against Robert Wainwright— LBJ's their target. When they lose they're not gonna stop. They're not going to go away. They're going to start looking around for the next thing, something to do with their time. And that's going to be state politics. They're going to start messing with me.

"I've gone to a lot of trouble here," Cobb said, "and you've spent a lot of money, building up what Russ

Stanley calls 'Cobb's coalition,' and I don't want to wake up some morning and find out I've got competition. There's not enough of us yet to survive internal fights. I got trouble enough keeping order, maintaining a group that'll do what I say, without any traitors and stragglers. Somebody sets up another machine, and I don't care how weak it is, I lose my sanctions—you see? If I say to a guy: 'I want you to do this,' and he says: 'But I want to do that,' I can't say to the guy: 'Hey, you do this, all right? Otherwise you're fucked.' Because he will just look me straight in the eye, and say: 'Fuck you. I'll go somewhere else.' Because he'll have somewhere else to go. Which he doesn't have, right now. It won't be enough to support him, and he'll get his ass whipped for him. But it will be enough to persuade all the others: it's okay to break ranks. Jesus," Cobb said, "now I know how Captain Bligh felt. And what he should've done. I got a mutiny on my hands here. Got to lash the bastards right now."

"So, what do you want to do, Ed?" Beale said. "You asking me if you should run?"

"No, I'm not," Cobb said. "And if you're asking me if I'd be willing to run, I'm saying 'No way in the world.' In the first place, Congress doesn't interest me. If the incumbent was Peter Rabbit, I wouldn't challenge him. I don't want the goddamned job. And this is a good thing, because Bob Wainwright's not a rabbit, and as long as he remembers what to do, breathing in and breathing out, he will be the congressman.

"What I'm asking you," Cobb said, "is for the name of somebody who can take out papers too. And then—yeah, then you'll be right—some money to support him. Not much. My guy in Washington, this's the guy

I called for Earl, he says he'll get me some dough from his people, if we get somebody that at least when we put him up, people won't laugh at him. So all I need is just enough to get him through the fucking primary, and beat this kid, Greenberg. Then we can cheap it out in the general, let Wainwright win, as he's going to. Tell Stanley at the paper that we're philosophical— 'Every journey of a thousand miles starts with a single step'—and we'll try again next time. 'gallant fight,' and all that shit. 'Really sorry that we lost.' But actually, we won."

"You know more names'n I do," Beale said. "You've done enough favors for people. There's not a state agency doesn't have your guys, loafing around for the paycheck. That's not what you're asking me."

"The names I know," Cobb said, "the names I know're guys that in the first place wouldn't do it, because they know what'd happen. And in the second place, the ones that would, nobody's heard of them. Which is why they've got nothing to lose. The first group won't run, and the second group's useless. At least that's what I think right now. Pretend we're back in college, staying up late and still talking. Make believe we've still got the office, long after dinner, we're there. Trying to figure out what's going on. 'What the hell're we gonna do now?' I always sharpened you up, then. I'm the one that told you: 'We shut down, and you sell cars, and I will run for office.' And goddamnit, I was right. Now you sharpen me up, all right? What the hell do I do now?"

Beale stood up. "Come on," he said. "Got something to show you. Come with me out to the back. I've got to think about this."

8

"It's sort of swoopy looking, isn't it?" Cobb said, studying the Mercedes from behind the left rear fender. "What the hell is it?"

"One-ninety SL," Beale said. "'Fifty-nine. It's not your XK One-twenty Jag or anything, but the fuckin' Huns did a good job with the looks. Can't get out of its own way, of course—little four-banger hauling two tons of iron. Practically has to go and lie down for a while, you ask it to go over forty. Gearshift's like a toilet handle; have to jiggle it around until you find what you want. But it's comfortable. Get a nice sunny day, put the top down, you're in no particular hurry? It's great. Even hear the radio. I dunno what the zero-to-sixty is. Probably about an hour. But it's a pretty little thing. You should buy it. Give you some class for a change."

"I don't need any class," Cobb said. "My constituents wouldn't stand for it. They love me as I am. Vulgar, low class, brute force and plenty of it."

"Gwendolyn'd love it," Beale said.

"Gwendolyn'd also love winters on the Riviera," Cobb said. "A charge account at Tiffany's, and caviar

86

for breakfast. But she didn't have good judgment. Married beneath her station. And there's a limit to how far I'm willing to go to pretend that she does. Or can, as far as that goes. Not on the salary I make."

"Hey," Beale said, "you had to know. Second wives can be expensive. You get no sympathy here."

"Speaking of which," Cobb said, "what're you gonna get for this thing?" He ran his hand over the fender.

"I don't really know yet," Beale said. "It's got a low clock, twenty-one thousand miles. And the broad who owned it obviously didn't drive it in the winter—not a speck of rust on it. I assume they use salt in New Jersey, and it does the same thing to metal down there that it does to metal up here. Probably six grand or so. Maybe more."

"New Jersey?" Cobb said. "How'd you get a car from New Jersey?"

"I didn't," Beale said. "Earl brought it to me. He's the one that got it. Some dame he knew from New York. She's some rich guy's mistress, and she wants to retire. Or else he is letting her go. So she's selling off all of her presents. Earl knew her from when he played ball."

"You took a car off of Earl?" Cobb said. "You took a car from Earl, a six- or seven-thousand-dollar item, and you let me touch the thing without asbestos gloves? What're you, *nuts?*"

"It's not hot," Beale said. "This broad's a honey that he used to know, back when he's still playing ball. He was down in New York last weekend, and he runs into her at a club. They cut up a few, the old touches, and she says she's selling her car, moving back to the city, as soon's she finds a guy with some cash. But apparently she's not telling the rich guy she's selling the presents he gave her. So she wants the car to be out of New York. And he asks her how much she wants for the thing, and she says about half what it's worth. So he gives her the three K, and she gives him the keys, and he drives the car up to me."

"Donald," Cobb said, "this car is hot. When'd you ever know Earl to have three thousand bucks in his pocket?"

"Several times," Beale said. "Several times, Ed, back when he was illegal. I never ask Earl, it's my policy, where he is getting his money. I've usually got a pretty fair notion, but I don't want it confirmed."

"And he'd lie if you asked him," Cobb said.

"Probably," Beale said. "He's lied to me in the past. In this life you get to pick friends. Not your brothers. Brothers, you take what they issue."

"Have you got a bill of sale on this thing?" Cobb said. "A paper that says that you bought it? From someone who actually owned it?"

"Not yet," Beale said. "That's why it's not for sale yet. Earl's getting the paper for me."

"Oh for Christ's sake," Cobb said. "I do not fuckin' believe this."

"Look," Beale said, "the fact that a guy does something once, and gets in the crap to his eyebrows, that doesn't mean that he did it again, or that's always what he is doing. Now think about it for a minute. Earl tells me he runs into this dame in a club in New York, and he knows her. Does Earl know the clubs in New York? He sure does. He knows clubs in New York that I never heard of, and wouldn't go into if I did. Does Earl know

88

the chippies in New York? You bet he does. Earl knows some broads in New York that'd set off a general alarm. Are those girls getting older? Well, you are, and I am, and Earl is, so it stands to reason they are. Do they get the boot from their meal tickets when they start to get long in the tooth? Sounds plausible to me. Who the hell else, 'cept for guys like Earl, would a rich bastard's girlfriend sell cars to? She wanted the cash. Earl had some cash. She wanted the car out of New York. Earl's going out of New York. She didn't happen to have a bill of sale on her. So that's coming to me in the mail."

"So why didn't he drive it to Boston?" Cobb said. "Put it on *his* dealer's lot?"

"Because Waldo sells cars to niggers," Beale said, "and some of those niggers're white. Guys who haven't got money. You're not gonna buy this little buggy with no unemployment check, and you're not gonna leave it sitting out on your lot in West Roxbury all night unless you really think it'd look a lot better with the top and the tires all slashed. There's a reason why Waldo took Earl on, you know. It's because the stuff that Waldo sells is cheap, so his salesmen don't make much money, and only desperate guys want the jobs."

"It's also because Earl's brother guaranteed Earl's draw," Cobb said. "And Earl's brother did it to get him out of here, and Waldo and Earl both know that." He frowned. "I hope," he said, "I don't think what I hope, but I'm hoping, that what I am thinking's not true."

"Like what?" Beale said.

"Like maybe this little item's connected to my errand that you sent Earl out on. You *sure* that he got this car from a broad that lives in New Jersey?"

89

Beale shrugged. "I'm sure he told me just what I just told you," he said. "I'm sure it had a Jersey plate on it, when he drove it in here. And I'm sure not going to sell it till I get that bill of sale."

"Because," Cobb said, "if that silly son of a bitch went down to Rhode Island Saturday, and clipped this thing off Battaglia, or someone Battaglia knows, he might as we"ve bought a gun, and one bullet, and just shot himself in the head. Or if he got it from Battaglia, and Battles gave it to him, he might as well've brought you a time bomb. Because something's very wrong. I wish I knew what Battles wanted done when he called me up. I mean, I know it was something shady, 'cause that's all that Battles does. But what it was, I didn't know. Just that he needed a guy in the car business, and that was all I knew. Earl tell you what Battles wanted done?"

Beale laughed. *"Tell* me?" he said. "He only bitched about an hour when he got in here. 'You and your fuckin' friends. Was it Ed Cobb, got me in this?' "

"Did you tell him?" Cobb said.

"I did not," Beale said. "He suspects it was you, and he's got more'n a feeling it was somehow tied up to Hank Briggs. But I know a lot of things about Earl, and I suspect even more, and I tell him nothing, myself. I know my brother pretty well. I'm sorry his life's in the sewer, and also his girl has to hook. But I still tell him no more'n I think's absolutely necessary. Earl's not trustworthy."

"He's worse'n that," Cobb said. "People also remember Earl. They remember the guy. When I called Battles back, he knew the name right off. Well, not right off—took him two or three minutes to place it.

Something another guy could do, and get away with it because no one remembers his face, well, if Earl does it, they do. Describe the guy down to his hangnails. What'd he want Earl to do?"

"Seems he's got a couple of pals," Beale said. "That's what he told Earl, at least. And one of them's a lawyer that does mostly wills for people, and the other one's an auctioneer. When the old people kick off, the lawyer hires the auctioneer to appraise the estates and then sell off the stuff. And the three of them've cooked up this scheme where the appraisals're too low, and the assets get knocked down cheap, to straws, and then the straws resell them, and these birds split the take. But apparently some of their people're getting kind of nervous. I guess some of the heirs've been suing, and they're afraid unless they change their patterns of doing business, someone's going to catch on, and nail them. So now what they're looking for's out-of-state buyers, that won't look like sidekicks of theirs. To buy up the houses and cars and that stuff, and they want Earl to take some of the cars. Or talk Waldo into doing it would be closer to the truth, since nobody in the whole wide world ever takes more'n one check from Earl. Anyway, it's strictly a fake paper deal, but it looks like the straight up-and-up."

"Is he going to talk Waldo into doing it?" Cobb said. "I've got to tell you, Don: I can't do it again. If Earl gets in the shit again, and gets convicted of something, I can't make it go away twice."

"Ed," Beale said, "Waldo's kind of a funny mixture of ingredients, like that stuff they sell for headaches— 'a combination of ingredients.' Only none of them match each other. He's got no compunction at all

91

about selling cars to people who can't afford them and should be getting new kids' shoes instead of buying a new car. And he runs the cheapest operation I have ever seen. But he's also got this mammoth motorboat that costs a whole bundle for gas, and he's still playing basketball with guys half his age, and cripes, you should see his wife's clothes. *She*'s pretty plain looking, but her clothes're gorgeous. Waldo knows exactly where the lines are, and he doesn't step over them. Waldo wouldn't touch a thing that even remotely smelled, and Earl knows this. Which is why he was so pissed off. Because he wasted a day going down to see Battles, and he blames me for making him do it. 'Just a good thing for me that I ran into Sally,' he said. 'Least I got something, this weekend.' "

"He's liable to get another spell in the cooler," Cobb said, "if this car deal's got something wrong. Jimmy's a real wrong number. Wished I never heard of the guy."

"What'd he do for you, anyway?" Beale said. "How is it you owe this guy something? He does not sound, to me at least, like your type of guy at all."

"Ah," Cobb said, "I'm not gonna tell you that much. I knew a guy that got in some trouble, one night down in Rhode Island. Nothing came of it, but it could've and it looked like it was going to. And he called me from the road and asked me if I could help him. Well, I didn't know anybody down there, really, but I knew my guy in Washington who knows everybody, everywhere, met him at the 'sixty convention, he was for Johnson, I wasn't, but we still got along all right. And I called him up and asked him, and he naturally knew somebody from Providence that could pull a string down there, and I called *him* up and he said 'Battaglia,' and he took care of it for me. I knew it was going to cost me. I didn't know when, and I didn't know what, but I knew it would, sooner or later. And now it did. Two things. This is the second thing, here. And now my guess is: I'm still not paid up, because Earl didn't do what he wanted. And I couldn't do the other thing. Or I'm not sure I did, at least, but I don't think I did."

"What two things?" Beale said.

"Ahh," Cobb said, "he wanted a guy that could do things with cars. And I of course thought of you. Which meant that I thought of Earl. And he wanted a guy, this was first on his list, that could do things with the army."

"The army," Beale said. "What'd he want? Some country invaded? Didn't he hear about the Bay of Pigs?"

"No," Cobb said, "his kid's in the army. And the kid wants to go to Vietnam. He's a hero, all right? He wants to prove it. And Battles thinks he'll get killed, and the kid has got this wife that Battles says looks like a toad, and she had a kid that Battles says looks like he should live under a bridge and live off of fish that he catches with his hands, and Battles says he doesn't care to support them and live with them, and if *his* kid gets killed, he will have to. So he does not want his kid to go to Vietnam, and he wanted me to make sure he doesn't."

"Can you do that?" Beale said. "You're gonna be the most popular pol in the country, if you can pull that stunt off. You've got the daddy vote wrapped up, my friend, if you can bring that one off."

"Of course I can't do it," Cobb said. "All I can do's what I said I could do. Make a call. And I made the call. To the guy I called in Washington, who is getting sick of these calls, that gave me the name of the guy in Rhode Island that knows Jimmy Battles. Which is how I got into the whole gonfalon in the first place. And the guy down in Washington laughed at me, naturally. So I said: 'Well, you see? This's why we need a Democratic congressman up here. So *he* gets all the calls, and *we* meet only for drinks.' But I did what I said I would do. And that is all I can do."

"So what happens when the kid goes to Vietnam and gets dead?" Beale said.

"Look," Cobb said, "that's what I'm trying to tell you. This car that you've got here. We know it's hot. You sell it and you get in trouble. You're going to sell it, and you'll get in trouble. This is *fait accompli.*"

"Hey," Beale said, "pretty good. You would've flunked French in college, if I hadn't sat next to you."

"Gwendolyn," Cobb said. "my wife, has culture. But the U.S. Army does not. The U.S. Army operates according to the principles of government management, which are that if it is possible to screw up, do it. The Battles kid puts in to win the hearts and minds of all those folks in Vietnam? He really wants to go? They may very likely say: 'Hey. Whoa. This kid is nuts. We're not sending *him* over there.' Or they may lose his papers. Or they may not lose his papers, but a guy that meant to stamp 'em 'Go' will stamp 'em 'Stop,' because he has to go to the bathroom, and besides then it's time for coffee. The kid doesn't go? I get the credit. The kid goes? I never said I could stop it."

"But Battles thinks you did," Beale said.

"Battles *wants* to think I did," Cobb said. "I can't help what Battles wants. I can help what you want, I hope, which is to sell this stolen car and get in trouble as a result. Will you listen to me, please?"

"How'd you get to know this guy again?" Beale said.

Cobb sighed. "I told you. I won't tell you."

"Henry Briggs," Beale said.

"What about him?" Cobb said.

"He's the guy that called you," Beale said. "Middle of the night. Has to be Henry Briggs. There's only about four guys you know who would think of your name when they got into some mess in a cheap motel somewhere else. And two of them you probably wouldn't help. You would help me, and you might help Paul Whipple, and maybe there's two or three more. But it has to be someone you knew a long time, which is Henry, and someone who traveled a lot, which is also him, and someone with a habit of getting into the kind of trouble that guys find in cheap motels. And that is also Henry. What'd he do? Screw an underage girl? Ball club would've liked that a lot, one of their players gets himself arrested for statutory rape."

Cobb said nothing.

"Jesus, Ed," Beale said, "you met the guy, 'd you adopt him? Is that what it is? I realize you grew up with the guy and all that, but how far back can the guy make you go? And when you get there, how the hell's he gonna pay you back?"

"Ah," Cobb said, "that forest warden job there, that was nothing. I'd put a word in on that job, for anyone I knew. And Henry really knows that stuff, the trees and the hairy woodland creatures. Besides, that was a very popular appointment. Everybody knows him, everybody likes him, and everyone that doesn't like him lies and says they do. I actually made friends with that. Henry's still a young man, you know, Don. Those ball players finish up early. They need something to do with their life."

"Yeah," Beale said, "they probably do, and you probably did. Make some friends for yourself for a change. But that's not what I'm talking about. What I'm talking about is: Henry's your man. Your guy to run against Wainright."

Cobb chuckled. "Shit," he said, "Henry wasn't even registered to vote, till I went and got him his job. 'Well, hell, Ed, sure I'll do it. It's something you want me to do. But why the hell do I have to? The animals won't care.' 'The animals in the woods maybe won't,' I tell him, 'but the animals where I work will, if I give out a soft job to a friend of mine, and he turns out another Republican.'"

"Ed, Ed," Beale said, "what're you telling me? That I should 'think creative'? That stuff you were saying about Earl there, remember that? What it was he did? Well, I doubt you're right, in ninety-nine cases out of a hundred. Maybe five out of a hundred remember the rigged games, and that some of the players went to jail, but only a real college basketball nut, one in a thousand, maybe, remembers the names of the players. And there's none of those guys around here. Dad went bullshit when Earl got arrested. Said it'd ruin the business, he'd be closing down in a year. You know how many people ever even mentioned it? Two. One was the basketball coach at the university, and he said he was sorry, and he bought a new car from us. The other one was Russ Stanley at the paper. Called Dad up and said he thought it was Saint Stephen's fault for bringing these green kids down from the country and not warning them about gangsters. Nobody up here follows that sport. Nobody knows who plays it. The Celtics, maybe. Some follow them. But otherwise our sport is baseball. Well, baseball and winter, of course.

"Now," he said, "the only guy I know of that ever came from here and made a big name for himself by playing baseball, well, that was Henry Briggs. Christ, the bars around this town, the veterans' organizations and the church groups—all that stuff? When he was with the Red Sox, and the Red Sox were in town, every single weekend I bet you could've had your choice of ten or fifteen buses, you'd've asked around statewide. I'd go so far as to say I bet Bob Wainwright's *not* the best-known man in his district. I bet Henry Briggs is that. And not everyone who knows Bob is a fan of his. He used to be a banker, remember, and bankers make people unhappy. He's been in Washington a long time now, and he's made some enemies, I'm sure, people who needed favors here."

Cobb did not say anything.

"This thing you got Henry out of," Beale said. "Is it the kind of thing, you know, that if it got out it'd kill him?"

Cobb shrugged. "A youthful indiscretion," he said.

"Meaning yes," Beale said. "Next question. How many people know about it?"

"Not many," Cobb said. "They don't *because* he got out. If he didn't get out, a lot would've. *Every*body, in fact. From sea to shining sea. But he did get out, so there's only, well, three, maybe five of us at the outside."

"Any of them include the guy in Washington?" Beale said. "Or the guy that knew Battles down there?"

"Nope," Cobb said. "All I told them was what I needed. The name of a guy that could help with a thing. Not what the thing itself was."

"How many can talk without hurting themselves?" Beale said.

Cobb pursed his lips. "I would say none," he said. "I can't. My friend can't. And Battles, he certainly can't. Not that he would, in a million or so years, but if he'd like to, he couldn't."

"So then," Beale said, "then it won't come out. And Henry's the pure driven snow."

Cobb nodded. "You're a very smart man, Donald Beale," he said. "I think, I think maybe in the next couple weeks or so, I'll visit a few towns. Talk to some people we trust. Get what their reaction is, to this crackpot idea."

"Good idea," Beale said, slapping him on the back. "And if it's what I would expect, well then, go talk to Henry. I bet you won't even need to remind him that what you want he has to do."

9

Earl Beale had the late shift at Centre Street Motors in West Roxbury on the Wednesday before Thanksgiving. He had been tempted, starting shortly after Roy Fritchie left at 7:00 P.M., to turn out the lights and lock up well before the scheduled closing time of 9:00, but after four straight successful "bagouts," as Penny called them, Waldo had caught him twice, and had promised to fire him the next time. "I get a base, you know, Earl," Waldo had said. "I know there isn't much business, some nights when we stay open late. But you never can tell, when impulse'll hit 'em, and those're the easiest sells. They get themselves a few beers, have something to eat, and all of a sudden they're hot to trot. Who knows what happens, that starts it? The old buggy wouldn't start without a jump, they went out to go to work inna morning? Their lousy fuckin' brother-in-law just got himself a new one and's rubbing their noses in it? There was a little snow, the ground, if it's wintertime, and they got stuck, their own driveways, and said: 'Screw it, I'm not getting new tires for this junker'? Or it's in the summer and the junker

99

boiled over? Who the hell knows, sets them off? But it happens, and when it happens, well, they got to get a car *tonight*. Half the time they don't even bother, try to jew you down. Just pay what the numbers are on the windshield. Those're the gravy commissions, and if we're not open to get them, my friend, someone else'll get them instead."

"Yeah," Earl had said to Penny the night before, "but I never get any gravy. And I'm never gonna, either, long's the nights they give to me're just before some holiday, three-day weekend or like that. Now you just look at me working till nine tonight. Nobody's gonna come in. You know where they're all gonna be? Down at the super, getting their turkeys, buying their veggies and ice cream. Stop-and-Shop and Star'll sell three trainloads of cranberries, and I won't sell any cars. Sit around on my ass all night, waiting for someone, come in."

"Take something to read," she had said. "That's what I'm gonna do. Sit around that damned courthouse all morning. Damn, who they kidding? I got to be there by eight forty-five, report to Probation and that crap, and I know I'll be lucky if I'm through by lunch. If my case is called before lunch."

"You should call up Nancy," he had said. "It was her grass anyway. Make her go waste her time, stand up when they finally call you."

"Huh," Penny had said. "Easier said'n done, I think, buddy. No one's seen Nancy in months. I run into Roberta, down at the hairdresser's, she's got a new guy named Arigo. And apparently this's gonna be his first, you know, Thanksgiving since he walked out, his wife. So, he doesn't wanna be around here, on the holiday and he doesn't have a real girlfriend yet, so he asked Roberta, go out of town with him. You ever heard of Aruba? Anyone going there, I mean?"

Earl had said he had not. "Well, that's where they're going, she tells me. 'This is gonna be good. Three years ago I'm cheerleading, right? Yelling that English beats Latin. Freezing my tight little ass off, going home to my mom's lousy turkey. And now here I am, it's Thanksgiving again, and I'm gonna be down in the sun. Down on the beach, South America way, they'll probably feed me a lizard.' " Penny had paused. "You know what, Earl?" she'd said. "That's what we should do."

"Go to Aruba?" he had said. "How can I go there, I dunno where the place is? And anyway, we're running out of money. I better sell a car pretty soon. I better sell three Cadillacs tomorrow night, is what I better do."

"Well," she had said, "if you didn't still insist on always betting on those games that you think you've got a lock, we wouldn't have that money thing, all the money problems. We had enough money, get us through Christmas. And you blew it all on football."

"Look," he had said, "just listen to me. There was not a thing wrong with those bets."

She had snickered. "Nothing wrong with them," she'd said, "except they were big losers."

"I had the right teams, those three locked games," he had said. "The only difference between me losing three thousand dollars—"

"Seven," she had said absently. "You bet one on the first, and then you lost that. So you doubled up on the second. And when you lost that, you did it again. Add up one and two and four—it isn't three you get, chum."

"I told you I didn't double down," Earl had said. "I told you I didn't do that."

"Earl," she had said, "you always do that. And, you always deny it. It's like you won't clean the toilet, and I mention it, and you say it isn't yours. You tell me that you go at work. It's the same with the betting's it is with the toilet: it's your shit but you won't admit it. If Allen didn't decide in October, take me that Chicago meeting, we'd've been right up shit's creek, 'stead of just getting by."

"Now there is a guy," Earl had said, "there's a guy that I'd like to be. There is a guy that leads a charmed life. The last time that Allen thought about money, he called up the people who print it. 'I'm thinkin' of going to Europe this summer. You guys gonna have enough stock?' "

"Yeah," she had said, "well just keep in mind that he didn't get it betting on dumb football games."

"The difference," Earl had said. "Those were good bets. I already told you that. The difference, you know what the difference was there? All three of those damned games combined? The first one I miss the spread because the Pats don't kick a field goal, and then don't score a touchdown, either. Field goal would've done it for me, but, no, they don't do that. The second one, Packers up by two, the fucking spread is four, they're practically at midfield and the clock is running out, and what do they do, go for first down, let the time expire? No, sir, they don't, they try the field goal, forty-five yards in the wind, *and they hit the goddamned thing*. The third one, I am in pig heaven, Giants up by two touchdowns with three minutes left to play, and they have got the ball. Fumble, score. Niners kick off, now I'm up by seven. First fucking play from scrimmage and they throw an interception which the Niners bring back and score. Now it's dead even. Got a push, okay, the money back. Niners kick off, less'n a minute, another goddamned fumble and another fucking field goal and I tear my ticket up. Those were not stupid bets I made. Those were damned good bets. It's just, nobody knows, you can't predict those things."

"Huh," she had said, "that's what you think. I happen, think you're wrong. I don't know the guy's name, and I don't know where he lives, but the guy who's got your money, I think he can predict. And he does pretty good at it. Pretty goddamned good, taking money from you of all people, think it's all on the up-and-up. Must give him a million laughs, too. You think he's just maybe smarter?"

"Ahh," he had said, "can it, willya? Now I'm gettin' all depressed. Isn't there something we can do, get our minds off all this shit we always seem to be in?"

"You wanna take in a movie?" she had said.

"Nah," he had said, "for something that costs money, it's too much like TV. Just leave me alone, I guess. I'll get over it. 'S funny, though. When I was in, especially after about a year, and I still had a long way to go, and it just hit me, you know? That I'd been in the can all this time, and I'd stood up pretty damned good, and I still wasn't even halfway, my release date. It seemed like I'd been in there all my life, you know? Doing the same things every day, wearing the same fucking clothes. Seeing the same fucking people, half of which're fucking animals, eating the same fucking food. When I was playing the ball there, about six weeks before the first practice, I used to go on the wagon, you know? No more beer for me. Go out running every morning. Lift the weights and all. Watch the diet, get my sleep, 'got to report in shape.' And then all through the season, I'd have two beers after games, never more'n two, and none the day before a game. I left more parties early? And it worked like a charm. And I hated it, and the only way I got through it was by knowing that when the grass started turning green, I could stop. Go and relax. So it was what? Five months? Six months at the most, and I was having fun. Prison I was not having fun. And it was not six months I'd been in there. It was a fucking year. And I wasn't even close to having fun again.

" 'If I can just last it out,' I used to think. "If I can just get through this, just make it to the end, someday I'll get out and I'll have fun again.' Then I'd think: 'Maybe I made a mistake. I must've made a mistake. I heard it wrong in court or something. They got the papers wrong. Or maybe I read them wrong.' And I'd get up off my bunk and go through them again, and nothing'd changed. It was still five to seven, and the minimum time to be served was still two and a half, and I'd still done only one. Jesus, it was discouraging."

She had frowned. "Two and a half," she had said. "Two years and a half? I thought you only did less'n two."

He had snorted. "Only less'n two," he had said. "Nobody who's done any real time says 'only.' I did nineteen months. They changed the guidelines for nonviolent crimes, 'less they were mob related. Which course mine was, but I wasn't sentenced under that part. It didn't exist, I went in. So I came under the new ones, and I got out about five months early. Which of course meant at least half the guys on the street thought I turned snitch in the can, and I'm lucky I wasn't clipped."

"Didn't they know, on the street?" she had said. "Didn't they understand that?"

"Honey," he had said, "you really want a tough assignment for yourself sometime, you try explaining, a guy with a gun, on a contract out on your ass, that the reason you're out is that *they* changed the rules. It's not because you turned rat. This is very difficult, a very hard thing to do. The guy with the gun is not thinking about Federal Prison Regulations. He is not even thinking about making you dead. As far as he's concerned, he's past that. You are whacked. Now the question on his mind is: Where's he dump the body? Are you too big, the trunk? His mind's not on regulations. It's on practical things. The practical problems he's got. I knew a guy in the jar that said he did a few guys. I think he was telling the truth, too. And he said to me: 'The worst thing, the very worst thing, you got to take a guy out, is when he figures it out. What you're there for. Well, it's natural, I guess. He tries to talk you out of it. He will not shut up. He simply will not shut up. I did a guy in a bar once. Right inna fuckin' bar there. S'posed to do him, the woods. And why did I do what I wasn't supposed to? Because he wouldn't shut up.'

"No," Earl had said, "your average hit man, from you he does not want a lot of conversation. It's a very tricky thing. I doubted I could pull it off. So the first thing I did, I got out, was go around and see a man and have a talk with him. Explain the situation, so nobody acted hasty, before they knew the facts. And he believed me, thank the good Lord for that, and His Blessed Mother, too, because I know for a fact he ditched two contracts on me from some real quick-tempered guys.

"But you know something?" he had said. "I still, I *still*, even after I was out and my ass was reasonably safe, I still wasn't having any fun. I didn't expect, you know, what I had. Before they caught up with me there. But, Jesus, at least some, now and then. It's hard when you haven't got money."

"I know what we could do," she had said. "I know exactly what we can do. You're not going home. I can't go home either. Us two, we just don't exist. But I can still cook. I know how to cook. And I'll fix us Thanksgiving dinner. Right here."

"We haven't got the stuff," he had said. "Don't you have start all that shit about a month ahead? My mother always did. I bet she still does. The onions and the stuffing, the soupy mashed potatoes and the goddamned squash. All that stuff. Relishes. Christ, I hated those relishes. Looked like a monkey threw up in a dish. Green stuff and red stuff and yellow stuff, and brown, all swimming around in this juice that looked like you stepped in cat puke or something. Supposed to dip the Ritz crackers in it. Yummy, yummy, yummy."

"Oh," she had said, "you can have all that stuff, if you want. But you don't have to. We'll keep it simple. Just a nice, small, frozen turkey. Not a chicken. A real turkey. But a small one. Eight, ten pounds. And some nice thick mashed potatoes, and some dressing and green beans. And maybe, this once, two whole bottles of wine. Wouldn't that be nice? It'll really be nice, Earl, you know? And then ice cream for dessert. We'll get some celery, and some dip, and a couple six-packs of beer, and you can turn on the TV, and watch the . . . Lions, is it?"

"The Lions," he had said, "always play Thanksgiving."

She had nodded. "My father always watched. I thought that that was them." She had waggled a finger at him. "But no betting on them, baby. You can't watch, you're gonna bet."

"Huh," he had said. "I never watched the games I bet on. 'Cept the ones I was in. Too damned nerve-racking. Besides, I got no money to bet, and Zack won't let me have credit no more."

"Oh," she had said, "this is going to be fun. The market opens at eight, right? We'll both get up early and be waiting there, when they open the door. And we'll both do the shopping, quick like a bunny, and then you can drop me back here. I'll put the turkey in the fridge to thaw, and the next morning when we get up, I'll put the bird in the oven. Show those relatives of ours: we can do things too."

He arrived at work on Wednesday twenty minutes later. "It was Penny," he said. "My crazy girlfriend. Last night she gets the wild idea in her head, all of a sudden, nothing on earth is going to be worth doing if we don't have Thanksgiving dinner. So, practically still dark out, we get up this morning and go to the store. The milkman's still making deliveries? That's how early it is. And as soon as it opens, we go in, and we fill up the fuckin' carriage with more stuff'n I ever bought in my life. The smallest turkey we could find

107

weighs almost fifteen pounds, for God's sake. We'll be eating it forever. And I drive her back home, help her carry it in, and that's why I'm getting here late."

Waldo forgave him. "You should marry that girl, Earl," he said. "She's a very good-lookin' head, and the two of you get along good. This hell-raisin' stuff is great when you're young, but nobody stays young forever. Settle down, pal, you still got the choice. Settle down, and have a nice life."

Right after lunch, Earl called the apartment to find out how Penny's hearing on the marijuana charge had turned out, but he got no answer. He imagined her pacing the hallways of the Brighton-Allison District Courthouse, chain-smoking stale Newports and swearing to herself. He called her again at 2:30, getting no answer, and then at 3:10, with the same result. Shortly before 3:30 a woman about nineteen with a bleached-blond boy cut, white vinyl Eisenhower jacket, tight, faded blue jeans, and low white vinyl boots with chromium chains across the insteps made what he called "a dreamboater" visit to the metallic maroon 'sixty-five Chevy Impala hardtop that occupied the featured place on a platform in the center of the lot. She stood beneath the red, white, and blue plastic pennants that flapped in the breeze over the car and admired the highlights of the sixty-dollar paint job Waldo had bought to conceal poor repair of serious collision damage to the right front quarter panel and door. She did not ask to sit in the car, and did not deduce, when they were up on the platform, that Earl had a reason for showing her the clean interior only from the driver's side—he was not sure she would be sharp enough to notice that the passenger-side door was badly out of

108

line, and made grinding, groaning noises when it was opened and shut, but he saw no point in taking chances.

"I figured," he said to Fritchie, when she left at 4:15, "that even though she obviously doesn't have the money, her boyfriend might. Or her father. And she might make such a pain in the ass of herself with that horrible sharp voice of hers, one of them might loan her the money, just to shut her up."

"Be all right if they don't decide to come down here, see it for themselves," Fritchie said. "Maybe even want to drive it, or something. That'll crease it, if they do."

"Oh, come on," Earl said. "The tires're new. There's no tread wear, tip them off. It's not like I'm gonna let 'em take out One-twenty-eight or something, and you don't even notice that shimmy till you get up to fifty or so."

Fritchie laughed. "I can't help it," he said, "but I love it when Waldo gets gypped on something. He brought that bucket in here from the auction down at Bridgeport, and he's really pleased, himself. 'Fifty bucks I got this for. Whaddaya think of that? Not a speck of rust on the thing. This is a Florida car.'

" 'I think you got took, boss,' I tell him. 'What'd they use to paint over that filler, huh? Finger paint like my kids get in school?'

" 'Ahh,' he said, 'I'll ship it over Mikey's there. He'll make her shine like new.' So naturally I'm the one who has to drive it over, but first I have to take Davey over the tire place, West Newton—he's getting snow treads on his wife's car, and he's gonna drive me back here. So we're running a little bit late there, and I take her out on Route Nine, and the fuckin' thing starts to

109

shake its guts out, soon's I get over forty. I'm fighting the wheel like it's a goddamned gorilla, and the goddamned gorilla is winning. So I say to him: 'Hey, you follow me, Mikey's, stay pretty close on my tail, right? See if what I think's going on, see if you see anything.' So he does that, and we get to Mikey's and he tells me exactly I expected. 'She runs like an old dog I had that got hit on the ass. Sideways, you know? You go in a straight line, that baby, right down the damned centerline, the front wheel's a foot closer to it'n the back wheel behind it is. That rat just ain't tracking right.'

"So we come back here, and I say to Waldo: 'Hey, I hate to tell you this, but before Mikey starts with the paint sprayers there, I think he'd better straighten the frame.' Not that I ever see one of those jobs that really did what it's supposed to. They put the damned chains on and pull it and haul it, but it never turns out so it's true. And Waldo just looks at me, and then he says, well I have got to be nuts. A frame job on that thing's a four-dollar bill, and he's not gonna part with the money.

"So, I don't know," Fritchie said. "I think Waldo might have to eat this one. Nobody smart enough to earn the kind of money he expects to get for it's dumb enough to buy it. And the ones stupid enough to buy it, they're too dumb to have the dough."

It was nearly 4:30 when Earl called the apartment again. The line was busy. He called again at 4:45. There was no answer. He called at fifteen-minute intervals between then and six, when he took his dinner hour for pizza at the Pleasant Café on Washington Street and stopped to buy two six-packs of Budweiser and two jugs of Almaden wine—one California Mountain Red, one California Mountain Rosé—at Barney's in the Square. He got no answer to the eight calls he placed between 7:10 and 9:05, time that he spent alone in the showroom before turning off the lights and locking up for the holiday.

The apartment in Somerville was dark when he opened the door, struggling with his bags from Barney's while he groped in the dim hallway light for the lock. He shut the door with his right heel and turned on the overhead light in the hallway with his left elbow. He went into the kitchen and put the bags down on the counter. There was a note taped to the refrigerator door:

Honey. I wasn't brave enough to call you. The court thing came out all right. I had Mr. Sweeney from the Mass Defenders, + he made the judge believe me that it wasn't my stuff. The judge asked me if I knew who's it was, + I just said my former roommate used to have all kinds of people in the apt., coming and going all the time, + that was the reason I stopped living with her, + it could've been anybody, really. So it was all thrown out, + that was pretty good, altho I did have to stay 'till after 3:30 + I didn't get home on the trolley 'till after four. Anyway, Allen was calling when I got here, + he had a big fight with his wife this morning, + he decided he wants to go to New York tonight + see the Celtics play the Knicks for a change, instead of always seeing the Bruins, + I told him I couldn't go, + about our dinner and everything, + he was upset + said I really didn't care about him, after how he's been

111

so good to me, + he would give me $15,000 to
go with him till Sunday, + I thought about how
we really need money, + so I finally said I would.
I'm really sorry, but I think we had to do it. I took
a cab to the airport + I'll find some way to get
home Sunday night, so you don't have to bother,
+ I hope you won't be too mad + lonesome, because I love you a lot. Love, Penny.

Earl opened the refrigerator. Penny had removed
the top shelf to accommodate the enormous turkey
thawing on the second shelf. She had relocated all his
beer to nooks and crannies among the pickle jars, cans
of Pepsi, the bunches of carrots and celery, the English
muffins and bread, and the cartons of cottage cheese
jumbled on the lower shelves. She had put three cans
on the shelves built into the door. He stared at the dis-
order for a while. Then he removed the turkey, cold
and wet in its plastic shroud, oozing water and blood,
and put it in the sink. He found the top shelf in the
space between the side of the refrigerator and the cabinet that housed the sink. He replaced it in the refrigerator. He put his beer back in its regular place: two rows
of six cans each stacked against the right inner wall of
the refrigerator. He went to the Barney's bags and took
out the two fresh six-packs. He stacked them next to
the old supply. Then he recovered the scattered Pepsi
cans and arranged them next to the beer. He took two
of the cold beers and shut the door. He went into the
living-dining room without turning on the light and sat
down in the chair at the end of the table nearest the
door. He cracked the first beer and drank half of it,

112

sitting in the faint light from the streetlamp outside, and thinking.

It was just after 2:00 A.M. on Thanksgiving when Earl went to bed. There were thirteen empty beer cans stacked in a five-four-three-one pyramid cluster on the lemon-scented polished table, with another, half full, balanced on the top. He did not undress, except for his shoes. He got up to urinate twice, once while it was still dark and once when it had begun to get light. He noticed that rain was driving against the frosted glass of the bathroom window, and that there seemed to be some crusted material on his shirtfront. He got up at 3:20 P.M., this time switching on the fluorescent light over the mirror in the bathroom. He was able to identify the crusted material as the semidigested remains of the pizza he had had for supper the night before. He removed the shirt and dropped it on the floor. He brushed his teeth and rinsed. In his stocking feet, pants, and undershirt, he went into the kitchen, noticing as he passed through the bedroom that the pillowcase, sheet, and blanket were also encrusted.

The turkey had thawed completely in the sink; he prodded it with his forefinger—the breast was soft and yielding. He opened the refrigerator and got two cans of beer. He returned to the living-dining room and turned on the football game. He sat down in his black vinyl armchair next to the window that looked out on Cedar Street. He put his feet up on the matching ottoman, opened the first beer, and drank. The game between the Detroit Lions and the Green Bay Packers was over. He watched the San Francisco 49ers play the Los Angeles Rams in brilliant sunlight in the Coliseum. "That's where I should be," Earl said. "Some place where it's fuckin' warm, and isn't raining all the time." As he drained each beer, he set the empty in the row he was arranging on the windowsill.

The news came on after the game was over. He learned that nine people had died in highway accidents in New England since the start of the four-day holiday, and that police, while pleading with motorists to drive carefully, had called out all available manpower to patrol the highways, looking especially for drunk drivers and speeders. A spokesman for Logan International Airport said that passenger traffic through the terminals had been light, and that the last departures and arrivals delivering passengers to family reunions at 1:40 that morning had justified Wednesday's traditional reputation of being the busiest travel day in the year. The Red Cross had announced that it was critically short of blood supplies, particularly type O negative, and urged all potential donors to report immediately to any one of seven convenient locations that would be open all night in the Greater Boston area. The cardinal archbishop of Boston had joined volunteers serving Thanksgiving dinner "with all the fixin's" to toothless, hairless, and confused residents of two Roman Catholic homes for the elderly; the diners gaped dazzled into the camera lights as the prelate held compartmented metal trays of food under their chins, and beamed into the lens. The weatherman predicted rain ending shortly after midnight, with the skies clearing and temperatures "in the balmy low sixties" for Friday and Saturday, but feared that another moisture-laden warm front moving up the coast from the Carolinas would bring more rain on Sunday, "just when most will be leaving for the long return trip home." He reminded

114

motorists that roads would be slick, and that police would be out in force. The sports reporter hurried over the professional football scores and said that the Celtics would be leaving in the morning for their game with the Knicks Friday night at Madison Square Garden, after enjoying two days off at home with their families; John Havlicek, who had suffered a slight ankle sprain in Tuesday night's game against the Pistons at Boston Garden, was expected to start. The announcer commented on film of the high school football games between Wellesley and Natick, and Brockton and Framingham, "played in a sea of mud," before introducing a long list of other scores in white lettering that crawled down a blue screen against background music—the fight songs first of Georgia Tech and then of USC.

Earl finished his last beer shortly after 9:30. He put it at the end of the row he had arranged on the windowsill beside him. After urinating for the fourth time since he had gotten out of bed, he returned to the kitchen and took the jug of rosé wine from the Barney's bag. He got the cork stopper out and took a tumbler from the cabinet over the sink. He put four ice cubes in the tumbler and filled it with wine. He replaced the stopper in the jug and put it in the refrigerator on the top shelf, on its side. He punched the turkey lightly and returned to the living room, momentarily and vaguely surprised to see that he had begun watching *The Sound of Music*. "Well, why the fuck not?" he said to the screen. "I'm a fuckin' human being. This is my day off. I got some fuckin' rights." He sat down in the chair again.

When he awoke there was a constant blizzard of gray snow on the screen, and an insistent, hissing buzz

115

from the speaker. It was dark outside the window. He was surprised again when he saw the jug of rosé, nearly empty, on the floor beside him. He lurched his way into the bedroom and groped on the bureau until he found Penny's alarm clock behind the upraised cover of her jewelry box. "Twenty past nine," he said. "Fuck it, so I'm late. 'You gonna do about it, Waldo, huh? You gonna fuckin' *fire* me? Well, fuckin' fire me, then get it fuckin' over with.' " He collapsed onto Penny's side of the bed and resumed sleeping almost at once.

10

Earl awoke shortly before 7:00 on Friday morning, sprawled on top of the quilt on Penny's side of the bed. He had a desperate urge to urinate, but held back until he had looked around the bedroom and identified enough objects to satisfy himself of where he was. His neck and shoulder muscles on the left were slighly stiff, and he felt somewhat groggy, but he knew what to do. He sat on the edge of the bed, his head lowered, and pressed the heels of his hands down against the mattress until his mind began to clear. Then he stood up and went into the bathroom. He relieved himself, and brushed his teeth twice, repeatedly rinsing with cold water and a gargle of mint-flavored mouthwash.

He shut the bathroom door. He took off his clothes and turned on the shower, three parts hot to one cold, and stuck the plastic curtain wetly to the pink tile tub enclosure in order to trap as much steam as possible. When the steam began to billow above the curtain rod, he stepped into the tub, shivering and flinching as the hot water sprayed over him, and gritting his teeth. "Poison goes out through the pores," he remembered, "poison goes out through the pores." He recalled his father's daily ritual of showering in cold water: "People ask me," he would say, at every opportunity, "how I stop my teeth from chattering. 'Why, it's easy. I leave 'em in the glass on the commode till I get out and dry.' " The old man was all right. Had been, at least, or would've been if Donsie hadn't set his mind against Earl.

The heat reddened Earl's skin and made him sweat. He put his hands on his pelvis and arched his back, bending and stretching his torso down-up, right-left, twenty times. Then he turned around and put first his right foot and then his left on the faucet that let water into the tub, tensing and relaxing the muscles in his calves and thighs; he did that twenty times with each leg. When he felt limber, he soaped himself all over and then shampooed, rinsing all the lather off at once. He shut off the water and stepped out of the tub, his skin very red, and grabbed the big, rough, white bath towel that Penny saved for her weekly sessions of bubble bath with oil. "Close those pores, close those pores," he muttered, rubbing himself vigorously and soaking the towel through. He wrapped it around his waist and opened the door to let the steam out. He returned to the sink and used Penny's facecloth to wipe the condensation off the mirror. He shaved and rinsed his face, splashing on heavily spiced Jade East shaving lotion. He dropped the towel on top of his dirty clothes and returned to the bedroom, naked. He felt wonderful, and hungry, and he dressed rapidly in khaki pants, a clean pink shirt, a maroon tie with narrow gold and silver stripes, and his maroon blazer, thinking of the $1.89 Special Breakfast served at Dean's Red Spot at

118

the intersection of Massachusetts and Western avenues in Central Square in Cambridge. He checked his wallet after he had slipped on his brown loafers. He had twelve dollars. He looked at his watch; he had plenty of time. He would have two Special Breakfasts. He gave the wet, soft turkey a friendly pat on his way out.

He was the first to arrive at Centre Street Motors. He carried his large cardboard container of coffee and his two morning papers in to his desk; he was studying the sports sections and drinking the coffee when Fritchie came in at 8:30. Fritchie had a bag of doughnuts and a container of coffee. "Jesus," Fritchie said, looking at the wall clock above Earl's head, "either I'm dreaming or the traffic this morning was worse'n I thought it was. What're you doing here first?"

Earl grinned. "Ahh," he said, "we had the big dinner yesterday afternoon, and then Penny gets it in her fool head, she's got to take the bus up to Portland, spend couple nights with her parents. Wanted me to drive her, but I said I hadda work. I tell you, Roy, I never been so glad I hadda work in my whole life. I never met her family, and from what she tells me, I got no ambition in that line. So anyway, the big dinner, and then I sit down in the chair, and I have the glass of beer, and I watch the football games, and then the movie comes on and I make a turkey sandwich, and I have a little wine, and then I have a glass of beer. The result of which is that I fall asleep in the chair, don't wake up until about two this morning, get in the sack and sleep till about seven. So I had, I dunno, maybe ten, eleven hours sleep. Wake up rarin' to go."

"See?" Fritchie said. He put the bag of doughnuts

and the coffee on his desk. "Gettin' old, just like the rest of us. Your younger days, feed like that, get up from the *table* rarin' to go. Go out, spend the night chasin' broads. Start getting a little older, best thing you can think of's a nap, and then get ready for bed. Doughnut?"

"No thanks," Earl said. "I must've stretched my gut yesterday. All I had to eat, and then I wake up this morning, it's like I didn't eat in a week. Ever eat, Dean's? The buck-eighty-nine breakfast?" Fritchie shook his head. "Well," Earl said, "it's three eggs; stack of three either buttermilk pancakes or blueberry; sausages, bacon, or ham; home fries; toast; all the coffee you can drink."

"Jesus," Fritchie said, "who eats there? The paratroopers or something?"

"Truckers, mostly, I think," Earl said. "The long-haul guys with those tandem trailers they can only pull on the pike? Have to leave them at the terminal over past the Coke plant there? Because there's a lot of those big tractor diesels with no trailers on them, parked in Dean's the morning.'

"Anyway," he said, "I had two of them breakfasts. Did have to leave some of the toast, didn't finish the second home fries, but now I really feel good. I think I'll sell, oh, about eight cars today."

Fritchie scowled. "One of us better," he said. "I heard Waldo on the phone Wednesday, you're out on the lot with that young chick? He was talking to his banker, I think. What I could get, Waldo's ass's growing grass, and the bank's thinking of buying a lawn mower."

"Jesus," Earl said, "I hope not. I had trouble enough getting this job."

"You oughta be in my position," Fritchie said. "This's all I've ever done. You at least had that time in the Peace Corps. That should be worth something, somewhere. And you're single, too, which I know single guys get sick of hearing from us married guys, because I didn't like it when I was, but the facts the matter still is: I got responsibilities. Three of them. Plus a wife that never worked. Never a day in her life. And Christmas is coming right up. What do I do, if Waldo goes under? Get fitted for the Santa suit, down the Salvation Army? Earn the money for their presents with a kettle and a bell? I'm telling you, Earl, I'm worried."

"You got me worried now, too," Earl said. "Jeez, and I really felt good."

"Well," Fritchie said, "maybe it blows over. Waldo's pretty quick on his feet. I seen him in corners before. Always gotten his dick out the zipper, just 'fore the guy yanked it up."

Shortly after 9:00 the young blonde in the white vinyl jacket all but pranced into the lot, followed reluctantly at a distance of about eleven feet by a short, fat woman in a threadbare black coat open at the front over a black flowered dress. She had gathered her gray hair under a yellow kerchief and she wore scuffed black shoes with bunion bulges at the first joints of her big toes. She clutched a worn black leather handbag with a tortoiseshell handle in both hands at her waist. The girl stopped at the platform and gestured animatedly at the Impala. The older woman looked at the car and tightened her lips. "Ah-*hah*," Earl said to Fritchie, "do I see two fish climbing into the barrel, or what? Time

121

to go out and start shooting," Fritchie shook his head and smiled. "You're just jerking off, Earl," he said. "It's okay if you like it, and you wash up afterwards, but it ain't gonna make you no babies."

Earl put his coffee aside and stood up. "That's what you think," he said. "What I think is different. I've got the hot hand today. I can feel it. Just gimme the ball and some room." He went out into the lot.

"Well," Earl said, as he approached the women, "good morning again, and a very nice one." He spoke to the girl in the jacket. "Come back for another look, did you? Hope you had a nice holiday."

The girl blushed. "I," she said. "I didn't want to bother you or anything. Coming back so soon. But I wanted my mother to see what I saw. So I asked her to come down."

"Look," Earl said, "you can't *bother* us, all right? This's what we do for a living. Someone spots a car, like this featured one here, wants to come in and ask questions? Well, why do you think we put it up there? And why do you think we're inside? Because we hope that folks will come in, and we're here to answer their questions. So, it's not bother for us." The girl smiled and the older woman said nothing, fixing her eyes on the car. "First thing, though, we should get straight: I don't know your name." He offered his right hand. "My name is Earl Beale."

"Oh," the girl said. "Well, I'm Charlene, Charlene Gaffney, and this here, Mister Beale, is my mother." The girl took his hand and shook it.

"Nice to meet you, Charlene, but please call me Earl." The older woman turned her gaze on him. He held out his hand toward her. "And nice to meet you,

Mrs. Gaffney," he said. "Thanks for coming down with your daughter."

The older woman stared at him. "Arnold," she said. "Gaffney run off, eighteen years ago. Just as well, too. He was no good."

"Ma married again," Charlene said to Earl. "That's why I'm Gaffney, she's Arnold."

"Mister Arnold," Earl said, "will he be dropping by?"

"Dead," the older woman said. "Sam was a good one, too. He'd roll over in his grave, he saw us in here today."

"Now, Ma," Charlene said. "We're just *look*ing, okay? Just wanted you to see the car. Sam wouldn't't've minded, us doing that. Not just *looking* at something."

The older woman snorted. "Huh," she said, "yes he would. Sam knew you better'n that. When you look at something, you want to buy it, and you haven't got any money."

"Mrs. Arnold," Earl said, "it's not like I want to argue with you, and I hope you understand that. But we hear that same thing from so many people, and more times'n not they are wrong. They don't *know* they're wrong, not when they say it, but that's what the fact is: they're wrong. And if they will listen, what we have to say, we can generally prove it to them."

Mrs. Arnold snickered. She nodded toward the Impala. "Mister," she said, "I don't know. I don't know what that car costs and I don't know what it's worth. Sam would know, if he was here. So would my son, Timmy. But Sam and him, they knew the score. Sam always knew the score before he got involved in something. And one the things he taught me was that

123

women don't buy cars. 'Men sell cars,' was what he said, 'and it takes a man to buy one. It isn't right, I don't say that, but that's the way it is. A woman goes to buy a car, unless it's from a woman, she's gonna get taken. That's the way it is.' "

Earl laughed. "Mrs. Arnold," he said, "bear with me, all right? Let me say what I think, just listen to what I am saying. You don't agree, when I'm finished? That's fine. All I'm asking for's some time."

Mrs. Arnold shrugged. "Go ahead, mister," she said. "You can talk all that you want. But when you get finished, we still won't've changed, and this girl still won't have any money."

"Mrs. Arnold," Earl said, "most of the people that buy cars from us, or buy cars anywhere else—most of those people don't have the money, least not the price of a car. Next to your house, car is your biggest purchase."

Mrs. Arnold laughed again. "Mister," she said, "we don't *have* a house, all right? We live second floor, a three-decker over on Balsam. The winter it's cold—landlord don't like oil bills. Summer's bugs—don't like buying screens. The last time it's painted, Sam did it himself, and Sam's been dead for six years now—you can guess how it looks."

"Okay," Earl said, "your furniture, then. The stuff in your bedroom. Your TV and your stereo. Nobody buys them for cash either, you know. Nobody has that much cash.

"Now I've been in this business for quite a long time—I know what I'm talking about. And what I say now may surprise you: *We* don't pay cash for cars either. You know how we pay for the cars you see here?

We borrow the money, that's how. And that means, well, we're on pretty good terms, with any number of bankers. All we're doing, we take you, well, any customer, see one of those bankers, say: 'Look, how does this hit you? These're honest people. We've got them checked out. Now basically what we want is you let them take our loan over. Let them make the payments now—their down payment wipes out ours.' And they almost always do."

Mrs. Arnold shook her head. "Mister," she said, "I don't care if you're engaged to marry them, those bankers you talk about. This child doesn't have a job. She's at home with me, and there's no one else in sight around there that has got a steady job. No banker drunk or sober's going to lend her fifteen cents, not when we haven't got a dime we can call our own."

Charlene chewed her lip. "We got Timmy's money, Ma. Timmy's money he sends home. He isn't gonna need it, not for a long time yet. He said that you should use it, if you needed something. We could do that, pay him back. Timmy wouldn't mind."

"No," Mrs. Arnold said. "Not touching Timmy's money. He earned that and it's his. And we don't *need* this car, young lady. Don't need any car."

"No, we don't," Charlene said. "And in the winter you either buy all our stuff at Harold's little store, the corner, and he steals us blind, or else you take cabs to the Star and spend it all on them. When you go to the doctor, Ma, for your legs and stuff, shouldn't have to take the *bus*, not in that cold weather. No, we don't need a car at all. Well I happen, think we do. I'll be working after June. I can pay Timmy back then. And make the payments, too."

125

Mrs. Arnold laughed. "Listen to her," she said. "Just proves she's never worked. I was the same way myself, I first went to work. It looks like so much money. 'I'll do this and I'll do that.' And then they take your taxes out, and Social Security, and Bond-a-Month, United Fund. And *then* you pay the rent.

"Don't get me wrong, mister," she said. "I had a good job, when I had one, and I worked hard at it, back when I still could. I worked at the post office. It was hard work, mopping those floors, people's dirty feet. Polishing the brass on the letter drops and tables, but at least the pay was good. Then my back and legs give out, and I hadda quit. Four years shy of a full pension. Got turned down for disability, which I never understood—how'd they think I got so sore, if it wasn't from my work? They think I work days in construction? Fell off of a roof or something? I said that to them, did they think that? They said no. But it didn't make no difference, and I got nine more years to wait until I start getting retirement—*some* retirement at least. And even that, it still looked like, well, maybe we could make it. Mister Arnold was a good man. They liked him where he worked. And when he first got sick, well, they took good care of us. But then he got pneumonia one day, and next thing we know, he's dead. And that was when I found out how come he did so good when he was sick: he never changed his plan over, the two of us got married. Just left it like it always was, when he was all alone. So when he went to meet his Maker, there was nothing left for us.

"Now this child here," she said to Earl, nodding toward Charlene, "this child here's got big ideas, and big eyes to go with them. Charlene's a good girl. No better

126

in the world." Charlene blushed and lowered her eyes. "But this child hasn't got no sense, and that's all there is to it. I've told her and I've told her: 'Charlene, get your education. Get yourself the diploma. Then go on some other school. I know you're impatient,' and I really do, I know, and I really understand, 'and you want to start out living, having fun and taking trips. But you got to put those things off awhile. The clothes, the cars, the boys, the fun: just grit your teeth and do it. And if you do, you will see, you won't be in my position and you will be able to.' Well," Mrs. Arnold said, "she don't want to listen. And I don't blame her any—I didn't listen either. And look where I am now."

"You're in school, Charlene?" Earl said.

She raised her eyes and nodded, chewing on her lower lip.

"Where do you go?" he said.

"Bunker Hill Community," she said. "I'm taking secretarial. I'm in my second year. It's just a two-year course. An associate's thing there."

"Are you good at it?" Earl said.

She shrugged and looked away from him. She looked down at the ground and scuffed the pavement with the toe of her boot. "Pretty good, I guess," she said. "Ma says I could be better, if I'd put my mind to it. And she is probably right. But I do pretty good, I guess. Sixty words a minute, shorthand—I was only forty last year. And almost seventy in typing. I guess I'm getting there."

Mrs. Arnold's expression combined pride and disappointment. "That's what's so hard to take," she said to Earl. "If Charlene really works hard, she does real good. But then it seems like she gets bored, and she don't do her work. Like she's got too much time on her hands, so she don't use none of it. She never really studies. Not the way she should. Listens to the radio, talks to all her friends, the phone. I bet she says 'Three hours' that she just spent studying, I bet she didn't spend a half one, working on her books. The rest was the music, talking to her girlfriends about boyfriends, the boys about the girls. She put her mind to it, like she should, this'd be just the beginning. If she kept at it, and really worked hard, she'd become a real legal. Work in one of them big law firms."

"They make good money, I know," Earl said. "My brother's a lawyer, used to have his own practice. Remember hearing him say that. Good legal secretary makes real good money. It's worth thinking about, Charlene."

"Oh, she's just like her brother was. Timmy. I kept after that boy, day and night. I said: 'Now don't stop with high school. Try out for a scholarship, something. Don't be in such a big hurry, finish your schooling and quit. Make something big, out of yourself. Get ready to have a career.' " Mrs. Arnold sighed. "He wouldn't listen. The minute he saw he was going to graduate high school, boom, signed up the marines. Like it was a big thing, you know, he got to wear his dress blues when he goes up for his diploma. He looked real nice, sure, but what's it all lead to? Nothing. Then more nothing after that.

"I can't understand it," she said. "I can't understand my own kids. If somebody'd said to me, when I was a girl over Saint Gregory's, all them years ago, if they had just said: 'Well, Florence, now what you should do, when you finish here, you should go to college, you know.' And without it costing no money? I would've jumped at the chance. But nobody said that to me. They didn't have that kind of college then, where poor kids with no money could go. So I got married, right out of high school, and look what happened to me."

"Oh, Ma," Charlene said, "Bunker Hill, all's they give you's that associate diploma. It's more like it's just, you know, two more years of high school. It's not like a real college thing. Timmy knew that, just as good as I do. But he was a boy, and he didn't have to, and I am a girl, so I do."

"Don't you tell me *that*, Charlene," Mrs. Arnold said fiercely. "I know the name of that place, and I been there. It's Bunker Hill Community *College*, and that means you're in college now."

"How do you get there?" Earl said.

Charlene snickered. "Same way we get anywhere, when we *go* anywhere. Down La Grange and wait for the bus. Four blocks and the thing never comes, so it's really fun in the winter. Take the bus down to Forest Hills Station. Get on the trolley car there. Take the subway into Park Street, change over for Charlestown. It takes me, it's taken me over three hours, the weather's real bad or it's broken. And even when the weather's good, and things're running right, it still takes way over an hour. And that's just after the bus comes. Sometimes that takes another thirty, forty minutes."

"So that's two hours a day that you spend, just commuting," Earl said. "How long would that take you by car?"

Charlene laughed. "*I* don't know," she said. "I never had one. I got my driver's license, high school? And all the time I'm studying, and then practicing the driv-

129

ing, all the time I'm asking myself: 'Why'm I doing this? I don't have nothing to drive.' And then I think: 'Well, we might get one, if I get my license. Maybe we'll get a car then.' And I knew that wasn't true. That was just pretending. What difference does it make, I know how? Might as well take pilot lessons, if that's how it's going to work. We might get a plane."

"Well," Earl said, "do you think you could make it in less'n an hour?"

"I don't know," she said. "What do you think, Ma?"

Mrs. Arnold shrugged. "I got no idea," she said.

"Well," Earl said, "but you'd know the way to get there by car. Isn't that right, Charlene?"

"Sure," Charlene said.

"Wait a minute," Mrs. Arnold said. "I don't know what's going on here. What does all this stuff mean?"

"Well," Earl said, "I'm not from around here, you see. I grew up, I lived in Vermont. I went to college in New York. When I got out, I was in the Peace Corps. So I know the way from where I live to here, and how to get back home again. And I know the roads around where I grew up, and the subways and trains in New York. And I know the dirt roads all over Kansas, because that's where I was in the Peace Corps. But from here to Bunker Hill College? I don't know how to do that, so that's why I asked her that question."

Mrs. Arnold's eyes narrowed. "I thought that Peace Corps thing," she said, "I thought that was just for places across the water. Coon countries, helping all them naked coons."

"They got all the publicity," Earl said. "The domestic branch, no one paid attention to us. But we still did our jobs, though—thanks or no thanks, made no difference, we still did our jobs."

"Oh," Mrs. Arnold said, "well see, I didn't know that."

"Perfectly all right," Earl said, "we're all used to it by now. But see, the reason I was asking that, asking about the way, is I think I'm seeing something here that maybe fits together. And I thought maybe, we took a ride, we might see if I'm right."

"*Yeah?*" Charlene said.

"Like what?" Mrs. Arnold said. "Like what might fit together?"

"Well," Earl said, "I've been listening very carefully here, to both of you. And it seems to me, well, I know that you, Charlene, really want a car."

"*That* car," Charlene said, gazing up at the Impala. "*That's* the car I want. That one sitting right there."

Mrs. Arnold grunted. "And you, Mrs. Arnold," Earl said, "you really want for Charlene to make the best of what she has. Realize her full potential. Have a better life than yours."

"That's right," Mrs. Arnold said, setting her mouth, "which she don't want to do."

"But," Earl said, "on the other hand, you wouldn't mind having a car, enjoying the convenience of it, if you thought you could afford it, and—*and*—you saw how it might *help*, help Charlene to do what you think she should. And what you think she *can*. Like legal secretary."

Mrs. Arnold barked a brief laugh. "Mister Beale," she said, "when I was a little girl, my Uncle Joe used to be able to find dimes behind my ears. Found nickels in my hair. Never found a lot of money, just enough

131

for ice-cream cones. I asked him once, guess I was six, how come he always stopped. Why he didn't just keep on, use his magic, make us rich. And he said, well, nightshift magicians for the Edison, they had just a little magic, just enough for ice-cream cones." She smirked at him. "Now Mister Beale," she said, smiling, "I don't know you very long. But if you've got some magic that not only gets us this car, but Charlene to do her work, well, good thing for Joe that he is dead. You'd put that poor man to shame."

Earl grinned and shook his head. He held up his hand in the stop-signal gesture. "Ah, Mrs. Arnold," he said, "you're a skeptical woman. But you're right: you don't know me. On the other hand, what've you got on your schedule today? Both of you, I mean. Charlene I take it's off from school, and you spend days at home. So why not take a ride with me—Charlene, you've got your license and you want to show it to me, don't see why you shouldn't drive. And what we'll do is get the ramps out, and—I'll back this baby down for you, 'cause that part can be tricky—throw on a set of plates, and go to this college. See how long it takes. Then stop, turn around, maybe come back a different way. And see how long the trip home takes. That could tell us something."

Charlene clapped her hands. "Oh, Ma," she said, "let's do it? Please please please please, *please?*"

"Like what?" Mrs. Arnold said, quelling Charlene with her right hand. "Just what could it tell us?"

Earl drew a deep breath. "What I'm hearing, Mrs. Arnold," he said, "is that Charlene here is spending about four full hours a day, going back and forth to school. Now, that's wasted time, ma'am, which means it's wasted money, too. You, she, could save that time, good chunk of it, at least, if she had a car. Maybe not *this* car, maybe a less expensive model. We have several in stock. But see my point? If she saves the time, and she isn't bored, it's likely that her grades'll go up, and that'd put her in a position to go for something better. Every morning I have breakfast at this place over in Cambridge, near where my apartment is. They've always got the signs up for waitresses and so forth. Desperate for help. Now that's pretty far from you, but there's other places, around here, must be the same position. If you spent the time working, you're spending traveling now—not all of it, but most of it—how much you think you'd make? Make in say a week?"

Charlene shrugged. "I dunno," she said. "My girlfriend Cathy, she works. Down McDonald's there. I think she works whole forty hours, but I'm not sure what she gets. Maybe brings home, I don't know? Ninety, hundred bucks a week? Something like that anyway. Maybe a little more."

"Call it that, anyway," Earl said. "Figure fifty for half-time, McDonald's, where they don't allow no tips. Figure fifteen, twenty more, in a place where they do tip, and a pretty girl serves guys the food."

Charlene blushed again.

"Now," Earl said, "I'm not even going to tell you what the price is on this car. No need of jumping into things, not until you're sure. But I can tell you right now, and I'm prepared to back it up, I *know*, I'm absolutely *certain*, I can put you in a car."

Charlene jumped three times and clapped her hands again. "Do it do it do it," she said, her eyes dancing

133

with her feet and the jangling chains on her white boots.

Earl went into the showroom and selected the Impala keys from the pegboard in Waldo's office. He took a screwdriver and dealer plates from the desk. Fritchie spoke to him as he emerged. "What're you doing to those people, Earl?" he said.

"Only what they want done," Earl said. "Only what they want." He went into the storage room and picked up the corrugated steel ramps and carried them, one under each arm, out to the parking lot. He fastened them to the brackets at the rear of the platform.

"Now," he said, dusting his hands together, "I'm going to back it down. While I'm doing that, I'd like both of you to think about some things I'd like to do. Give me some help on this." He nodded toward the Impala. "I haven't driven this car myself. It's a southern California car, only two years old. The owner drove it here, to school, and then he had to sell it to get money for expenses. So I know it's got no rust. But what I don't know is how it handles. We put on new tires; maybe it needs alignment. Maybe after that long trip, it needs a shot of oil or grease—may be some creaks in it. The mileage is low—even going coast to coast, that once, it's still only got about eighteen thousand miles on her. Anyway, watch and listen all the way, what you see and hear and feel. And if there's the slightest thing wrong with it, well, I'm sure we can take care of it. Okay?"

"Uh huh," Charlene said. Mrs. Arnold said nothing.

"Let me see your license, Charlene," he said. She displayed it. "Okay, good," he said. "Now, just one

134

more thing: our insurance says no customer testing over forty. Will you keep her under that?"

"Uh huh," Charlene said.

"Promise?" Earl said.

She nodded. "Cross my heart to die," she said.

Mrs. Arnold shook her head. "I wished Timmy was home," she said, "'stead of over in Saigon there. I wish he was right here now. Timmy would know things."

11

Roy Fritchie before eleven thirty had invoked both
seniority and elementary justice as his entitlements to
oust Earl from the early lunch break. "It isn't fair,"
Earl had said. "I didn't want it when I first come in
here. I told you and Waldo both I never ate my lunch
until around twelve thirty, so. And it was gonna get
my stomach all screwed up. But you both said I hadda
take it because I was the new man, and the one that
was here first got to pick which one he wanted, and
you happened to like eating your lunch later on. I'd
get used to it, you said. So that was that, and my stomach did get all screwed up, and I lost about ten pounds.
But I did get used to it, and now my stomach wants
lunch early. So now what are you telling me? I got to
eat lunch late."

"It's just today," Fritchie had said, getting into his
jacket. "And it's your own fault anyway. You had me
thinking about eating ever since this morning, telling
me about all that breakfast you scarfed up. I'm going
over Hyde Park there, the other Eire Pub, and have

myself about a dozen hot dogs, all with onions, and ten beers. Maybe a hot pastrami, too."

"Yeah," Earl had said, "well fart your ass off there, okay? Before you come back here. And don't *forget* to come back here, like you been known to do when you went that place before. I don't see your ass in that chair by five past one, the latest, I am calling Waldo up. Speaking of which, where the hell is he? Waldo coming in today?"

"He called up while you're out with that honey," Fritchie had said. "Told him it's quiet, nothing much going on. He said he'd be in, around two or so, but I bet he never shows up. He was on his way to the boatyard, getting things all set for winter. But that always takes him more time'n he thinks. I doubt we see Waldo at all."

Shortly after noon a middle-aged man in a shapeless gray suit drove a 'fifty-five Ford Crown Victoria into the lot. It had come out of the factory two toned, the body divided by a thick chromium strip that swooped down from the crests of the front fenders into a fat silver line ending at the taillight assemblies. The lower part of the car had been painted brilliant turquoise; the upper half, including the roof, had been blinding white; another thick chromium strip went over that to create what Ford had advertised as "a tiara effect." Earl got up from his desk and watched as the man stopped the car in front of the door, shut off the engine, and got out. Earl opened the office door for him.

The two of them stood in silence for a minute, the man staring at the car as though unfamiliar with it, Earl making notes in his head. After a while he went out into the lot and walked around the car, running

137

the tips of his fingers along the trim strips, stooping to rap his knuckles lightly on the liners inside the wheel wells, noting the fit of the removable skirt over the right wheel, placing his hands on the trunk and then on the hood to jounce the car on its springs, touching the treads of the tires, opening the driver's side door and examining the jamb and sills, getting in and looking at the odometer reading, starting the engine and listening to it while he turned the steering wheel from lock to lock, stepping on the brake pedal, and running his hand over the white upholstery. Then he shut off the engine and returned to the office.

"What do you think?" the man said.

Earl shrugged. "Same thing you probably do," he said. "You wouldn't be here, otherwise. Owned it since new?"

The man nodded proudly. "Original owner," he said. "Got the bill of sale in the glove box. Complete service records on her, too. Taken damned good care of that car."

"Yeah," Earl said, "I believe it. Taken pretty good care of you, too. I assume the clock's on the second time around, right?" The man nodded. So did Earl. "Hundred forty thousand—that's damned good for any car. She's plumb wore out now, of course, but New England'll do that. Do that every time. But stood up a lot better'n most cars I've seen, driven that far around here. I'd go back to the guy sold me that one, buy another one, I was you."

The man's face crinkled into the kind of reluctant smile that Earl had seen on the faces of very tough men the nights before their release dates at the end of long terms in jail, when other inmates heckled them about bedding wives and girlfriends blind before the next sundown. The amount of mail and visits he had had from the women that he'd known had told him what the chances were of such things happening. "I lived in New Bedford then," the man said. "I think he's out of business. And if he isn't, I am—that kind of business, at least. I paid thirty-one hundred bucks for that car, two thousand bucks in my trade-in and cash, and the rest I paid off in a year." He paused. "I could do that then. Spend it all on a car, I mean. I was single. I'd earned it. It was all mine to spend like I wanted." He looked at Earl as though seeking approval.

"And now you're not," Earl said.

The man lifted and dropped his eyebrows, tilting his head slightly, and making a small gesture with his left hand. "And now I'm not," he said.

"What've you got in mind?" Earl said.

"I don't know," the man said. "Well, like I said, I know damned well I'm in no position to buy me another new car. But she said to me, my wife did, this morning, I'd better face facts pretty soon. Because winter's on the way." He sighed. "And she's right. I know that. I've got to get on the stick here."

"Do you know what you want?" Earl said. He nodded at the Impala, back up on the platform. "I've got a customer looking at that, but it isn't sold yet. Committed. I don't personally think it's likely to give you the service you got out of this one, but it is ten years younger, eighteen on the clock, and you'd still have that, well, sporty look. How much you figure you can spend?"

The man shook his head. "I wouldn't want that one," he said, squinting at it. "You can see it from here—it's been hit. And as for the sporty thing, well facts're facts: my sporty days're behind me. Least for damned certain now, I can tell you, and as far's I can see up ahead. I think what I'm looking for's what they put under the old 'good transportation' flags there. Something three or four years old, kind of dull, with low mileage on it so far and good mileage on the gas. I'd like a radio and heater—well, I'd like a lot of things but I really do need those."

"We've got some, might meet your requirements," Earl said. "But I still can't be sure till I know, about how much you can swing."

"Well," the man said, "I won't know that until I know how much my car there's worth in trade. How much I can swing on another one depends a lot on that."

Earl stared at him. "You mean," he said, "you don't know? Is that what you're telling me here?"

"Well," the man said, somewhat defensively, "I mean, I know it can't be much. It does have a lot of mileage on it, and I know it's twelve years old. But it still starts and everything—it runs. I put new tires on it last year. And it's had new shocks, and a tune-up. I know it won't stand up much longer, someone drives it to work every day, or needs a car in his work, as I do. But for somebody who just needs it for doing errands, maybe retired, going to the store and so forth, or to get to the nearest subway stop, well, it might last someone like that quite a good long time. It must be worth something. Had no trouble passing Inspection."

"Mister," Earl said, "don't give me 'Passed Inspection.' You had that done by the guy sells you gas. He'd pass a camel, you had one. No, you just got a common sickness. Some people get it from getting too close to their dogs. Or their cats. Canaries. Some people get it from boats, so I heard anyway. And some people, like you, get it from cars. You fall in love with your dog, you just can't face the fact the dog's gotten old, and it's sick, and it's got to go to sleep. The cat, same thing. The bird. The people who get it from pets: their vets all drive big Cadillacs. The people who get it from boats: if the old tub doesn't just sink and drown them, the guy that repairs it gets rich. And that's why where cars're concerned, you don't fall in love with the things. Gets in the way of your judgment.

"Now," he said, "it does start. Starts when it's hot, at least, and the weather isn't too cold. But it doesn't really *want* to start, even when it's warm. You had it tuned? Well, it was either a while ago, and you've been driving it a lot in city traffic, or else it's burnin' more oil'n both of us think, because those plugs in there're all fouled. And the tune-up did not include a new starter motor, which pretty soon is my guess is gonna cost someone most of what's in a C note. New shocks? Cheapies, then, or else you've been driving on dirt roads—they're shot. Tires're bottom-the-line Sears, and you were smart to save your dough because the front ones're all scalloped and the back ones're all scuffed. It needs a new muffler, and a new tail pipe, and a new resonator—you drive it with the windows closed, like people do, the winter, you're at least gonna get a bellyache from the exhaust fumes seeping up from that system through the floorboards. If you're lucky and don't die—because my guess is those boards're all rusted out, just like the rockers, and the wheel wells, and the sills, and all the panel welds that

141

I saw just in my few minutes. Which means that anyone dumb enough to dump a lot of money into parts and labor on that thing is only saying he's determined to make sure that when it falls apart, it will be at least moving.

"So, mister," Earl said, "I hate to hurt your feelings, but I got to tell the truth. We've had some junkers on this lot and in time we got them sold. But your car if it was a horse, the place to take it, way it is, would be the dog food factory. It's shot. It's not worth anything, except, maybe, to you."

"Gee," the man said wistfully, "I really didn't expect much, no more'n a few hundred dollars. But, nothing? Nothing at all? I got to have a car, my job, I never know, I'm gonna need it, but it's got to be around."

Earl spread his hands. "What can I tell you?" he said. "Whaddaya want me to do? You want me to hike up the price on something that'll do what you want, need a car for? We got what you're looking for, I think. At least one and possibly three. We got a nice 'sixty-three Falcon, out in the yard in the back. Why's it out back, instead of out front, if it's such a bargain for someone? Because most of the people, come in off the street, they come in when they see the hot stuff. Convertibles, hardtops, real jazzy wheels: that's what brings them in here. When we get a Cadillac, right? Or a Lincoln, big Chrysler or something—if it can be polished, it goes out in front, and better cars, not flashy but better, they go in the back.

"Now," Earl said, "this little Falcon, it's white and it's got Fordomatic. Which means it's a two-speed, hitched to a six-banger, and quick off the line it is not. It'll go sixty, go sixty-five, but you'll have to be patient

142

getting there. If some cop arrests you for seventy-five, go to court and you'll get acquitted. The most it'll ever do, running flat out, is seventy—that takes a week. And the downside of a steep hill with a good stiff wind behind you. Thrilling this car is not."

The man smiled weakly. "No good for picking up girls," he said.

"No good at all for that," Earl said. "You might get an old nun, you trolled long enough, but otherwise, no hope at all."

"What's the mileage?" the man said.

"Twenty-seven honest thousand," Earl said. "You doubt that, I suggest you check the carpeting, the seats, and the inside of the trunk. All the usual stuff, and all original, that most people never learn is how you tell if the clock's honest. It gets, at least they tell me, it gets nineteen miles the gallon."

"And the old lady who owned it drove it just to church on Sundays," the man said.

"We don't know who owned it," Earl said. "We got it at an auction when a big dealer out in Holyoke got himself overextended and had to Chapter-Eleven his inventory. All I can tell you's that he sold it new to whoever it was, and whoever it was'd just traded it when the guy's show went belly-up. His nameplate's still on the trunk. You got a toothpick or something, you can run it along the letters and peel off the dried paste wax that owner missed with his rag. This car had good care. But good care don't go out front."

"How much is it," the man said.

"That's what I was getting to," Earl said. "I got to look it up in our book—which I'm not gonna show you—because I really don't know what we own it for, or what we're asking for it. So my question is, when I look at those numbers, what do you want me to do? I tell you your car is worth nothing to us—your unit is ready for Goldie's. You drive it down there, it's right down in Braintree, if it'll make it that far, and Goldie might give you two tens and a fin, maybe five tens if he's in a good mood and he knows a guy desperate for 'fifty-five Ford chrome parts—your chrome does look pretty good. If I stick to that statement, that we don't want your car, is that gonna hurt all your feelings? Hurt them enough so you go somewhere else, get someone to tell you nice lies?

"Because I can do that, you know," Earl said, smiling. "I tell lies with the best of them. And if that makes you happy, happier at least, just say so and I will get going. I'll get down the book and I'll look at the numbers, and then I'll add three hundred bucks. And then I'll say to you, a completely straight face: 'Well, sir, I'll go this far for you. Two hundred bucks is the best I can do for that fine antique car you drove in.' And you can tell me that that's not enough, you got to have four at the least. And I'll cough and I'll shake my head, shake my head lots, and do some more math on my pad. And then I'll say: 'Look, this is it: two fifty on yours for the Falcon.' And you'll say: 'Three fifty.' I'll say: 'Split the difference.' You'll grin and then we'll shake hands.' And you will end up paying eight hundred dollars, if that's what we *do* have to get, and Monday or Tuesday the boss'll tell me: 'Your lunch hour today, drive that clapped-out old Ford down to Goldie's, and keep what he gives you, yourself. I'll pick you up, my way in.'

"So what's it going to be," Earl said. "Eight ball, nine ball, straight pool?"

The man forced his smile again. "Let's go and look at the book," he said. "And if that's in the ballpark, the car."

The man said he was impressed with the Falcon. He sat in it and looked under the hood, repeating the inspection steps he had seen Earl perform on the Ford. "I really don't know why I'm doing all this," he said, standing up after rapping the rocker panels lightly with his fist. "I just saw you do it, so I know there must be a reason. Makes me feel like I know what I'm doing."

"Well," Earl said, "if somebody asks you sometime, you ever do it again, the reason is that's how you tell if you got rust starting under the paint, coming from inside out. If it's solid, there isn't, or there probably ain't—if it isn't, there certainly is, and it's not gonna be long before you can see it, which is when you say 'bye-bye' your dough."

The man dusted his hands off and looked critically at the Falcon. "It's pretty much the way you described it," he said. "I'd like a test drive, though."

"Well," Earl said, frowning, "you oughta get one, of course. But my problem is, I'm here alone, and I can't leave the office, but our rules say I got to ride with you. That way if the car doesn't come back, neither do I, but the cops take kidnapping more serious'n they do plain auto theft. That's if the boss isn't mad at me that day, so he decides not to report it."

The man laughed. "Well," he said, "is anyone else coming in?"

Earl looked at his watch. "He was due back from lunch twenty minutes ago," he said. "But that doesn't mean what you think. Roy don't do it often, but every now and then he gets to having a glass of beer with his sandwich. And then he has another one, and sometimes he comes back pretty late. Like maybe two or three days."

The man looked crestfallen. "I'm sorry," Earl said. "If you think I'm pulling something on you, you're wrong. I really want to sell you this car, and I'd like to close it today. Because I think you like it, and I'm off tomorrow, and I will bet you will come back. Which will mean Roy will be here, and he'll close the deal, and he'll get at least half commission. When I was the one that made the damned sale, and he's getting paid for beer drinking."

"Well," the man said, "suppose we do this: Get all the paperwork done now, and I'll give you a deposit. Then I'll come back tomorrow and road-test the thing, and if it's okay, I'll pay the rest."

Earl studied him. "How you planning, pay for this?" he said.

The man shrugged. "I'm not going to borrow the money," he said. "If that's what you're thinking about. I've seen too many people, much better off than I am, get themselves in trouble taking out loans. Even when they manage to pay them off on time, it's always a struggle. And it's usually because they weren't able to control themselves, and decided to spend more'n they could afford—Cadillacs on Chevy wages—so that they got in too deep. I've got no self-control, either. Well, not much, at least. Just enough so I don't even go to new-car places, and tempt myself. I shop for bargains, where bargains're are sold, and I only carry as much money as I can safely spend. I carry that much in cold cash."

"But you've got the checking account, I assume," Earl said.

"Sure," the man said, "but there isn't much in it, I'm sorry to say. Maybe two or three hundred bucks."

"Okay," Earl said, "how about this? We agreed on eight hundred plus your car. Which looks like I'm giving you a hundred but is actually fifty big bucks. Now this little Falcon is cheap to repair—not that I think it needs work. If the front end is shot, or the thing's out of line, the most it can cost you's a hundred. You give me seven in cash, and your regular check for a hundred. I can't deposit the check until Monday, so you can stop it before then, or let it go through, get the car fixed yourself. And that means we do the deal right this minute, and my thirsty friend gets no divvies."

The man smiled. "Excellent," he said. "Where there's a will, there's a way."

Back at Earl's desk in the office, the man produced his checkbook and the registration for the Crown Victoria. He wrote the check to Centre Street Motors for a hundred dollars, and Earl filled in the serial and engine numbers of the Falcon on the standard bill of sale, along with the description of make, model, and year. He signed it. He said, "Hey, all of this, we've been talking all this time and I wish to God all my customers were like you, but I never did get your name."

The man had taken out his wallet and was counting crisp new hundreds onto the desk, making seven of them into a fan. "Make it out in my wife's name," he said. "I'm in the process of putting all our bigger assets in her name. In case I should drop dead or something.

147

Get more conscious of that possibility, I find, as you get closer to forty. Eleanor D. Forrest. With two *r*s."

Earl paused. "Yeah," he said, "well, I hope the Ford's in your name, though. Or else she signed that registration over."

"No, no," the man said. "The Ford's in my name, all right. Like I told you, I bought that little beauty when I was a single man."

"Good," Earl said, writing in the woman's name. "I could just see this falling through at the last minute because of some piddly thing like that."

"Nope," the man said. He endorsed the back of his registration to Centre Street Motors, and signed it. He pushed the currency and the check and the registration across the desk to Earl, who handed him the bill of sale. "Looks fine to me," they said in unison. They both laughed. They stood up.

"Well," the man said, folding the bill of sale and putting it in his inside jacket pocket, then extending his hand to Earl, "a pleasure to do business with you." He laughed again. "And I never did get your name, either."

Earl laughed. He shook hands. "Earl Beale," he said, turning the registration over with his left hand. "Mister Forrest." He looked up, still smiling, but frowning. "Chatham?" he said. "You live in Chatham? All the way down on the Cape? I thought you lived somewhere round here."

Michael Forrest shook his head. "No," he said, "well, fairly near here. I live, well, *we* live, north of Boston. Up in Andover. We register the car in Chatham because the insurance rates're lower."

Earl rolled his eyes. "Well, I know," he said, "but

isn't that taking a chance? I mean, where you register the car, where you insure the car, it's supposed to be where you keep the thing, and where you do most of your driving. You get in an accident, and they find out, you're actually up Andover there, and there's where the car is garaged, well, your policy won't be no good."

"Oh," Forrest said, "that's no problem. We have a house in Chatham. A summer house in Chatham. And that *is* where the car's garaged. And that is where we use it. In the summer Eleanor moves down there with the kids, and I lead the bachelor life. On weekends I just take the bus from in town to the Cape. So I have our car up here, if I happen to need it—most days I take the train—and she has, or had, the Ford down there, for errands and the beach."

"Well, jeez," Earl said, "we didn't advertise that Falcon. Why come all the way down here to buy a car? Andover's quite a ways. Or if the Cape is where you use it, why not just buy one there?"

"Simple," Forrest said. "In Andover everyone knows exactly what I do. If someone hasn't told them, all they do is look it up. In the town directory. And to a lesser degree they also know, down there on the Cape, though it matters less down there. On the Cape all the dealers inflate prices when they sell to summer residents, because that in their estimation is why God created them. On groceries and stuff like that, we have to sit and take it. But not on cars, uh uh, not when we're buying cars."

"Then why not Andover?" Earl said. "That's a pretty nice town, isn't it? Should take some good trades in up there."

"Because of what I do," Forrest said. "On the Cape

they screw me on general principles. In Andover it's specific, because of my assignment. I'm a government lawyer. People don't like us a lot."

"That's a new one on me," Earl said. "The guy that . . . what do you do? Put people in jail?"

"Oh, no," Forrest said, picking the Falcon keys off Earl's desk, "I don't do that. Okay to drive this around and swap the plates out front?"

"Sure, sure," Earl said. "Well, what do you do?"

"I'm just a counsel, in-house counsel," Forrest said. "An office lawyer, that's all. Just a standard drone."

"Well, who do you do this for?" Earl said.

Forrest smiled at him. He took out his wallet again and gave Earl a business card. It read: "U.S. Department of the Treasury. Internal Revenue Service." The seal of the United States was embossed in gold below the agency name. Below it was the man's name, and below that, in the lower-left-hand corner: "Regional Counsel. Northeast Region." A Boston address and a phone number were listed on the lower right.

"Oh," Earl said.

"I'm surprised you didn't guess," Forrest said, smiling.

Earl snickered. "No, you're not," he said. "You know you're cute enough to do it, fool dumb clucks like me."

"Oh, yeah?" Forrest said. "Look, the deal's done now. You want to level with me? How much's my car actually worth, that you think you'll get for it?"

Earl shrugged. "I dunno," he said. "Some kid comes in, looking for a new Corvette with three hundred in his pocket, I might get a couple hundred. Leave him enough, insurance. Chances of that happening aren't

150

good, I'll tell you that. But I could turn a quick dollar. If I should get lucky."

"And how much," Forrest said, "was your honest-to-God rock-bottom on the Falcon? What you would've sold it for, if you had to move that car?"

"Just what you paid for it," Earl said, looking him straight in the eye. "And you know why? Because I *did* have to move that car. We got inventory problems here, and we're hurting for cash."

"Do I believe that?" Forrest said.

"In your line of work," Earl said, "I'd tend to doubt it, myself. Your habits're probably pretty strong now. But I did tell you the truth."

Forrest nodded and headed toward the back door. When he had left the office, Earl picked up the card from the desk, and put it in his pocket.

When Fritchie returned from lunch at quarter of three, he resisted Earl's suggestion that he sleep it off in the storeroom. He mumbled something about "new fuckin' junker out in front. Waldo'll have your ass for that one." He took off his jacket and sat down at his desk and gazed into space, moistening his lips from time to time. Then he rested his forearms on the desk and gazed. Finally he folded his arms on the desk and rested his head on them. Earl let him snore softly for ten minutes. Then he got up and gently pulled Fritchie's chair away from his desk, easing Fritchie's arms and head up and back so that his head lolled gaping-mouthed to the right and his hands lay on his crotch. Earl wheeled him slowly and quietly through the office and into the back room where the tools and ramps were

151

kept, pushed him into the darkness, and shut the door He returned to his own desk.

The phone rang just as Charlene Gaffney and her mother appeared at the front door. He picked up the handset and said: "Centre Street Motors. Hold a minute, please?" He put the line on Hold. He went to the door and ushered the two women in. "On the phone," he said, pointing to his desk. "Come in, sit down. Just be a minute." He went back to the phone. "Centre Street," he said, "thank you for waiting." Then he said: "Hey, sorry, boss. Had some customers come in, same time as your call. You told me the rules, old buddy. Customers got to come first. No, it's been pretty quiet. Roy took the late lunch. Isn't back yet. So I'm here all by myself. Yeah, uh huh. Yup, one. The Falcon. Guy wanted it, his beach place. No, didn't give me any trouble. Nice clean sale, for just what we wanted. I don't think you need to, really. Roy should be back in an hour. This is his late night. Okay, so I'll see you on Monday. Yes, I do, boss, don't kid me—I have got tomorrow off." He hung up the handset.

"Mrs. Arnold, Charlene," he said, "why don't you two all come with me and sit down. Tell me what I can do, help you out." He got up and ushered them into Waldo's private office. They took chairs facing him at the desk.

Charlene wet her lips and looked at her mother. Mrs. Arnold in her black coat sat without expression, her black bag clenched in her hands. Charlene looked pleadingly at Earl. "Mister Beale," she said, "I hope maybe you can help us. Me. We, after we went home, I started calling people? The restaurants, like you said? And they do have some jobs. But I got no experience,

152

so I get starting pay. And, it isn't very much. After what Ma tells me."

Mrs. Arnold shook her head once. "I tried to tell her that," she said. "God knows how many times. I guess this is better, though. When someone that she don't know, that's got no reason to protect her, tells her the exact same thing, well then, at least, she listens."

"How much is it?" Earl said. "What does it come to?"

Charlene licked her lips again. Mrs. Arnold answered. "By the time they get through," she said, "taking things out, and the hours that they'll let her work, she'll be lucky she brings home fifty a week. And that's working almost full-time that place. It's criminal what they can do."

"It isn't much, is it," Earl said. "How long would the starter pay last? And what would you make after that?"

"Three months, they said," Charlene said. "Then I would get fifteen more."

" '*If* there's an opening, after three months,' " Mrs. Arnold said. "They didn't promise you, would be. I told her and told her, and told her again. I said: 'Charlene, that's not enough. If Timmy was here, instead of Saigon, Timmy would tell you that, too.' I don't know who's, which one of them's taking the biggest chance. Her over here, mooning at cars that she just can't afford, or Timmy over there with people shooting at him."

"Oh, Ma," Charlene said, "cut it out. Timmy's an embassy guard. He's not out where the fighting is, people're getting shot. You read his letters, Ma, and you know, Timmy's just plain bored."

Mrs. Arnold said: "Huh. Timmy doesn't know enough, get scared when he should. Don't surprise me, he isn't. He's got no sense, either. Not an atom of sense. Just like the people in charge of the country—not an atom of sense. Americans should mind our own business, just stay home and go to work. What those Chinamen're up to shouldn't bother us at all."

Charlene sighed. "Mister Beale," she said, "do you see any way? Any way at all?"

Earl cleared his throat. "Charlene," he said, "and Mrs. Arnold, let me assure you something. There's no point, I've got no reason, sit and lie to you." Charlene looked hopeful. Mrs. Arnold showed a small, grim smile. Earl shook his head. "No, Mrs. Arnold," he said, "now you've got to listen, now. This is the truth I'm telling you, no matter what you think. If I sell you a car that I know you can't afford, and I help you get financing, knowing you can't keep it up, well, that won't do me any good. It will hurt me, in fact. If you default on a loan that I vouched for you to get, the next time that I take a buyer in to get a loan, the bank is going to turn him down, no matter he can pay. And why will the bank do that? Because you didn't pay on yours. So there's no percentage in it for me, get you in some big fat mess. This is how I make my living, day in and day out. I'd rather lose a nice commission, I can live without, 'n get it and then find out that I can't make any more.

"Now," he said, "Charlene, I got to be honest with you. I know you love that neat hardtop. I want you to be happy. But this job that you're describing won't carry the payments until you graduate in June and go on, a better job. Unless, and I don't know this, you can

154

make a big down payment. Just how much can you pay down?"

Charlene glanced at her mother again. She looked back at Earl. "I," she said, "Ma finally said, if you could find a way, she would let me borrow some of Timmy's money. Not all of it, but some."

"Which Charlene has got to pay back," Mrs. Arnold said, "before he gets home, October. And that's how I decided how much I would let her use. By figuring up just how much is the most she can pay back, along with the bank payments."

"You don't need to tell him that, Ma," Charlene said. "He don't care about that stuff."

"Well, and how much is that, then?" Earl said.

Charlene said, "Five hundred dollars, sir."

"Okay," Earl said, "let's do the numbers." He moved his pad in front of him and took his ballpoint out. "After you folks left today, I went and checked the book. I wasn't sure the figures, so I went and looked them up. That car out there that you drove is a 'sixty-five. It's only two years old, and the mileage on it's low. This is good news for some buyer, but it may not be for you. That car listed new for thirty-eight, almost four thousand dollars. The Blue Book, which is what all the dealers use for prices, the Blue Book says that model, year, in good condition runs around twenty-six hundred bucks. Which isn't chicken feed." He wrote the figures on the pad. Mrs. Arnold scowled. Charlene continued to look hopeful.

"Now," he said, "you don't have a trade-in. Most people don't know this, but I'll let you in on a secret. If we don't have to take your worn-out car in trade, and maybe lose some money on it by the time we get it fixed enough to sell it, someone else, we're in a position to sweeten things a little. Which means"—he paused and looked at them—"I can knock two hundred off that twenty-six I mentioned." Charlene smiled.

Earl held up his right hand in the Stop gesture. "Don't smile yet, Charlene," he said. "I haven't finished yet. You've got five hundred dollars. Good. On twenty-four that's a good start—at least it looks like one. But I wouldn't let you put it all down on the purchase price, the car. Because you're going to need insurance, plus the fees for number plates. I'd be on the safe side and make sure I had enough. Since you're under twenty-six, and you'll be driving it, even if your mother owns it—which is what I would suggest—those insurance costs are high. I'd say put down three hundred." He wrote that on the pad. "Which means you finance twenty-one. Twenty-one hundred dollars."

"Now," he said, "twenty-one hundred at eight percent for two years, just let me check the tables here." He opened the top drawer of his desk and took out a plasticized card. "Is one-oh-one fifty a month."

"Eight percent?" Mrs. Arnold said. "I seen an ad in the paper, and on the TV too, that auto loans are cheaper's that. Six or seven, I thought."

"On new cars, Mrs. Arnold," Earl said. "That hardtop's used. And that's for three years also, thirty-six payments, which the banks won't write for used cars—two years, twenty-four months, is the highest they will go.

"Now, Charlene," he said, "you're going to need gas. Car with no gas in it, well, won't get you very far. You're going to need snow tires pretty soon, too, which

156

that car, coming from California, doesn't have. Snow tires are expensive. You're going to have to have the oil changed, and filters, and all that sort of thing. And all that stuff costs money. Next year about this time, you'll get a new insurance bill. And there's the excise tax you pay, just for owning it. Now, you may not've thought of this, but I think you really should. Owning a car, keeping it up, costs money. Steadily. If you get through a given month without having to spend at least sixty, seventy dollars, in addition to your payment, you can count yourself lucky. And if I was you I'd save that money, for next month when you may need it."

Mrs. Arnold shook her head. "Mister," she said, "I don't care what you say, and I don't care what she says. This girl cannot afford that car. There's no two ways about it: she just can't afford that car."

Charlene looked at Earl. Her eyes were brimming. "She's wrong, isn't she," she said. "There is a way, I know. I just got to have that car. You showed me yourself, you showed her, how much easier it'd be if I had a car for school." She turned to her mother. "And I mean it, Ma, I will work. And I will get better marks." She looked back at Earl. "Tell her that she's wrong, please? Tell her there's a way. You just left something out. Tell her that she's wrong."

Earl shook his head. "She's dead right, Charlene," he said. "I hate to say it but it's true. You can't afford that car, and even though I'd make some money, selling it to you, I have to tell you I don't want to. I think it's a big mistake, and I left nothing out."

Charlene slumped in the chair and covered her face with her hands. Her body shook and she made quiet sobbing sounds.

157

Mrs. Arnold's face showed mingled triumph and anger. "I knew I was right," she said. "I knew it all along. And I'm glad you finally told her. But I got to say I don't thank you for stringing her along." She put her arm around her daughter's shoulder and patted her on the arm. "There, there, darlin'," she said, "you'll get over this. Stop your cryin' now, just stop. And tell yourself that come next summer, you get a *good* job, then you can get yourself a car." She looked at Earl again. "This was a bad thing to do, mister," she said. "You got this poor girl's hopes all up, and then just smashed them for her. I'm glad you finally wound up on my side in this whole thing, but I sure God wished you didn't have to rile her all up first."

"Mrs. Arnold," Earl said, "you haven't let me finish. I meant every word I said, to the both of you. I do think Charlene could get better grades in school, if she had a car. I think that your life would be easier at least, if she had a car. I'm on her side, not on yours, where those things are concerned. Charlene's dead right about your need. You need to have a car."

Charlene put her hands down. Her cheeks were wet. "Ma's right," she said angrily. "You just strung me along, and now you're doing it some more. What good's it do for you to say that, about how I'm right? You just told us we're too poor for me to have a car. Well, we knew we didn't have much. Didn't need you, tell us that. And we don't need you now, you bastard, to sit there and rub it in."

"Charlene," Earl said, "you're not listening. You do need *a* car. You can't swing the Impala. But that Impala's not the only car outside this office. There's *a* car that you *can* afford. It's right outside the door. The man drove it in here today, right after you folks left. He told me that his mother needs to have an operation and he had to sell his car to get money now, today. I bought it from him on the spot. And you can own that car. You can drive it out today, if you can get insurance and the plates." He looked at his watch. "Although it's pretty late for that. I doubt you could pull it off. Well, still, it can be yours today. I'll put a set of plates on it and drive it to your house. I can't let you use the plates this weekend—that's against the rules. But on Monday, when they're open, you can get yourself insured, and then go down and get your plates. By noon I'll bet on Monday you can drive out and have lunch."

Charlene jumped out of the chair and ran to the door. She left it open when she went out into the yard, squealing. Mrs. Arnold scowled at Earl. "All right, mister," she said, "you got more tricks in your bag'n even I dreamed that you had. Just what would the payments be on this new goddamned temptation?"

"Nothin'," Earl said.

She stared at him. "Nothin'? What new kind of bunk is this? What're you pulling on us now? Treatin' us like suckers."

"Same answer," Earl said, "nothin'. Zero payments, zero months, and zero interest, too."

"There's a catch in here somewhere," Mrs. Arnold said. "There's got to be a catch. I know that there's a catch in there. I just can't see what it is."

"Mrs. Arnold," he said, "there's no catch, believe me. That Ford, that's a Ford there she's looking at, that Ford is twelve years old. True, it's only got forty-odd thousand miles on it, but it's still an old, old car. And to someone who's been a little luckier than you

159

and Charlene've been, someone who's got some free cash, well, they just won't look at it. It's got some rust. It needs a new muffler. It just isn't as pretty as that maroon job that she first saw, and somebody with that kind of money, who can afford to spend it, well, he wants pretty too.

"But," Earl said, "and I won't deny this, I had Charlene in mind when I bought it from the guy. For someone in Charlene's position, and in your position, too, that Ford hardtop out there could be just about the perfect car. It runs all right. Does burn some oil, but all old cars do that. It's got a new inspection sticker so the running gear's all right—if it wasn't all right then the car would not have passed. I don't know but I would guess when it gets cold, new battery.

"But still," he said, "add all that up: a Midas muffler, okay? Fifteen bucks, including labor, cheaper'n I can sell one. A battery from Western Auto? Maybe eighteen more. If she can learn to keep the oil up, and buy cheap stuff by the case, maybe forty cents a week'll keep it fat and happy. Can she drive it to New York every day? Nope. Can she drive it to school every day, and you to the doctor, and store? Sure can. What'll the excise tax probably be? Ten or twelve bucks, I would guess. And since no bank's involved in the deal, you don't need collision insurance—price there drops to about sixty bucks. Will it last her three, four years? No, indeed it won't. But will it last her until she can get a job, and a better one? If she's careful with it, sure. No trouble at all."

"And what about your price, to buy it?" she said. "I bet I know what that is. I bet I can guess it right

160

off. To the penny. Your price right down to the penny."

Charlene came bounding back into the office. "Oh, Ma," she said, "come and see it. It's just beautiful, it's just beautiful. Can we start it up, Mister Beale? And maybe go out for a ride?"

Mrs. Arnold turned to face her. There was a small smile on her face. "Charlene," she said, patting the chair, "now you just sit down here a minute. Mister Beale here and I, we've just been having a chat. And I want to finish that chat here and now, because he's got me real curious."

Charlene sat down. "You mean it, Ma?" she said.

Mrs. Arnold nodded. She patted Charlene on the thigh. She looked back at Earl. "Okay, Mister Beale," she said, grinning, "did I guess right? Yes, I did."

"This isn't fair," Earl said. "You want me to tell you if you guessed right. But I don't know what you guessed."

Mrs. Arnold nodded serenely. "That's all right," she said. "Im an honest woman. Been one all my life. You just tell me what the price is, and I'll tell you, I guessed right."

Earl shook his head, smiling ruefully. "Well, Mrs. Arnold," he said, "I'm glad they're not all tough as you. I suppose you don't believe me if I say when I bought that car, that I had Charlene in mind?"

Mrs. Arnold smiled broadly. "Probably not," she said.

"And that when I bought it, just an hour or so ago, I made up my mind on the spot that if you two could swing it I would let it go to you for cost plus twenty bucks? Because I like this kid, and I do think she needs a car?"

Charlene bounced in the chair. "Charlene," Mrs. Arnold said, patting her again, "now you just be still now, while Mister Beale's soft-soaping us. No, Mister Beale," she said, "I don't think I would. But I will be polite now, and I'll say: 'Of *course* I do.' How much does it cost?"

"Three hundred bucks," Earl said.

Mrs. Arnold stared at him. Charlene's mouth dropped open. Earl grinned. "Now it's my turn, Mrs. Arnold, and you promised you'd be honest. I told you twenty over my cost, which was two hundred eighty bucks. If you think that's a funny price, well, I can't say I blame you. But here is what happened, how I got to that: I gave him two seventy-five for the car itself. The other five was for the gas he just put in. Two eighty plus twenty's three hundred. Three hundred's my price to you."

"And there's no catch," Mrs. Arnold said. "You're not gonna spring something later. Something that costs us more money."

"Nope," Earl said, "that's all there is. Three hundred and she's yours. Take her home this afternoon and get her out of here before my boss comes in tomorrow, and makes me raise the price. And since you still haven't told me your guess, I'm gonna guess at your guess. It was five hundred, right? Five hundred bucks, on the nose?"

Mrs. Arnold swallowed and nodded. "That's what it was," she said. "Once you knew how much we had with us, that's what I figured it was."

"Well, you see, Mrs. Arnold," Earl said, getting a

162

bill of sale from the drawer, "I agree that you sure can't trust many, especially my line of work. But now and then, you got to agree now, one of us plays by the rules. Some of us do tell the truth. I happen to think it's the only way. I need my conscience clear to sleep."

The driveway of the brown three-decker on Balsam Street in West Roxbury was two tracks of cement leading in from the street. Earl crouched to remove the dealer plate from the Crown Victoria. When he stood up with the plate under his arm, Charlene grabbed him, spun him to face her, hugged him, and stood on the tiptoes of her white vinyl boots to kiss him repeatedly on the face, ending with the lips. The last one was a fairly long kiss, that she emphasized with her tongue, and by writhing against his torso.

Mrs. Arnold took her by the shoulder and pulled her away. "Now you cut that out, Charlene," she said. "You just cut that out right now." Mrs. Arnold's face was very red as Charlene, without letting go of Earl, stepped back half a pace. *"Honestly,"* Mrs. Arnold said.

" *'Honestly,'* " Charlene said, mimicking her mother, and then, "Thank you, thank you, thank you, Mister Beale. I love you lots and lots. Oooh, thank you just so much." She gave him another hug, and a more chaste kiss.

He gently disengaged her hands from his upper arms and stepped diagonally back from her. He tried to look sheepish. He looked at Mrs. Arnold. "Well, Mrs. Arnold," he said, "I've sold a few cars in my time, and like to think at least I've pleased some of my customers. But I've got to tell you, ma'am, she's the first one, ever kissed me."

163

"Yeah," Mrs. Arnold said, getting a restraining grip on Charlene's arm. "Well, I appreciate it, too. Not quite that much, but I thank you. I might have misjudged you. I'd invite you in for coffee, but I'm afraid what this one might do."

He laughed. "It's okay," he said. "I've got to start back anyway. The boss in special situations like this doesn't mind us putting the sign up, but it does say twenty minutes is how long that we'll be closed. So I do have to start back."

"Do you want us to call you a cab?" Charlene said.

"Huh," Mrs. Arnold said, "walk to Worcester and back, 'fore he'd get here."

"No," Earl said, "but thanks for asking. I hope you enjoy the car."

On the walk back he stopped at a doughnut shop and bought two large coffees, one black and one with cream and sugar. He carried them back to the office, unlocked the door, and went in. He did not remove the CLOSED sign from the door; he locked it behind him. He put the bag of coffees on Fritchie's desk, opened it and took out the one with cream and sugar. He sat down at his desk, opened the container and began to drink, staring vacantly straight ahead, his forehead furrowed. Then he nodded once and put the cup down.

He opened the drawer and took out a blank bill of sale. He took the pink and yellow office copies of Florence Arnold's bill of sale and tore them into eight pieces. He put those in his left front pants pocket. He picked up the copies of the bill of sale made out to Eleanor Forrest for the Falcon. He copied the information onto the blank bill of sale, omitting the notations

164

listing and describing the Crown Victoria as the trade-in car. He entered the purchase price of the Falcon as $600. When he had finished, he tore off the top sheet and ripped it into eight small pieces. He put them in his pants pocket with the shreds of the Arnold document. He reached into his left-inside jacket pocket and took out two packets of currency, kept separate with paper clips. He removed the clip from the bundle of fifteen twenties Mrs. Arnold had given to him, and put thirteen of them in his wallet. He removed the clip from the seven one-hundred-dollar bills that Forrest had given to him and counted out three that he put in his wallet. He clipped the remaining four together with the two twenties he had held out from the Arnold sale. He reached back into his jacket and got out Forrest's check for $100; he clipped that with the currency remaining from the sale. He took a brown manila business-size envelope from his desk drawer; he folded the copies of the Forrest documents to fit it, dropped the clipped currency and check into the last fold, and put all of it into the envelope. He took his pad and wrote a note. It read:

Waldo. I thought I had the sprained Chevy sold, but they couldn't raise the dough. Sorry. Thought they were live ones. I did, like I told you, move the Falcon. I would've gone to $550 if the guy'd asked me, but he was in a hurry, I guess, and didn't haggle me. I took the ten percent you said we could have for moving that one, long's you didn't see it still here before Santa Claus comes in. I hope you don't mind, but it'll come in handy for me—I had a call from my brother's lawyer's secretary up in Burlington, and I guess there's some kind of problem with a deed or something to my Dad's land that I got to sign or something and be in person when I do. So I got to go up there this weekend. I hope I'll be back Monday but I probably won't. So I'll see you Tuesday. You can give me my draw then, okay? Hope you had a nice holiday. Glad we at least got rid of the Falcon. I was sick of seeing it too. Sincerely, Earl.

He put the note in the envelope and sealed it. He wrote "Waldo" on the front. He took another sheet of paper from his pad and printed on it: "Waldo—In the safe—Earl." He got up and went into Waldo's office. He put the note on the desk. He bent and opened the small combination safe and put the envelope on the first shelf inside. He closed the safe and spun the dial.

He returned to the door, unlocked it, removed the CLOSED sign, and turned on the outside floodlights. He looked at his watch; it was nearly 4:30. He turned on the interior lights and went back to his desk. He took his wallet out and counted its contents and the coins in his pocket. He had $575.38. He did the arithmetic in his head: $4.58 for two breakfasts with tip and 30-cent coffee to go at Dean's, 50 cents for the two doughnut-shop coffees. He was satisfied. He put the wallet back in his pocket, his feet up on the desk, and clasped his hands behind his head. He drank lukewarm coffee and smiled while he thought. He fished around in his jacket pocket until he had located Forrest's card. He read it again, and smiled more; he put that in his wallet, too. Outside the darkness came rapidly. The

Impala gleamed in the floodlights and the red, white, and blue pennants flapped lazily in the evening breeze.

At 4:45 he got up and went back into the storage room. He opened the door and groped for the light switch. He heard Fritchie snoring away in the gloom. When the naked bulb on the ceiling came on, Fritchie stirred sluggishly, swallowed three times, licked his lips, shifted position slightly, and then resumed snoring. Earl turned the chair around. Fritchie had drooled on his tie, and he stunk, but otherwise he seemed all right. Earl took him by the shoulders and shook him. Fritchie made feeble flapping motions with his hands and uttered meager growling sounds. "No, no, Sleeping Beauty," Earl said, "no more nappie-time now. Time for work now, Thirsty Boy. Lunchtime's been over for hours." Fritchie's eyes snapped open after about thirty seconds of Earl's agitation. "Hey," he said, licking his lips. He looked around in confusion. "Good for you, Roy," Earl said, straightening up, "knew you could do it, just knew it."

"What time is it?" Fritchie said.

"Almost five," Earl said. "*Way* past the lunch I never got."

"Gotta go the bathroom," Fritchie said. He lurched out of the chair and stumbled past Earl out the door and across the hall into the toilet, switching on the light as he entered. He did not shut the door behind him.

Earl went back into the front and sat down at his desk. Fritchie took a long time getting noisy relief in the bathroom, punctuating the steady plashing of his water with belches and coughs and dry hackings. The principal noise diminished into intermittent dribbles,

167

finally stopping. Earl heard Fritchie close his zipper, and then the toilet flushed. After that Fritchie ran water in the basin, making more splashing sounds followed by the squeaking of the paper-towel dispenser.

Fritchie walked unsteadily out into the office, his tie pulled down from his opened collar. He was using a brown paper towel to rub the back of his neck. He had put water on his hair as well. "Jesus," he said, "I feel awful."

Earl nodded toward Fritchie's desk. "I got you some coffee," he said. "Probably stone cold by now, I went out and got it round four. But it's still black, and it's still got caffeine. Might shape you up some, at least."

"Thanks," Fritchie said. He took the container from the bag and removed the lid. "You went out?" he said. "What'd you do?"

"Put the sign up," Earl said, "locked the door. What else could I do? You in your coma in there. I hadn't've done that, someone could've come in, had his pick of the lot."

"Yeah," Fritchie said, "but you shouldn't've done that. Waldo don't like it, shut down." He drank some of the coffee.

"Oh go fuck yourself, Roy," Earl said. "Thanks to you I missed lunch, you and your beer. I needed at least a cup of coffee. You want to tell Waldo I ducked a few minutes, and *why* that meant we were closed? Go ahead. Leave anything out, though, and I'll fill in the gaps, soon's I see him on Tuesday."

"Tuesday?" Fritchie said. "How come you won't see him till Tuesday?"

"I left him a note in the safe," Earl said. "I had a

168

call from Vermont. My brother's apparently selling some land, and I got to sign off on it. Something."

"Should've called Waldo," Fritchie said. "He doesn't like getting notes."

"In the first place," Earl said, "Waldo called from down the boatyard, around three o'clock or so. He said he was staying there. So how could I call him? You got the number, the pay phone?"

"What'd you say to him?" Fritchie said, looking up at Earl quickly.

"About you, you mean?" Earl said. "I said you came back from lunch totally shitfaced, so I stashed you out in the back." Fritchie licked his lips. 'Roy can't come to the phone right now, Waldo. Roy's out in the back, all passed out.'

"Come on," Fritchie said. "You didn't tell him that."

"No, but I should've," Earl said. "I told him *you* took the late lunch, and weren't back yet. Which as a matter of fact, you did do. You took *my* late lunch, you drunk. I should've reported you, him. That's always been my worst fault. I'm just too nice a guy."

"Yeah," Fritchie said. He finished the coffee. He said, "Well, look, I'm sorry, all right? I'm sorry you missed your lunch. And thanks for protecting my ass. Tell you what I'll do: I'll stay here for you, while you go and get yourself dinner. Just try to get back around seven."

Earl stood up. "Roy," he said, "you never quit. I got to give you that. Well, nice try, pal, but it won't work. This's your night in the barrel. And since I didn't get my lunch, I'm having a big dinner. I'm going down to Rosoff's, Rosoff's Town Terrace there. And I am going to get myself a nice big piece of roast beef, and about six good, cold beers. And then I'm driving to Vermont, and I will see you Tuesday."

"Rosoff's?" Fritchie said. "You can't afford Rosoff's. Not on what you make."

"Tonight I can," Earl said. "Tonight I go first class. I sold the Falcon while you're gone. Whole deal in forty minutes."

Fritchie slumped back in the chair. "You bastard," he said. "I practically had that car sold. You know I practically did. You sell it that wife of my butcher there, Hyde Park? She come in while I was out? That commission is mine, sonny boy, if you did. That was my customer that I developed."

"Talk to your priest about it," Earl said. "I don't know the butcher's wife. I sold it a guy who lives in the Cape. He dropped in while you were out getting smashed, and he had the money in cash. The lady comes in, tell her she is too late, just like you were, my friend."

"You cocksucker," Fritchie said. "Just kissing ass for Waldo, the same time you're screwing me. Probably so if he decides, he's got to fire somebody, he'll fire me instead of you, 'cause you just sold a car. What'd you let it go for, just to pull this nifty stunt? Five fifty, huh? I bet you did. Sure, I bet you did. Just to cream his jeans."

"Eat your heart out, Roy," Earl said. "I got the six we wanted. The five forty's in the safe." He started toward the door.

"Bullshit, Beale, just bullshit," Fritchie yelled. "You sold that car five fifty. And then you cut your commission so Waldo'd think that you got six. You're a pussy,

170

pussy kid. You know that, Beale? You know that? Just a pussy, pussy kid."

Earl paused at the door. "You know, Roy," he said, "that is not a bad idea, now you mention it. Penny's out of town and all, and I got some extra cash—after I have my roast beef I might look for some of that. See you on Tuesday, Snuggles."

12

Earl drove Penny's Dodge from the dealership to Tallino's Restaurant near the intersection of Hammond Street and Route 9 eastbound on the Brookline-Chestnut Hill line, arriving well before the bar patrons had finished dealing with their thirsts. He finished a large salad, an eighteen-ounce sirloin steak, a baked potato with sour cream, and three draft beers before 6:15. His check came to $9.40. He put a ten-dollar bill on the table while his waitress was picking up an order in the kitchen, and left the restaurant before she returned. The hostess, a middle-aged woman in a black beaded dress, stood aside as he reached her station, but did not wish him a good night.

He parked right in front of the walk leading to Penny's apartment in Somerville. He shut off the ignition, got out, opened the trunk, and pulled Penny's train case toward him. He dug out the camera and rewound the film inside it. He opened the back and took out the cartridge, closing the camera and replacing it in the train case. He shut the trunk and dropped the exposed film in his pocket.

The couple on the first floor were in the preliminary stage of their weekend argument when he climbed the stairs to Penny's place. He let himself into the dark apartment, noting as he switched on the kitchen light that the turkey had begun to stink. He took a tablespoon from the drip-dry rack on the sink and tapped the bird's breast with it; it was spongy, and seemed to have started to discolor. He had the refrigerator door open before he recalled that he had drunk all the beer on Thanksgiving. He saw Penny's quart bottle of Tab in the vegetable bin behind the lettuce and squash they had purchased to go with the turkey. There was a fresh half gallon of milk behind it. He took the Tab out and set it on the table. He got a tall glass from the cabinet next to the refrigerator and filled it with ice. He shut the refrigerator door and poured Tab into the glass.

He carried it into the bedroom and put it on the bureau. He got down on his hands and knees and moved the bedclothes so that he could reach under the iron frame supporting the mattress and spring. His fingers touched large, dry balls of dust, and the sensation made him flinch, but he kept at it until he had located Penny's cache of nips of rum and scotch, served to her but not consumed on her trips with Allen. He hoped for rum, but settled for the first three he touched: two Dewar's White Label and one Haig & Haig Pinch. He got to his feet, putting the White Label on the bureau and pouring the Pinch into his Tab. He took the mixture and drank half of it.

On the floor at the rear of the closet, under the hems of Penny's long dresses, there was a Bostonian shoe box. He pulled it out and put it on the floor behind him. Next there were two pieces of soiled maroon nylon luggage: a medium-sized duffel with a white shoulder strap, and a shapeless two-suit hanging bag. Each of them was stenciled "St. Stephen's University" and had been featured in pictures composed by *New York Daily News* and *Post* photographers assigned to see him off on the marshals' blue bus headed for his first stop en route to Leavenworth. Two of his former teammates had written to him in prison, querulous letters indignantly demanding to know why he had seen fit to add that small disgrace to the major dishonors he had brought to the program, thus confirming his earlier judgment that they were too stupid and naive to trust. He straightened up, holding the two bags, and dropped them on the bed.

He picked up the shoe box and opened it. There were eight of the business-size manila envelopes inside, each of them thick, dated on the front with the occasions covered by their contents. He chose one at random—"Prints 9-8-66-1-3-67"—and opened it. He leafed through the contents, three-by-five-inch black-and-white photographs of Simmons and Penny made in airport terminals, under hotel marquees, emerging from or entering restaurants, sitting very close at Bruins, Celtics, and Patriots games. He replaced the prints in the envelope and returned it to the box. He zipped open the duffel and took at random from it one of the two compartmented white plastic negative files dated for the last three months of 1966 and the first three of 1967. The 35-millimeter negatives were intact in their glassine protective wrappers. He closed the file and returned it to the duffel. He picked up his glass and raised a silent toast to the shoe box and the duffel.

Fewer than fifteen minutes were enough for him to

174

collect and pack his one gray suit, his blue blazer, his tan slacks and his three chino slacks, four dress shirts, three neckties, four polo shirts, a windbreaker, and all his underwear—enough socks, handkerchiefs, T-shirts, and shorts for six days. He left his dirty underwear and socks—three sets—in the bathroom hamper. The Dopp Kit went on top of the underwear and the shirts in his duffel; his black loafers and his sneakers went into the bottom of the hanging bag. He took the eight envelopes out of the shoe box and layered them between his sets of underwear in the duffel. He took his raincoat off the closet hanger and tossed it on top of the luggage. He put the top back on the shoe box and moved to replace it in the closet but hesitated; he held on to it and went into the living-dining room.

Penny kept her bills, canceled checks, three-format checkbook, and bank statements in a small, gray steel filing box under the dining table. He pulled it out and opened it. He took out four envelopes of canceled checks and put them in the shoe box. He opened her checkbook and tore five pages of blank checks from the back of it; he left them on the table in front of his pyramid of beer cans. He closed the case and replaced it under the table. He returned to the bedroom with the shoe box and put it back in the closet. He picked up his luggage and carried it into the living room. He sat down at the table and took his ballpoint out. He wrote a note to Penny on the blank backs of the checks:

Dear Penny: As you probably have guessed, I have left in a pretty big hurry, and I am sorry to leave the place in such a mess and that I didn't have time to do anything about the heat either. I had

to turn it up all the way on account of the landlord's not sending it up enough, or else the boiler's
broken or something and it was still pretty cold.
So I hope it's okay in here when you get back Sunday night (this is Friday night). But I think after
you read this and you see what else is here, you
will see that I didn't really have much choice but
to light out and you will not be mad. This Forrest
guy showed up today at work when Roy was out
and it was obvious he wasn't there to have some
laughs with me, or even to buy a car! It was me
he came there to see, and I finally got it out of
him that was what it was. It took me a long time.
But he finally said well he knew all about me, and
naturally I just said So What and that I did my
time and I don't have any reason to be afraid of
him or anybody else. I thought he was a cop or
something, maybe a private cop. But he said No
he was with the IRS. And I said So What? again.
Which I guess he isn't used to people talking to
him like that, especially if they been in jail and
they think they are going to be afraid of Government. Well, I wasn't and I let him see that. And
he said Well it wasn't Me exactly, what he wanted
was to know if I knew Allen, and I said I did a
little because I met him through a mutual friend
and he asked me if that was you. So I had to say
Yes because if he had your name and everything,
it didn't seem like there was any reason not to.
And where could he find you did I know? And
I said I didn't. And then he asked me some more
questions a lot like the ones before, and then he
left. But when I went over to the doughnut shop

later, I saw him sitting in his car up the street a ways where he could see what I was doing if I left the place and he sort of squatted down like that meant I couldn't see him but of course I already had. And I figured what that meant was that he was either going to follow me and see where I was going, if it might be to see you or maybe even Allen or you might lead them to him.

The main point is that I don't know what is going on here and what I just wrote down is all of it I do know. But I think if some guy like this is smelling around for Allen, well something must be pretty wrong and since I got a record I'm not doing either of you no good by hanging around here, and I better get going. I told them at work I had to go home for a few days because I got to sign some papers that apparently Don's selling some land that our father left to us—want to bet how much money I would get for that if Don ever sold a foot? Nothing. Ha ha, as if I would go all the way up there to do something for Don. But that should keep them quiet until Tuesday, and then I can always call them from where I am, and say it's taking longer. Which I will probably do. So if Waldo calls or Roy, just tell them I am still tied up and I said I will call them. As soon as I have a number someplace where you can get in touch with me, I will send you a letter with it in it because I shouldn't call you on it here because I think you better not call me from your phone on account it might be tapped and they are listening. You should probably tell Allen that too, you can only use pay phones until this mystery just blows over. If you want the truth, it looks to me like Allen's wife or something or maybe one of his business partners must've gotten mad at him and said he's spending lots of money on his fancy girl-friend or something because lots of people do that when they get pissed off—the very first thing they do is call the IRS and just turn the poor guy in and give them his name, even if he didn't do a goddamned thing or anything except to them. You should both be pretty careful from now on, I think, because these guys are really mean and if they get the slightest thing well it's like being in hell.

So I got to sign off now and go, and I love you and will see you soon and I hope you had a nice Thanksgiving. But in case I don't, here is your spare car keys and the door key.
Earl.

He took his key case out of his pocket and unclipped the car keys and the door key and dropped them on top of the note. He put Michael Forrest's business card on the note as well.

He went back out into the kitchen and found Penny's big glass ashtray in the drip-dry rack and a pack of matches in the drawer beneath the counter. He put the ashtray down on the counter, but the stench of the turkey in the sink was strong and he noticed that its plastic wrapper had begun to expand away from the carcass. He took the ashtray back into the living-dining room and put it on the end of the table opposite the note. He struck a match and took the torn documents from his left pants pocket. He burned the Forrest registration first, allowing the ashes to drop on the glass. Then he burned the carbons of the true bills of sale. When he was finished he used the stapled end of the matchbook to pulverize the ashes, and then carried the ashtray into the bathroom and flushed them down the toilet. He wiped the ashtray clean with toilet paper and flushed that away as well. He urinated and flushed again. He took the ashtray back into the kitchen and replaced it in the rack. He stood over the sink and calculated whether the gases from the rotting turkey would burst the plastic bag before Penny returned Sunday night, and decided to take no chances. He took a paring knife from the counter drawer and slit the bag down the top center, releasing a wave of gas. He stepped back and wiped his eyes. He thought a moment and then opened the refrigerator door partway; he reached in and took the milk out, opening the sealed spout and pouring about a quarter of it into the sink, letting it seep down to the drain slowly under the turkey. He put the carton back in the refrigerator and left the door ajar.

He returned to the bedroom and took a last look around. He picked up the two nips of White Label and put them in his pocket. He went into the living-dining room and reset the thermostat from 62 degrees to its maximum of 90. He picked up his baggage, putting the duffel strap over his left shoulder and hooking the hanger bag with his left thumb and first two fingers over his back as well. He carried his raincoat over his right forearm. He turned the light off in the kitchen as he opened the door, and made sure the lock snapped home behind him when he closed it. He was halfway down the stairs when the door of the first-floor apartment opened and the woman who lived there came backward fast through it, slamming her buttocks against the radiator next to the front entryway. She was wearing a blue satin Fraternal Order of Eagles tanker jacket over her yellow pedal pushers. *"Bastard,"* she yelled. She put her hands back on the radiator to launch herself back toward the door. *"God-damn,"* she shouted, yanking her hands away, "oooh, god-*damn*, god-*damn, goddamn."* She put her hands to her mouth and licked them. Her husband appeared in the doorway. He was wearing a white Celtics T-shirt. "Oh stop makin' the fuckin' noise and *go* out drinkin', you dumb cunt," he said. "What's all the racket about now?"

She had bent over and was pressing her hands between her thighs. "I burned my fuckin' hands on the fuckin' radiator," she said. "Is that all right with you, you shit? What'd you do? Turn up the heat again, so we can't pay the bill? Asshole."

"No," he said, "I didn't think of it. I'll go and do it now." He slammed the apartment door shut, leaving her bent over in the hallway. "My hands my hands my hands," she said.

Earl made his way down the rest of the stairs. At the bottom he said, "Excuse me? Could I get by?"

She looked at him as though surprised. "What're you doing here?" she said. "I didn't see you standing there. What the hell do you want?"

"I want to get by," he said.

She straightened up. "Oh, sure," she said. "Never mind how I feel. Just as long as you get by." He edged past her toward the exit. "Takin' a trip, huh?" she said. "Or are you finally leavin' that whore up there?"

He paused at the inside front door. "Mrs. Bonfiglia," he said, "I got some business, all right? Business out of town. Is that all right with you?"

"What," she said, "are they makin' you travel now, collect the unemployment? You're not here when De-Lisle's goon comes for the rent Tuesday, might's well not bother comin' back."

"Good night, Mrs. Bonfiglia," he said. He closed both doors behind him and went out into the chill. He walked eleven blocks southwest into Central Square in Cambridge and descended into the Red Line of the subway to Park Street. A large group of teenagers in Rindge Technical High School varsity letter jackets were noisy on the platform, exchanging semiplayful shoves of each other toward the pit where the third rail stood ten feet away. Earl went down to the far end of the platform and stood smelling urine and stale tobacco smoke until the blue-and-white train rumbled in. The first car was empty when its doors sighed open, and he was alone in it when they wheezed shut. He put the garment bag over the seat beside him and rested the duffel on top of it. At Park Street Under he climbed the stairs to the upper level and waited fifteen minutes while three two-car trolley hitches pulled in and took on passengers for Lake Street-Boston College; a single trolley promising Cleveland Circle arrived about eight thirty, and he got on, leaving it at Coolidge Corner.

A light, cold rain had begun. He removed the duffel strap from his shoulder and set the bag on the asphalt sidewalk. He draped the garment bag over it and put his raincoat on. He picked up his bags and crossed the eastbound side of Beacon Street, turning to walk west, the rain at his back. Just beyond the intersection of

181

Beacon and Chiswick there was a three-story brick building set back from the sidewalk behind a low privet hedge and a carefully raked lawn, distinguished from abutting buildings, also three-story brick, by a small blue sign with white letters, illuminated from within. The larger block letters at the top read "HOTEL BEACONVIEW." Below that in script was "The Tattersall," and below that "Lounge and Dining." There was an oval metal sign suspended by chains from the bottom of the lighted sign; it reported the recommendation of the place by AAA. Earl turned left onto the walk and then left again close to the building, where another lighted sign directed Tattersall's patrons down a short flight of stairs to a red door.

The coatroom was closed. Earl went through the foyer with his bags and descended two more steps into the bar. In the southwest corner a woman with puffy ringlets of carmine hair was playing a medley of songs from *Showboat* and *Carousel*. The ceiling was low, allowing men of normal height perhaps four inches of clearance but requiring Earl to stoop slightly to avoid feeling his hair brush against the stippled plaster. Two men sat at the small round table in the semicircular booth nearest the piano. Six similar booths lined the western wall. There was another to Earl's right, tucked in against the partition dividing the entry from the bar. Three of the booths were occupied by men who drank alone. To Earl's left there were two dozen freestanding small tables, with iron-back chairs and candles guttering in glass chimneys. The bar had room for twelve on stools. Behind the bar there was a large print of Robert the Bruce in armor, holding his helmet under his left hand and effortlessly reining his rearing black stallion with his mailed fist against a backdrop of moors and a threatening sky. Three men sat at the bar, each of them drinking alone. Two of them had luggage on the floor next to their stools. The bartender had his back to the room and seemed to be reading something.

Earl went to the fifth booth from the piano and deposited his luggage on the floor, stowing it as neatly as he could while at the same time leaving it visible. He eased himself into the booth and used his hands to mop his damp hair.

After a while a slim young man with long, wavy blond hair entered the bar from a door at the southerly end. He wore a white button-down shirt, a tartan kilt, a large white-fur sporran belted at his waist, white stockings that came to his knees, with a sheathed bone-handled dirk stuck into the top of the left one, and black shoes with dull silver buckles. He carried a small tray; on it was a bowl of something that steamed. He stopped at the service end of the bar and picked up a pint flagon of beer, his gaze roving the room and noting Earl's arrival as he glided from the bar to the third booth and served the man seated there. Earl heard him ask if there would be anything else; he could not hear the man's answer, but gathered it had been negative. The waiter immediately backed away from that booth and came to Earl's.

"Good evening, sir," he said in a somewhat breathy voice. "May I get you something to drink?"

"Yes," Earl said. "I was thinking of John Courage. It's been a long time since I had it, and a friend of mine told me you sometimes had it and this was a good place to get it."

The waiter twinkled his eyes and made a very small

nod. "Yes," he said, "well, we often do. But we have no imports tonight. Just the domestics, I'm sorry. Still, all in all though, your friend was right. Our domestics are all very good. I take it you're not from around here?"

"Well," Earl said, "actually I get around so much I hardly know myself anymore where I'm from. My friend who told me about this place, well, he's someone that I met in Kansas."

"Kansas," the waiter said, "my. We don't get that many from Kansas. You must travel a lot. That must be a very, well, lonely life. Always moving around."

"It is," Earl said. "I have to fly out tonight in fact."

"Oh, my," the waiter said, "but not that soon, I hope."

"No, no," Earl said, "not at all. The late plane, out to the Coast. I'm sure I have time for a drink. A good couple hours or so. And if the drinks make me feel like it, I can always leave in the morning."

"Well, good," the waiter said, producing a white cotton towel from the back of his kilt and wiping Earl's table down quickly. "I'm sure we'll find something that'll satisfy you by then. Is there anything else you might like to drink?"

"I think so," Earl said. "A Smirnoff blue label. A double. On ice. Rimmed with a small twist of lemon. Oh, and an extra glass of ice, and water back. Okay?"

The waiter smiled and glided away. "Back in a jiffy," he said. He went to the service bar and stood tapping his left toe until the bartender looked up and walked down to him. The waiter talked to the bartender while the bartender fetched the 100-proof Smirnoff and prepared the drink in an on-the-rocks glass. The waiter filled one tumbler with ice and another with plain water. When they had finished, the bartender looked over toward Earl's table, nodded to the waiter and started back along the bar. He paused between the first and second men seated at it, placed his hands on the rail, and said something to them. Each of them ostentatiously delayed before sipping some of his drink and then feigning some muscular discomfort or idle curiosity that required him to move on his stool and chanced to bring his eyes into contact with Earl's. Both of them languidly returned to their drinks, as did the third bar drinker after the bartender had spoken to him.

The waiter returned with Earl's order. He set the glasses down and said, "Just let me know now, sir, right away, if I can do anything else. Our rest rooms are right over there. Right behind the piano there, second door in the back." Earl thanked him. The lady at the piano played Hoagy Carmichael tunes. The two men who shared the first booth got up to dance. When the waiter went into the kitchen and the bartender had returned to his reading, Earl poured half the vodka into the glass of ice and refilled his drink from the water glass.

By 9:30 five more men had come in. Two, one in his late fifties and the other in his late twenties, arrived together and took one of the freestanding tables in front of the bar. The solitary drinker farthest from the service bar accepted their invitation to pull up a chair and join them; the third arrival replaced him at the bar. The fourth walked slowly to and from the men's room, looking over Earl and the other men seated alone in the booths. On his return he detoured from the bar and joined the man in the booth next to Earl's. Earl heard soft conversation but was unable to understand what was said. The fifth man came in drenched, removing his sodden raincoat as the inner door swung shut behind him. He was in his early forties, average height, somewhat overweight, wearing a blue glen plaid suit. He had dark hair and long, bushy sideburns, and he wore a dress shirt with blue, yellow, green, and red stripes against a tan background, set off by a wide white silk tie patterned with heraldic devices. He draped the coat over the table in the vacant booth to Earl's left against the partition and fluffed his wet hair with his hands. "Wow," he said. "Coming down in sheets out there." Earl smiled. "Christ," the man said, "no rain all day, I'm in the car, or else I'm in appointments—not a bit of rain. I finish up, plenty of time, I think I'll have a drink. Okay so there's no place to park for maybe half a mile. It's only a light drizzle coming down by then. A hundred yards from the car and what happens? Boom, the skies unload."

"Yeah," Earl said, "but look at it this way. You can wait it out here. Stuff that heavy doesn't last long. Me, I got, first I got to find myself a cab. Then I got to ride the airport and take a plane in all this crap."

"You're going out tonight?" the man said. "Me too."

"Yup," Earl said, "the Coast."

The man nodded. "Lemme get myself a drink," he said. "Mind if I come back and join you?" Earl said he did not. The man went to the bar and had a conversation with the bartender. The bartender talked while preparing the drink. The waiter came out of the kitchen again, and the bartender beckoned him over. The waiter glided up to the man and they walked

186

awhile. The man turned back to the bartender and said something; the bartender took the Smirnoff blue and poured a double shot over ice, rimming the glass with a twist of lemon. The man took both drinks and returned to Earl's table. "Saul knew what you were drinking," he said, setting two rocks glasses on the table. The one in his right hand was dark liquor, straight up. "Didn't know if you're ready, but you're anything like I am and you got to face an airplane on a dark and stormy night, well, I'm always ready, pal. For another drink, I mean." He raised his glass. "Cheers," he said. Earl raised his first drink to his mouth, saluting the toast.

The man eased into the booth on Earl's left. "So," he said, "my name's Ed. I'm in sales. Office systems. Communications, you know? What's yours?"

"Don," Earl said, offering his hand. They shook. He grinned. "I guess, you want the truth, sales's what I'm in, too, but they don't call it that. They call it something else."

"Like what?" Ed said. He sipped his drink, but he sipped greedily, so that the level in the glass diminished almost as rapidly as it would have under showier drinking.

"I sell a college," Earl said. "Well, I sell a piece of a college. The athletic department. The basketball team."

"You sell tickets?" Ed said, looking puzzled.

Earl smiled. "In the end, yeah," he said. "That's the whole point of it. And I guess if they told me I hadda, I'd probably have to do that, too. I mean: stand behind the counter and sell the actual tickets for the game. But what I do, I'm doing now, 's a combination of two things. See, I used to play for the team myself. And I had, well, I figured the most I had was an outside shot, the pros, and what hell, I was young, and all idealistic, and JFK was up there getting everybody steamed up, so when I graduated, well, I made the noble choice. Didn't even wait to see if I'd get drafted. Went right in the Peace Corps, the domestic version of it, and naturally when I came out, well, if I'd ever had a chance to play some ball for money, well, it was long gone by."

"Was that that VISTA thing there?" Ed said. He finished his drink.

"VISTA?" Earl said.

"Yeah," Ed said, "that Volunteers in Service to America thing there. Had a cousin was in that. Spent about two years or so down in Arizona someplace, teaching the Indians how to grow stuff off of rocks. I don't know. Never made any sense to me. Kid from Metuchen, New Jersey, and they send her out the desert to teach Indians to farm?" He shook his head. "Course a lot of things the government does, makes no sense to me." He finished his drink. "Anyway, was that it, VISTA? What'd they have you doing?"

"Oh," Earl said, sipping his diluted vodka, "various things. I set up this skins 'n' shirts basketball league for three little towns about thirty miles between them. What I was actually doing was spending maybe five, six hours a day, driving around from one the next. Coaching them, back in the car, and on to the next town. And I helped with some other stuff, too. Teaching junior high, mostly. And yeah, it was VISTA. I misunderstood you. I thought you said 'Vassar' or something. Not many people ever heard of it."

Ed grinned. "Vassar," he said. "Wouldn't've liked going there, myself. Nothing but women around."

Earl grinned back. "Me neither," he said. He raised his glass and took another sip, looking at Ed over the rim.

The waiter appeared. "Can I get you something, Ed?" he said.

"Oh," Ed said, "yeah please, Randy. Johnnie Red twice, straight up. No vegetables or nothing." He looked at Earl's array of glasses. "I'd offer you one," he said, "but you're drinking slow."

"Hey," Earl said, "I was here a good hour before you walked in. Beside, I can't sleep on planes, and passing out don't do it. I've got a long flight, ahead of me tonight. Got to pace myself."

The waiter went away. "So," Ed said, folding his arms on the table and gazing into Earl's eyes, "you, ah, you think, well, what'd you accomplish out there, the VISTA thing, I mean? My cousin, I asked her that, and what she said was: 'Nothin'.' Not a goddamned thing. Just a total waste of time. Those kids have any talent? Stars I heard of since?"

"No, not a single one," Earl said, "except for being farmers. There's very few people, kids or big—one the things I do now when I'm out selling the college is I scout the high school players. Our team plays two nights a week, although of course I never see them, because I'm always a week ahead, scouting next week's opposition. And that leaves me three nights or so, four if I'm on the road, when I go to the high school games, see we ought to keep close tabs on. Worth a look, I mean. Well, maybe a look, but very few people got talent. Not kids, not bigger people. Not in anything, re-

189

ally, any line of work you name. In basketball what you almost always find is that the ones that *can* run, and *can* handle the ball, well, they got the reputation in the little towns they live, but that is all they've got. And it's all they're ever gonna get. Because the basic reason that they've got it's usually their towns and schools're *so* small and so tiny that not many kids're playing. And they just happen to be that year the ones that are the best. Or the ones that can shoot, or play defense—same thing. The worst player on a tar court at some school with broken windows in the jungle up in Harlem could take on three of them at once and outscore them ten to two. And if they got the two, they'd be lucky. What they're playing against, they *are* pretty good, but you stack them up against some kids can *really* play, which is what happens, college, they're gonna eat their lunch for them. It's just the way it is.

"And then," Earl said, "now and then, let's say that I get lucky and the kid turns out be great. A little rough around the edges, and he needs a lot of coaching, needs to work out with the weights and maybe grow a couple inches, but after all, he's still a kid, he's not finished growing yet. A good prospect, in other words. Not a real barn burner, but you don't expect to find those on the kind of trips I make—basic prospecting, you know? In New Hampshire and Vermont. There isn't that much gold out there, and you don't expect to strike it. This is where you're browsing, sort of, for your 'pretty good' kid, the one that you can look at and say 'not a bad little player.' But definitely worth approaching, worth taking a look at. So the way you do that's generally by going to see his coach. Tell him who you are, recruiting and you'd like to try this boy out on a little one-on-one."

The waiter returned with Ed's second double. Ed took it from his tray and drank half of it. He put the glass down and folded his arms on the table again, gazing at Earl's face. "Oh," he said, "I bet you could do that, all right. You're in terrific shape. At least you sure look like you are."

"Ahh," Earl said, "My weight's all right. But my muscle tone's lousy. Being on the road so much, you can't keep up a program. And my wind's shot, too, if you decide to run me like these damned teenagers do."

"I wouldn't do that," Ed said.

Earl grinned. He patted Ed's hand. "Now, now," he said, "we barely met. Let's get to know each other."

Ed looked contrite. He drained his glass. He aspirated the whiskey. He began to cough violently, his face turning crimson.

"Here," Earl said, handing him the extra-ice glass containing the half of his first drink and water from melted cubes. Ed took it and drank all of it. His coughing subsided. He held the glass in his left hand and studied it. "Whew," he said, "was that vodka?"

"Oh, my God," Earl said, "I thought I was giving you water. I meant to give you the water."

Ed smiled. "Oh," he said, "no harm done. I just wasn't prepared."

"You're all right now, though," Earl said.

Ed nodded. "Fine, fine," he said. "Just let me get another drink." He signaled to the waiter, who nodded understanding. He looked back at Earl. "Go on, go on, Don," he said. "This is very interesting."

"Well," Earl said, "most coaches in most schools,

well, they like nothing better 'n some scout a well-known college drops in of an afternoon, oils 'em up a little. What a fine job they're doing teaching kids the fundamentals—coaches love it when you say that: 'Damn but that impresses me, way you teach the fundamentals. Very few guys do that now, and it's the secret of the game'—and is there any chance that you could maybe get your gear on, try out this kid that's his tall forward, put him through his paces on the give-and-go? Just the simple stuff. Might lead to something for the kid, and of course the coach is thinking: 'And maybe that's not all—maybe something for me, too, like a college assistant's job.'

"But St. Stephen's," Earl said, "well, we got problems. Not fatal but no fun, either. Being well known doesn't help you, if it's for the wrong reason."

"I don't know anything about the place," Ed said. "I mean, I've heard of it and all, living in New Jersey, and I know they have a team." His eyes were bright, and his face remained deep crimson.

"I bet," Earl said, "I bet if I asked you, you'd know what we're famous for. But I won't make you guess. We had some kids fix games."

Ed opened his mouth wide. "I *do* remember that," he said. "It was some years back—that right?"

"A few," Earl said. "But the bad taste lingers on, at least in the sport itself."

"I felt so sorry for those boys," Ed said. "I have sons of my own, and of course, I know quite a few . . . Well, I know I'd be terribly upset if it happened to someone I knew. Didn't some of them go to jail?"

"Three of them," Earl said.

"Did you know them?" Ed said. "Were any of them your, you know, special friends of yours?"

"No," Earl said. "Oh, I knew a couple of them. Slightly. The ones who were seniors during my freshman year. But not very well." He sighed. "I still felt sorry for them, though. It seemed like, you know, that, well, they got hit awful hard for what wasn't really very much. Not that big a thing. From the team's point of view, I mean. We didn't lose any of the games we played when they did that. Beat the spread. Or made sure we didn't beat it. So what if some people won bets as a result?"

"Well . . . ," Ed said, his eyes moist and sweat appearing on his cheeks.

"I know, I know," Earl said. He toyed with the glass. "They said it was all for protecting the integrity of the game. But people still bet afterwards on games, and they always will. Nobody punished them. And the bookies that made money on the games those kids were playing, they're still making money on the games the new kids play. And don't kid yourself the colleges and the universities aren't making money on them too. You think the coaches, the assistants, the people behind the scenes that you never hear about, the people like me? You think we don't get paid? We don't get paid much, that's for sure, but we do get paid. And when we go on vacation, or our doctors send us bills, those things get paid too. You think that money doesn't come from the games that those kids play? And it's lots of money, getting bigger every year, with the TV stuff and all. Why should it be just the people who actually do it, actually do the work, spend all the hours at practice, and really sweat their balls off? Why should they be the only ones that don't make any money? Doesn't seem quite fair."

He sighed again. "But that's the way it is," he said. He toyed with his first rocks glass. He picked it up and finished the drink. "It isn't going to change. We just have to live with it, and so when I go into one of these jerkwater high schools, and ask if I can see some kid and work him out a little, well, if I was from UCLA, or Villanova, Indiana or DePaul, Duke or N.C. State? They'd fall all over me. But the minute that I tell them that I'm from St. Stephen's, that's when even if they have got someone reasonably good that might make our second team, I know I'm just wasting my time. It's very discouraging. Just a waste of time." He picked up his second drink and raised it to Ed. "Well," he said, "bottoms up. Great way to spend your holiday, huh? Just jerking around."

"It could be something more," Ed said. "Will you come in the men's with me?"

"You've got a plane to catch," Earl said. "You said you had a plane."

"The Shuttle," Ed said. "The eleven o'clock Shuttle. All I have to do's drop off the car at Hertz, and go and catch the plane. I'll be cutting it close, sure, but I'd really like to, you know—it's only ten fifteen. Just a little quickie, Don? At least one good thing this weekend that's been so lonely for you?" He licked his lips and spread them in a sudden grin. "You know what we could do?" he said. "I know what we can do. Your plane, what time does your plane leave? Is it the last one for the Coast?"

"Eleven thirty," Earl said. "Or eleven thirty-five. I haven't got my ticket. It's there for me at the desk.

194

This was a late change they made. Without telling me. The guy that was supposed to scout Loyola tomorrow afternoon and San Fran tomorrow night got sick, so he can't go. So instead of me going to New Orleans Sunday night, and staying here the weekend with my sister and her kids, I have to fly out on short notice. Yeah, I do deserve a treat."

"Well," Ed said, his eyes bright, "here's what we can do. You drive and drop me off at Easter. That way I can make it easy. And then you drop off the car for me. I'll give you all the paperwork, it's all completely done. And just go and catch your plane. It won't be as much time as I'd like to spend with you, won't be time enough to hump. But you can let me blow you, Don. We've got time enough for that."

After he saw Ed safely inside the Eastern terminal at Logan International Airport, Earl took the exit ramp and stopped the rental car at the airport gas station. He used the pay phone to call the Hertz twenty-four-hour number. Referring to the rental agreement, he identified himself as Edmund R. Cornell, the driver-customer of a dark green Pontiac Le Mans coupe, Massachusetts registration K76-333. "No, no," he said, "no troubles at all. Car's running fine in fact. It's just that something came up, and my plans've changed, and I didn't want you people to think I'd swiped the car. I'd like to return it instead of tonight sometime either Tuesday or Wednesday. Yes, still at the airport. Uh huh. Thanks very much." He returned to the car and drove it out of the airport, taking the right fork leading to the Mystic River Bridge, marked "NORTH SHORE N.H./MAINE."

13

At 7:30 on the Tuesday evening after Thanksgiving Donald Beale was still in his office. Oakes looked in. "Rough day?" he said. "You still up here and all?"

"Yeah," Beale said. "God made gin for days like this."

"Bank?" Oakes said.

Beale shook his head. "No," he said, "the bank's all right. We're fine in that department. The line of credit I took, the one they didn't want to give me but they did anyway, well, it turned out I didn't need it after all. Detroit's not shipping as many as they threatened to. So the payments I've already made're out of whack as usual, but in *our* favor, for once. I ran into Mace Brookens at the Rotary today, told him I wasn't sure I can afford to finance the bank like this. So no, nothing to do with the business. Just that about the middle of the afternoon, it was like things started to get a little bit out of whack, you know? Like when you dream about a funeral, the way Lincoln's supposed to've done, and you keep going through this big house hearing people crying, and finally you come to the room where the

196

body's laid out, and you look down in the casket, and it's you. Well since it's you that remembers the dream, you must be awake, and if you're awake, and remembering, then you can't possibly be dead. But it's kind of upsetting, you know? It *has* to mean something. You almost want to *make* it mean something, even bad, if that's what it's going to take. I dunno. Feel like I'm losing my grip."

"What happened?" Oakes said.

"Oh," he said, "I was sitting here, going over payroll. I know, and you know, Elio's a crackerjack service manager, and he's such a stickler for getting things right the customers think he's God. But damn it all, when he makes Rudy stay till nine because somebody's car still knocks, Rudy gets this idea in his head that he's earning overtime. So all right, Rudy's not too bright, and if he was determined to go in the car business, he should've stuck to pumping gas, and maybe changing oil. But we need four guys out there, and three good ones're all we've got, so Rudy's where he shouldn't be, doing what he doesn't know how, and Elio is screaming at him, making him miss dinner, and *I'm* paying for it.

"Elio forgets that. He acts like he thinks Rudy gets paid by the job. But Rudy knows better'n that, so the worst mechanic that we've got is making close to the most money. Which isn't good for morale. But what do I do? Fire Rudy? Leave us short a man? Tell Elio just to let Rudy's crap work go out of the shop, and get my customers pissed off?" He sighed. "When it's quiet," he said, "like it was today, like it always is, this time of year, I like to bang my damned fool head against minor problems I can't possibly solve.

"Well," he said, "God saw my situation, and He took pity on me. Not completely, oh no. God doesn't believe in making things *too* easy. Just a little something to get the old heart pumping away, you know? A call from Earl's pet hooker. I didn't even know her name. He's always called her Penny, when he's mentioned her at all. 'Mary Slate,' the switchboard girl said. 'Says it's personal.' 'Personal?' I say. 'How the hell can it be personal if I don't even know the name?' But I took it anyway. Should've known it meant trouble. Should've ducked the call."

"Oh my God," Oakes said, "what's that little shit done now?"

"Well, that's what I mean about God," Beale said. "When God sticks it to you, you don't get full particulars. God likes to tease you some. I don't know what Earl's done, and neither does she. Which is why she's calling me, to see if maybe I do. What Earl's apparently done, I guess, is skip out on her. 'I was out of town for Thanksgiving,' she says. Crying, of course, which I guess is supposed to make me think she's telling the truth. I don't, naturally. Partly because I know she's been shacked up with Earl quite a while, and only another natural-born liar could stand that, and partly because there's no good reason for her to tell me that. The minute she tries to make sure I know she was with her family, that minute I know she was out working when Earl flew the coop. Why she cares what I think, I don't know. Why she thinks I care what she thinks or she does—that I can't answer either.

"So I'm a little short with her," Beale said. "I say: 'I hate to tell you this, miss, but Earl's got a history of that. Skipping out on people that trust him. Did he take something from you or something? Because I'm not making it good. If he got your jewelry, or he took your money, well, I'm sorry, you know? But your best bet's to call the cops. I don't insure anyone against Earl. I don't trust the bastard myself."

"Well," Beale said, "surprise, surprise. At least as far as she can tell, he didn't take a thing. Except his clothes and shaving gear—only his own stuff. 'You checked your car since you got back?' This is what I say to her. 'Car still where you left it?' Yup, right where it's s'posed to be. The only bad thing that he did was leave the apartment filthy. 'It really stunk in here,' she said. 'He left some steaks and stuff just rotting in the sink, and the refrigerator open so it all got spoiled in there. And the bed, I hadda change it. I think he threw up. Probably from too much beer—he left all his old beer cans and stuff dumped in the living room.'

" 'Well,' I say, 'that's in character for him too. My mother swears to this day that the swollen veins in her legs came from following Earl around, all the time he was growing up, bending over and stooping down to pick up all his garbage.'

" 'But I don't care about that stuff.' This is what she tells me. 'All I care about is Earl. If he is all right. And that's why I finally called you. To see if you know where he is.'

"I tell her I don't," Beale said. " 'Did he leave a note or anything that might give you a hint?' And that was when she said he did, that he left her a note that said he had to drive up here and see me about some important family business. Something about seeing a lawyer and signing some papers. 'And I called the people where he works, and he told them the exact same thing.'

" 'Well,' I say, 'that takes care of one possibility then, which was pretty remote anyway—that some kind of fit took hold of him or something and he told the truth for once. Nobody from here called him, and if there's some important business going on that concerns my family, I don't know about it and I kind of think I would. My guess is that the law *is* involved, though, or will be before too soon.' So she says, she gives me another dose of the crying there, just to see if maybe I do know, and I'm holding back on her, maybe covering for him, and she says: 'I guess you can't help me then.' And I said that was how it looked to me. And she says: 'If he gets in touch with you, will you at least tell him to call me? Get in touch with me?' Well, there's small chance of that happening. If Earl gets himself in a position where he decides he has to call me, one call's all he'll be allowed to make, and it'll be to get him a lawyer. But I said: 'Sure, sure I will.' And she hung up."

"Well," Oakes said, "if that was all there was to it. Maybe it's just a case of Earl ducking out on another girlfriend. Like you say, he's done it enough before. And not just on girlfriends, either—family, friends, Earl plays no favorites. Maybe that's all it is—he was sick of her, and he didn't have the guts to face her. That would be typical."

"I've kept trying to tell myself that," Beale said, "ever since I hung up. And I couldn't get it down. Couldn't choke it down. What little I know, that I got from her, it's *got* to be more than that. I know he's gone—that part's true. I know he left in a hurry, and a mess behind him. Like you say: typical. I know she doesn't know where he is, and I know Waldo that took him on doesn't know, either, if he thinks he came up here.

"What I don't know," Beale said, "is why he left a false trail. If he hadn't've left her the note, and gone to all the trouble of giving his boss a load of shit, then I'd be worried about him. Somebody from his noisy past finally caught up with him after all these years and grabbed him, to settle an old score. But he knew he was going. And he had time enough to write the note, and time enough before that to spin his yarn at the car lot. This wasn't some kidnapping thing. This was something Earl planned. And it was something, it was something he planned without letting her in on it. This girl is no virgin. It wouldn't bother her if something was illegal, if it looked like she could do it without getting caught and make some money at it. Hell, that's how she makes her living. Her job's doing something that's against the law, peddling her ass for money. So if Earl didn't tell her what he was up to, and did lie to her about it, then it figures it was either something pretty dangerous, or else it wasn't dangerous but he didn't want to share the loot with her. But it was still illegal."

"You sold that car, didn't you?" Oakes said. "You sold that Mercedes. You sold it to that flashy dame from over in Manchester."

"I had the bill of sale," Beale said. "Earl did send me that. Kathie Derwood. Morristown, New Jersey. To Earl Beale. Notarized. And another one, also notarized, from Earl to me."

"I farted once, in a high wind," Oakes said. "Worth about as much. Lasted about as long."

"Well," Beale said, "that deal was down the line. But this call put me on tenterhooks, and I've been on them ever since. The suspense is what does it, you know? If Earl's doing something, Earl will get caught. The only real questions're when, and for what. So that call amounts to an early Christmas card from Earl: 'Happy holidays, Don. Guess what I'm up to, and how I'm gonna screw up your Christmas.' "

Oakes frowned. "I hope that's all it amounts to," he said. "For your sake, I mean. That lady from Manchester, she's not from here."

"Nobody's from here anymore," Beale said. "They all came from some other place. For some reason I don't know, her husband's sick of her. She bought him the car to revive him. Revive her. It won't work. It never works. But I owned the car, and I sold the car, and she bought the car, and she gave it to him. That's all there is to the thing."

"I hope so," Oakes said. "I sure hope so."

14

Ed Cobb was not sympathetic. He sat in the chair in front of Don Beale's desk in the upstairs office and let his displeasure show on his face. "There is one situation where we get in trouble, you and me," he said. "It is when we have talked about something, and we either have not agreed on what to do about it, or else we *have* agreed on what to do about it. And then one of us goes out and does something that the two of us didn't agree on. Oakesie tells me you sold that car."

"Look," Beale said, "the car is the least of my worries. Hell, it's none of my worries at all. The car is fine. It's Earl that's my trouble."

"That car came from Earl," Cobb said. "Earl is trouble, and what comes from Earl is trouble, and you're telling me that you got trouble with Earl? You better hope that woman's husband is one lucky, damned good driver. If he ever gets a parking ticket on that thing, and some rookie cop, going by the book, runs a title check on that thing, there'll be shit flying through the air like confetti, and all of us'll get some on our clothes."

"Leave me alone," Beale said. "You said it was Briggs on your mind."

"It was," Cobb said, "until Oakesie told me you sold the car, and you told me Earl's on the run. Here I've been out on the road like a sheriff, taking my good friend's advice, and finding as usual, like I always do, his advice is pretty damned good. And then I come back, to thank my good friend, and what do I learn's going on? My friend's been ignoring *my* good advice, and absolutely jeopardizing all the possibilities that something good'll happen, because I followed his."

Beale sighed. "Ed," he said, "If it's good news, let me have it. I could use some. Just give it to me. Don't make me pay for it. All right?"

Cobb exhaled loudly. "Shit," he said. "In my next life I'll do something simple, like my mother said. Be a jewel thief or something. This business of dealing with people's beginning to get on my nerves.

"I did what you made me think of," he said. "The first thing I did was sound out Danisi and Shaw: what'd they think of this idea. And they loved it. They both said the same thing that you said. That Henry's the best-known guy in the Second, better'n Wainwright himself. And I said: 'That's fine. Glad to hear it. But that just means people know him. Does it mean also they'll vote for him?' And both of them said: 'Why the hell not? Since when did the voters vote for a guy because he's the best qualified? They vote for the guy because they like the guy, not 'cause they think he's the best. They like him the best? Then he *is* the best. And everyone likes Henry Briggs.' 'But,' I say, 'sure, but like him enough? Like him enough to beat Wainwright?' And they say: 'Who cares? What difference

loes it make? They like him a lot more'n Greenberg.'
See, I'm losing sight of my own object here. What
we've got to do is beat Greenberg. And when they remind me of that, well, okay, I'll go and see if they're
right.

"I went down to Occident," Cobb said. "I went
down and I saw Paul Whipple. There're other people
I'm going to see there, but Paul is the power in Occident. It's okay to talk to the rest of the people that
know things and keep up on things, but if you talk to
them before you talk to Paul, then Paul will not talk
to you. So I went in his IGA store there, and I had
a cup of coffee with him. And I told him what it was
I had on my mind, and I asked him what he might
think.

"He looked at me like I had two noses. 'For *Congress?*' he says. 'Henry Briggs?' I said: 'Yes. He's an old
friend of yours, right?' It was like you had him to dinner, and he ate it, and then you told him you just served
him a casserole of his cat. 'Well, Jesus Christ,' he said,
'I don't know. Don't know as I ever considered it.'

" 'You grew up with him too,' I said, 'just like me.
You know him better'n I do. Did you ever think, when
we were growing up, well, let me put it to you this way:
Did you ever think, when we were growing up, that
Henry'd pitch for the Red Sox?'

" 'No,' he said. 'I knew he was a good ball player,
but, no, I never did.'

" 'And he did, didn't he?' I said. And Paul said:
'Yup.' And I said: 'All right, then why shouldn't he run
for the Congress?'

" 'Well,' Whip said, 'well, for one thing, Henry

205

practiced the baseball. I never knew Henry to practice the politics. Never knew him to do that.'

" 'And if he had,' I said, 'you'd look at him like you look at me, an' you'd call him a damned politician.'

" 'Yup,' says Whip. 'And you'd vote against him, for that,' I said. 'Wouldn't vote *for* him,' Whip said. 'Do you think most people feel that way?' I said. 'Couldn't say,' Whip said. 'Never know what people're thinking.'

" 'Well,' I said, 'take a stab at it. If I could get Henry, think about this some, would you say that he had a chance?'

"He got this strange look on his face. 'Guess I would,' 's what he said. 'Guess I'd have to say that. Henry's got friends all around here. Don't know as there's enough, to win an election, but Henry's got friends all around here.'

"I went over to Charlotte, saw Father Morissette. Asked him the same sort of questions. And I got the same kind of answers. Nobody ever thought about voting against Bob Wainwright. No one's ever done it, really. Never had the chance. Now if they happened to get one, and the man was someone they liked, well, sure, they'd give it some serious thought. And many'd come down for Henry.

"I only talked to about ten people," Cobb said, "but those ten people represent just about every kind of life we've got, in the Second District. And all of them deal with the public, every single day. What struck me was just what you said: everybody likes Henry. They all know who Henry is, and they all admired him. He'll leave that Greenberg kid for dead, in the primary. He's a natural."

206

"Good," Beale said. He rubbed his forehead. "Like I say, I was in the market for good news."

"Yeah," Cobb said, "but what you did could turn good news into a hurricane warning. Do you know where that car came from?"

"New Jersey," Beale said, yawning.

"If it came from New Jersey," Cobb said, "it came from New Jersey because Battaglia sent Earl to New Jersey to get it, and there's something wrong with it. And if that something wrong floats to the surface someday, Battaglia's going to float up with it, and that's where Henry's vulnerable. The people that like Henry now will not like Henry if that wop begins to run his mouth."

"Ahh," Beale said. "It'll never happen. The lady gave it to her husband. It's his brand-new toy. Go and talk to Henry now, and put the boots to him. I'd like to see Bob Wainwright's face, when this news gets to him."

15

The bar and billiard room at the back of the third floor
of the Wampanoag Club on Boylston Street in Boston
was empty when Allen Simmons emerged from the
wire cage of the elevator shortly after 7:30 in the evening. The Oriental rugs and the tapestries hanging
from the oak paneling of the walls of the broad corridor
and wide staircase absorbed most of the conversational
noises and muted the occasional rattle of dishes and
silverware from the dining room overlooking the street.
He found the switch for the fluorescent lights that illuminated the stainless-steel sinks and Formica working
space under the ornate oak bar; that and his own memory enabled him to locate the bottle of Campari on the
back bar, and the ice maker enclosed next to the sinks.
He took a bottle of club soda from the refrigerator next
to that and mixed the drink with a long silver spoon.
There was another panel of switches to the right of the
bar entrance. He chose one at random, and a hundred-
watt bulb shrouded by a green-glass circular shade
threw all of its glare onto the green baize surface of
the billiard table in the corner farthest from the bar.

wo cue sticks and a wooden triangle lay at the far end
f the table; the cue ball was against the near rail. He
vent over to the table and put his drink on the sill of
he high window near the farthest end. He bent to re-
rieve the balls from the bin under the table, racking
hem in no particular order except for the eight ball,
vhich he placed at the center. He hung the rack on
he peg under the far end, and put one of the cues in
he holder on the wall behind him.

He had broken the formation with a sharp shot that
lispersed the balls, sinking both the thirteen and the
wo, when Sidney Roth entered the room. Simmons
lid not look up at his soft entrance; he chalked the tip
of the cue and lined up a combination shot, intending
o sink the three ball in the corner pocket by caroming
he seven ball off the cue ball, dropping the three, and
eaving the cue and the seven lined up for his next shot
it the same pocket. Roth put his attaché case on an
oak chair next to the entrance and hit the switch to
nis left that turned on the lights overhanging the bar.
He went behind it and poured white rum into a rocks
glass, adding two cubes of ice and a twist of lemon from
the shot glass at the service area. He joined Simmons
it the table as the seven ball kissed the three too hard
and slightly off the angle he had chosen, so that it rat-
tled against the edges of the pocket and halted on its
brink; the seven rebounded from the cushion at the
end and stopped amid a cluster of balls near the center
of the table. The cue ball came to rest against the rail.
Simmons straightened up and studied his situation.
Roth set his drink on the windowsill and took a cue
from the holder. Simmons stepped back from the
table. Roth chalked his cue, frowning. He leaned over

the surface of the table and tapped the end of the cue on the corner pocket farthest from him on the right. He drew his shot to put overspin on the cue ball and hit it sharply, so that it struck hard on the twelve ball, sending it crisply into the pocket, and ricocheted into the cluster at the center of the table.

"Nice," Simmons said.

"Misspent youth," Roth said. He chalked again and tapped the side pocket to his left. He struck the cue ball softly, so that the eleven rolled slowly into the side pocket and the cue ball came to rest against the ten. He tapped the corner pocket on his left at the other end and executed another soft shot, sinking the ten and leaving the cue ball still at the center. Walking quickly to the side of the table opposite the window, he sank the fourteen in the corner opposite to the one at which Simmons had left the three, the carom sending the cue ball off the rail in perfect position to drop the nine in the side. When that clunked home, the cue ball was precisely positioned to drop the fifteen in the corner, the white ball stopping after that shot at a tough but possible angle to sink the eight ball in the far corner, or a three-rail shot into the side pocket nearest him. "What the hell," Roth said, chalking, "faint heart, fair lady, all that kind of shit." He tapped the far rail, the near rail, and the far rail again, and said, "Eight the side." He hit the cue ball crisply and launched the eight hard against the far rail on precisely the path he had wanted. It moved back and forth across the cloth three times, as he had predicted, changing its angle slightly with each impact, slowing gradually until it lay poised on the lip of the side pocket. "Come on, come on," Roth said. The eight ball dropped. He straightned up, his face disappearing into the gloom above he lamp, and looked where Simmons stood near the window in the gloom. "Now," Roth said, "my secret's out. Now you know what I was really doing all those cold winter nights when I should've been studying Real Property."

Simmons went over to the holder on the wall and put his cue stick away. "If what I wanted was a guy who knows the Rule in Shelley's Case," he said, "I would've called somebody else." He returned to the window and retrieved his drink.

Roth put his cue in the holder and joined Simmons at the window. "We take a seat?" he said, nodding toward the tables and the captain's chairs grouped around the bar.

"Might as well," Simmons said. "You up to dinner afterwards? I told Mario I'd be coming in."

"Good," Roth said. "Man cannot live by airline snacks alone."

"It's very simple," Simmons said when they were seated. "The facts, I mean, are simple. What to do about them—that's where it gets complicated."

"Start with the facts," Roth said. "That's where I always feel more comfortable. The law's what you go looking for when you've decided what you want to do, and when you want it done. Lots and lots of law. You can almost always find some that'll suit your purposes. Facts're the hard part."

"There's no question what's being done to me," Simmons said. "Neither is there any question about who is doing it. Or trying to, at least. A man is trying to blackmail me. He may or may not be in cahoots with a woman I've been dating."

211

"Screwing," Roth said absently. "This'd be the bounteous Miss Slate. Penny wise, pound foolish—didn't I read that somewhere?"

"Screwing," Simmons said. "That man's name is Earl Beale. At least that's the one he went by when I met him, and he didn't change it. If he was lying, he was at least consistent. And I recognized his voice when he called me on the phone."

"You met him," Roth said. "More than once?"

"Every time she went away with me," Simmons said. "Well, at least every time since she took up with him. Originally I met her through Nancy."

"Whom you were also screwing," Roth said.

"Sid," Simmons said, "I didn't ask you to come here and ratify my life."

"That's good, Allen," Roth said. "Because I'm not doing that, and if I'd thought that's what you wanted, I would've stayed in New York. Because I'm not up to it. But we are gonna call things by their right names here, Allen. You've been playing with the pros a long time now, ever since I've known you. When you've asked me for advice, I have given it to you. You never asked me for advice on that subject, so I never gave it. If this is that request, well, I think it's kind of late but I'll do the best I can. What was this Earl's function, as near as you could tell? Did he act as her pimp or something? Is that what you're telling me?"

"Not to my knowledge," Simmons said. "He moved in with her after Nancy moved out. Initially, though I've sure changed my mind since then, I was glad when this all happened. Nancy was a very busy lady. And I was never sure exactly what their relationship was—hers and Penny's, I mean."

"Wouldn't be unusual," Roth said. "I've seen more'n one guy fall ass-over-teakettle with a pair of sculptured marble tits he rented out in Vegas, and turn completely oblivious to the obvious fact that she considered men work, and other women fun."

"I never fell in love with Penny," Simmons said. "If that's what you're suggesting."

"I understand that," Roth said. "You thought of it as business. What you weren't prepared for was that she, or her pal Earl, might approach it the same way. Strictly business. Object's to make as much profit's you can. As fast as you can. Pure and simple. What've they got? Pictures, I assume. Tapes? Did this jezebel come to your bed with a tape recorder running in her cosmetics bag?"

"No, no tapes," Simmons said. "If they ever tried to make any, they'd be useless. I never promised her anything except money for sex. That's all. No marriage proposals or anything. I've already got a wife."

"Yes," Roth said. "Does Phyllis know about this? I mean this new development? She had to have a pretty good idea what you were up to, I assume."

"In a manner of speaking," Simmons said, "it was Phyllis's idea. The year after I became a member of the firm I got into some trouble with one of the secretaries. She had to go away and have an operation. We didn't have much money then, and what we did have Phyllis watched pretty carefully. I don't mean I wrote a check to the kid, but there was no way a thousand dollars could come out of our income without Phyllis noticing. And she did. So I had to account for it, and she was very calm about it. Said if I felt I had to do things like that, well, she guessed there wasn't much

213

she could do to stop me. But sooner or later she was afraid there'd be a real scandal that a thousand dollars wouldn't fix. She was very practical about it. She reminded me that I refused to let her hire unskilled people to do work around the house because it never turned out right, and we always ended up paying to have it torn out and done again by someone who knew what he was doing. 'If you feel you have to have this variety in your life,' she said, 'stop using amateurs. It won't cost any more for you to give some other woman fifty or a hundred dollars for the use of her body each time than it will for you to go around sneaking the same amounts to save up for a gold bracelet or something for a secretary. And the one you come right out and pay won't get it into her silly little head that she's going to take my place.'"

"Phyllis always struck me as a real down-to-earth lady," Roth said.

"She's pragmatic," Simmons said. "Her father kept a mistress most of his adult life. Her mother knew about it, and in time so did his kids. She wasn't shocked when she found out I was attracted to other women. More or less expected it."

"Well," Roth said, "then if that's the case, what's the problem? Tell the extortionist to go to hell and show your wife the pictures."

"The problem is this," Simmons said. "Part of the deal with Phyllis is discretion. I wasn't to bring home any diseases, which I haven't, and I wasn't to appear in places with a woman where our friends'd be sure to spot me. Well, my interests and Phyllis's are quite different, so that was never a real problem. I did occasionally run into one of her friends' husbands, but there the benefit of mutual silence was so obvious we didn't even need to discuss it. The society reporters may go to the parties down at Keeneland before Derby Day, and they're all over the place when the America's Cup's being contested at Newport, or the Museum has a special show, but those weren't the kind of events where I took my ladies. Where I took them, most of the men were about my age, and most of the women about the same age as Penny, and nobody in attendance saw much wrong with that. It was sort of like getting to the age where you could afford a beach house or a private plane or a big yacht with a crew. If you had the money, and you wanted a girlfriend, well, you certainly had the right." He paused. "I've seen a lot of famous men at the places I've taken her. Faces you would recognize. Pro athletes, U.S. senators, show people, prominent businessmen—you name it. There may be some risk involved in that kind of amusement, but when someone that you've hired to sleep with you tells you that she slept with the president of the United States back when he was running, and people who know confirm it, well, it's not the kind of risk that seems to stop anybody."

"I suppose not," Roth said.

"Unless it caused a ruckus," Simmons said. "And that's what seems to have happened to me."

"How much do they want?" Roth said.

"I'm not sure it's 'they,'" Simmons said. "He says it's just him, and that Penny's not involved."

"You don't believe that, I assume," Roth said.

"I didn't when *he* said it," Simmons said. "I figured that was just his way of trying to protect her. He collects the money, and then she flies off to meet him on some Caribbean island. But then *she* said it, and the way she said it? I don't know. He left a note for her, this was Monday morning, before I heard from him, and if what she read to me over the phone was what was really in that note, and he left the place in the shambles she said it was in, it could be that she's telling me the truth."

"What exactly did the note say?" Roth said.

"I can get you a copy," Simmons said. "Basically he claimed some IRS guy'd been by the place where he worked, asking questions about me. And for some reason or another, that scared the daylights out of Earl, and he decided to hit the road. Said he'd made up some phony story for the people at work, something about a family matter back wherever he comes from, and he advised her to alert me and then he hit the road. Well, that didn't make any sense. Not to me at least. If it, if he'd said it was a guy from the SEC or something, well, that might make me nervous. But the IRS? Pretty unlikely. My taxes, well, you know how pure and honest they are. What do I pay in taxes that I could probably beat? Quite a lot. And they've audited me three years in a row, right? With three 'No change' letters in a row? They have to leave me alone for a certain amount of time now, unless they can prove going in I did something. No, it's not the IRS.

"So," Simmons said, "I told her that, and I said: 'Look, there's something going on here that either he's not telling me, or you're not. And I want to know what it is. What're you leaving out?' And she assured me there was nothing. And this horrible thought struck me, blackmail was involved, and I asked her if there was anything, any kind of evidence, that he had of our

216

relationship. That he could show, or threaten to show, to somebody else. And she said: 'No.' And that she was going to call his brother and see what was going on.

"She did that this afternoon," Simmons said. "Apparently it was a waste of time. She reached his brother up in Vermont and got nothing out of him. 'He's just as stupid as Earl always said he was,' she said, this is when she talked to me. 'I almost can't believe it. They haven't heard from him. They don't know where he is. And they don't really care.' And I said: 'Look, Penny,'—this was just a hunch—I said: 'Look, Penny, you're keeping something back from me. I can hear it in your voice. I believe you don't know where he is. But I don't believe you have absolutely no idea of what he's up to. Is there anything, did he take anything you know about that could link the two of us?' And that's when I found out about the photographs."

He laughed. "On the one hand," he said, "I feel like a sap. Here's this goniff thief snapping pictures of us every time we take a trip, and here I am, man of the world, and I never even noticed him. All those times I shooed those goddamned nightclub photographers away from our tables in San Juan, out in Nevada, wherever, and all the time this piece of human shit's been pointing a lens right down my throat.

" 'And you knew it,' I said to her. 'You knew very well what he was doing. You didn't tell me. You not only didn't tell me, you probably helped him. Let him know where he could spot us.' Who the hell pays any attention to people taking pictures in an airport? Long-lost relative comes home. Kid comes back from college. Happy couple going off on their honeymoon. There's always some idiot grinning into space while his moronic relatives fire flashbulbs in his face. I mean, who the hell'd want a picture of a middle-aged man and a woman getting off a plane, or going into a hotel?" He grimaced. "A two-bit crook with a long-range plan, that's who," he said.

"And then you heard from him," Roth said.

"Late this afternoon," Simmons said. "Right after she called to tell me about talking to his family. First there was an envelope by messenger service. He must've been somewhere around the building, where he could see the messenger come to deliver it. Probably in the lobby. Took a gamble that whoever took the elevator to my floor, and looked like a messenger, carrying my envelope, was the guy he'd hired. The phone rang about three minutes after I opened the envelope. One picture of me and Penny. Some airport or another—most likely Kennedy. She's leaning on me and taking her shoe off." He sighed. "We certainly made a handsome couple."

"And he wanted money," Roth said.

Simmons laughed. "He didn't open with that," he said. "He worked his way up to it. He hated to bother me at the office. He hoped I understood the only reason he was doing it was because he was desperate. He said Penny didn't know where he was which of course is what Penny'd told me, and that she didn't know what he was doing. Or'd been doing, for that matter, for the better part of a year and a half. I cut him off. 'Earl,' I said, 'I'm a busy man. Let's just dispense with the bullshit you gave your boss, and the bullshit you also gave Penny. I know about the pictures. What do you want?'

"Well," Simmons said, "that sort of threw him off

218

stride for maybe a second or so. Lost his place in his script. But he recovered pretty well. 'Mister Simmons,' he said, 'the next time I call you, I figure I won't be able to talk very long, because you'll have something on your line.' "

"Not entirely stupid, then," Roth said.

"Right on the money, in fact," Simmons said. "If he'd taken thirty minutes instead of three to call me after that envelope arrived, our security people would've had a tracer on that line and the cops on alert to grab him. 'This is true,' I said.

" 'So,' he said, 'I got to tell you what my situation is.' And he started this long, involved fantasy about how the only reason he's doing this to me is because he got in too deep with the bookies and the loan sharks, and they're going to have him killed, if he doesn't pay up. I asked him how he managed this, to get himself in such a mess. Very contrite. 'Gambling, Mister Simmons. I've always been, well, I guess what I am is a degenerate gambler. It's like a sickness with me.' And I asked him how much, and he said: 'Well, a million dollars.' "

"Fellow thinks big," Roth said.

"Too big," Simmons said. "I laughed in his face. Well, if you can do that over the phone. I said: 'Come on, Earl, be serious, willya? A million bucks? What do you think I am, the federal government or something? That I can just *lose, misplace,* a million dollars, and no one'll ever notice? My wife, or maybe the auditors here, or the guy who does my taxes—you think they wouldn't see it and say: "Ahh, Mister Simmons, hate to bother you, you know, but do you have any idea where this million dollars went?" What am I going to say? "Gee, honey," if this is my wife that asks, "I really can't imagine. Must've left it in my other suit, before it went to the cleaners." Come on now. Be realistic. Tell me something I can at least pretend to believe.'

"He swears again it's true. 'Bullshit,' I say. 'I never heard of a bookie or a shy that'd lend a guy in your class, or let him get in debt, a million U.S. dollars. If you told me five, or maybe ten, maybe ten thousand dollars, that I would believe. But you in hock for a full mill? Couldn't happen in this world.'

"He backtracked some. 'Okay, okay, it's more like half that. But I aslso got to get myself lost, and I got this opportunity in southern California, to go in partners with this guy I know that's building shopping centers. So I need a fresh start. A stake is all I need.'

" 'Earl,' I said, 'really, now. I like a good laugh as much as the next guy, but this is ridiculous. Now let's see if we can trim this thing down to manageable size here, get so we understand each other, and maybe just eliminate a lot of frustration and delay for both of us, all right?

" 'You want money and you think I've got it. Conceded. I haven't got anywhere near as much as you obviously think, but it's more than you've got, and I've been in that position myself. Not as extreme, maybe, but in my time I've found myself a lot times in a situation where I had to get my hands on some money, and the only way I could do it was by yanking it away from somebody else that had more. So this is fun for you, I know.

" 'The thing of it is, you've got to be, like I said, realistic. There's no point in my giving you a sum of money that's so big explaining where it went, and what for, 'll put me in a position just as awkward as the one that I'd've been in if I didn't give you one thin dime and just said: "Go fuck yourself." Which is what I'd like to do, of course, but I'm willing to be reasonable, and that's what I'm telling you, see? We both have to be reasonable here.

" 'If you send those pictures to my wife, she'll throw me out. Again. You hearing me, Earl? You soaking all this in? She will throw me out *again.* We've had our little differences in the past about my choice of companions, and I've spent my share of nights living in hotels alone. It's inconvenient, and the word always gets out on the street, and people that I'd ordinarily never try it figure I'm distracted and start getting cute with me. So I have to mash their fingers, and that's a damned nuisance, and while I'm doing it I'm not making any money.

" 'You still with me, pal? You can cause me some trouble, granted. But not a million bucks' worth. Not half a million bucks' worth. Not a quarter of a million bucks, or a hundred thousand bucks, or even fifty grand. Don't get yourself confused about what you are, Earl. You're not a scorpion that can kill me. You're not a German Shephered that can tear off my right leg, and you're not even a bedbug that can cover me with welts while I'm unprepared and sleeping. What you are is a mosquito. If I'm not quick enough to swat you, you can make me itch. You nip me once—this the once—the chances are I won't be quick enough. You hang around for refills, seconds, thirds, a buffet, the chances are, I will get quick, and I will swat you good. So I'm making you a counteroffer, and if you're smart, you'll take it. We still on the same song?'

221

" 'I'm warning you, Mister Simmons,' he says. 'You may think this is funny, but I can tell you that it's not.'

" 'No problem there, Earl baby,' I say, 'this ain't laughter that you hear, and these aren't jokes I'm telling you. You put all of the pictures, and all of the negatives, in a box or something, and you leave that box in a baggage locker someplace. Keep the key on you. Train station, airport, the bus station on Saint James Street. Don't matter shit to me. I'll meet you in the nearest coffee shop. I will have two keys. The first key will be to a locker in the same place. In it you'll find an envelope with ten big ones in fifties. You give me your locker key. I give you my first. I'll go to your locker and get the damned box out. If it's got in it all the stuff you're saying that you've got—no fair keeping something back—you get the second key I've got, to my second locker. And in it is another pack of fifties—fifteen large. That's twenty-five I'm offering and I'm not going up. I'm your only buyer, Earl, your only customer. Twenty-five to go away, tomorrow afternoon.'

" 'Shit,' he says, 'you must think I'm an asshole.'

" 'As a matter of fact, I do, 'but the world is full of assholes, as I learned long ago, and sometimes I do something dumb and have to deal with one. Well, I admit it: I did that. And you lucked out and caught me at it. Okay, spilt milk. So I pay up. Get it over with. Forget it. On to the next thing. But once. Once is all I pay. Tomorrow. Twenty-five thousand. Take it or leave it.'

" 'Fuck you,' he says.

" 'Sleep on it, pal,' I say to him. 'Give me a call in the morning.' And that was my fun for the day."

"Umm," Roth said. "Off the top of my head, I

doubt that he'll take it. You made the same mistake he did. He started too high, and you started too high."

"Too high?" Simmons said. "I would've thought you'd say: 'Too low.'"

"Oh," Roth said, "you had the right idea. I'm not saying that. But you're misjudging him and his situation much the same as he is yours. He thinks you've got a raja's purse; you know very well you don't. But when he says he's broke, you think his broker's pushing him for ten grand more in margin and his cash flow's been off lately. Nada. Nothing. Zilch. If you're willing to give him twenty-five K to get rid of him, and you call him a mosquito, the mosquito gets the idea he must be a goddamned vampire and you're really scared of him. That is big dough to this punk, and if you think it's chicken feed you really must be rich."

"Ahh," Simmons said. "So tomorrow when he calls me, he'll still be demanding more."

"That's my guess," Roth said.

"So what do I do?" Simmons said. "Call the FBI?"

"How eager you are to testify, first to a grand jury, then in court?" Roth said. Simmons scowled. "That's what I figured," Roth said. "Well, that's the only way you get J. Edgar's men to help you. They're not like the gallant firemen that come and rescue you down ladders, and then don't expect a thing from you except you buy ten tickets every year to the Firemen's Ball. They go out and grab a bad guy that is causing you trouble, they really want—insist, in fact—that you make sure he stays grabbed."

"I know some guys," Simmons said. "Well, I know some guys that claim they know, some other guys I don't. That ocassionally do things for guys like me. I could feel them out. See if that's all talk."

"It isn't," Roth said. "You put out feelers for them, you will find it's not all talk, and find out real fast. But later on you'll find out there's a price for what they do. A price much higher, I would guess, than what this bozo wants, and one that you'll have to pay. Pussy's still against the law, unless you marry it, but nobody enforces that law. Accessory before the fact of some fatal event, well, that's a different matter. That is one you can't laugh off, and if you don't pay up large money, you'll have cops, not patient Phyllis, waiting for explanations."

"I think I'd better sleep on this tonight too," Simmons said.

"I'd recommend that," Roth said. "I'd put that trace on, too."

16

Shortly after 10:30 in the morning of the last Wednesday in November, Earl Beale used a telephone booth outside the train station in Gloucester to call Allen Simmons on his private line at his offices in Boston. Earl had awakened in his bed at the Harbor Cove Motel an hour before to a double dose of audible bad news; rain thrummed steadily on the metal casing of the window-unit air conditioner and blood pounded in his head through vessels that had tightly constricted as he slept and his body burned up the booze he'd had the night before. At first he had trouble remembering whether he had spent the night alone, and was about to search for his wallet. Then he recalled that the spike-heeled woman from the dim pink neon barroom, shockingly late-fortied in the unforgiving glare of the sodium streetlamps, had passed out still leaning on his arm six blocks away. Gradually he remembered easing her down slowly, allowing her to fold herself into a fetus crouching on the soapstone step before a doorway, and that led him to the explanation for the abrasions on his right hand—he had used it to fend off the brick-walled buildings that encroached on his unsteady walk back to the motel.

Getting those things sorted out he had recognized that no coffee ever made would supply what he needed. He had pulled on his clothes and raincoat and gone out into the rain, finding a bar where fishermen whose teeth were missing lamented through gray stubble and accents from ports near Lisbon the North Atlantic weather, engine trouble, absent fish, cranky Coast Guardsmen, and torn nets; they drank PM rye whiskey with beer chasers for their lunches during breakfast and commuting hours for people who worked on land, and they showed tolerant contempt for the shiftless drunk he was. He drank three shots of Mr. Boston rum and put the fire out with glasses of ginger ale.

"Mister Simmons, all right?" he said, when the secretary answered, the sound of his own voice reminding him of how the dust had felt on his fingers when he'd searched under Penny's bed: furry and threatening. She said, "Just a moment, please—I'll see if he's come in," and put his call on hold.

In the office, Allen Simmons sat at his desk. Sidney Roth sat on the couch, a yellow pad before him, his head bowed down by earphones wired into a double phone jack on the wall behind the couch. Next to him a man in a brown suit and tie perched up close to a black metal console, staring at its seven dials; it was wired into the wall jack. He had a spiral notepad and a red felt-tip pen. Two men in dark gray uniforms, also wearing earphones, pushed test-panel buttons on a Uher reel-to-reel recorder wired into the speakerphone next to Simmon's left hand. One of them had a notepad and a pencil in his hand. He nodded to Simmons,

226

who switched on the speakerphone. "Simmons speaking," he said.

The echo effect of the room on the receiver's microphone caused the speaker to reverberate, making Roth and the two guards wince. The phone lines up to Gloucester and the tinny hangover still resonating dully between Earl's eardrums amplified reverberations. *"Jesus,"* Earl yelled into the handset while the rain ran down the booth, "turn that goddamned gadget off and use a goddamn honest phone. I don't need your showing off."

"Sorry," Simmons said, making the sound waves crash again. He picked up the handset, and the speakerphone shut off. "Here I am again." Roth and the two guards relaxed.

"You said I should call you back," Earl said. "Okay, I'm calling. Let's hear it. What you got to say?"

"Me?" Simmons said. "I don't have anything to say. I said what I had to say yesterday." The man at the console leaned forward intently and began making notes, tapping each of the seven dials in order, left to right. When he reached the last one he stood up from the couch and took his notepad from the office, walking silently, opening and shutting the door without making any noise.

"You son of a bitch," Earl said. "I know what you're tryin', do, and it's not gonna work. I won't be on this long enough. So either you either talk to me now, or else I hang up."

The man in the brown suit took the handset from Simmons's secretary and spoke into it. "Herbie," he said, "take this down." He read seven digits off. "My guess is that's in Gloucester," he said. "Could be Marblehead. Wife's family used to have a summer house up that neck of the woods. Think I remember that exchange." He paused. "Yeah, hanging on."

In Simmons's office, Simmons said into the phone, "Earl, you can hang up anytime you want. The way I left it with you last night was that you said you had something to think over. You accept my offer of twenty-five thousand dollars, today, the way I outlined it, and I get all the pictures, and all the negatives. Or, you turn it down. Take it and you get it. Turn it down, do whatever you like. This is our last conversation.'

"You fucking bastard," Earl said. "You must think I'm fucking stupid. You give fucking Penny fifteen thousand fucking dollars for a fucking long weekend, and that's it, it's over with, like you just bought a dinner. And then you got the fucking nerve to tell me, knowing what I've got, and what I can do to you, you got the fucking goddamned nerve to offer me just ten lousy fucking more? I could wreck your fucking life. I oughta blow your fucking car up. I could do that, you know. Fucking asshole big shot—who the fuck you think you are?"

Simmons did not say anything. "*Hey,*" Earl said, "answer me, you fuck. I asked you who the fuck you think you are, you fuck."

"Earl," Simmons said, "any horse that had you for his ass'd break his leg, so someone'd shoot him fast. You know what Penny says about you? Do you know what she thinks? I asked her once about you, just, oh, who the hell you were. This was when you first showed up. I was curious. And she said: 'Oh, Earl's kind of fun. Fun to have around. But there are times he's a champ, a real champion asshole. Someday's he's gonna bore

228

me, and I know what I'm gonna do. I'm gonna get a whole big barrel of Preparation H, and rub it on, all over him, and he'll shrink and disappear.' That is what she said."

"You're a fucking liar," Earl said. "Penny did not say that."

The man in the brown suit opned the door from the outer office and entered silently. He went to the couch and displayed his notepad to Roth. It read: "Gloucester number. Opposite train station. Friends on force there on their way. Will folo and ID." Roth read and nodded. The man in the brown suit mouthed, "That okay? No arrest?" Roth nodded. He wrote on his notepad: "Just follow—no arrest." The man in the brown suit left the room as he had come.

"Okay," Simmons said, "have it your way, then. But now we both agree on at least one way Penny talks, because you just told me what she told you that I gave her for last weekend. And I tell you: I did not."

"You're a fucking liar," Earl said. "You're fucking lying to me. She left a fucking note for me. Fifteen thousand fucking dollars. That's the only way she went, the only way you made her go. You gave her five more thousand'n you usually do. Regular ten plus five more. That was why she went."

"I did not," Simmons said. "I have *never* given Penny ten thousand dollars at one time, any time she went with me. I haven't given her a dime, until just this past weekend. Not once, Earl, not until then, did a dollar pass between us. From my hand to hers. And that is the truth, my friend. You can count on that. So, if she told you otherwise, otherwise than that, well, I guess she lied to you. Didn't you see what she got?"

229

"Whadda you mean, you bastard?" Earl said. "I know she got that money. The time you went Barbados there, the times you went San Juan? Las Vegas, all those fucking trips? She got ten big ones every time, and five on top for this one."

"Earl," Simmons said, "believe me, it didn't happen. Do you seriously think I could disguise large cash payments of that size, without my wife finding out? Nonsense. Penny was on the payroll here. She was a consultant. She got five thousand bucks a month, whether I called or not. Winter, summer, spring, and fall, sixty grand a year. To be at my beck and call. I did tip her the five extra, because it was Thanksgiving and she told me you had plans. 'An early Christmas bonus': that was what I said to her. I appreciated her loyalty, her loyalty to me. And to you, too, if you'll believe that. She's a very loyal girl."

"Bastard," Earl said. "Bastard. You're just making all this up. I'm gonna kill you, doing this. Fucking goddamned bastard. You mean Penny always had money, and she got more every month? Just like she had a job or something? She wasn't flat broke like she told me, summertimes and stuff? It was like she had a job?"

"It wasn't *like* she had a job, Earl," Simmons said through a large smile. "She *did* have a job. It wasn't maybe one you'd look for in the newspaper, or through an agency, but it was still an honest job. Salary for service. Same as any other job. You know what we called it, Earl? On the corporation books? 'Physical therapy', okay? For the tense executive. We have several Pennies. Some for us and some for clients. Yours just happened to be mine. And selected friends of mine, but I screened them carefully."

230

"You son of a bitches," Earl said. "The fucking pair of you. She's got this job, she doesn't tell me, she says she's got no money. And all the time, *and all the time*, she's getting fucking money every goddamned fucking month."

"She *was*, Earl," Simmons said. "Up till now she was. She, when I hired her, well, I was pretty damned specific. I didn't say to her: 'And, oh, I'd like my picture taken. A few keepsakes to show my wife. Think you could arrange that, too? Have someone just show up and do it, while you're entertaining me?' That wasn't in the job description, those extra services. I wasn't planning a wedding here. She says now of course that she didn't know. Had no idea what you were doing, and I would expect no less from her—she is such a loyal girl. But, you see, I don't believe her. She's just too damned loyal, to too many men at once. And when those loyalties get crossed, well, she doesn't tell the truth."

"Bullshit," Earl said, "fucking bullshit. Fucking god-damned bullshit. All your fucking fancy phone is good for's talking bullshit. Think you're a big fucking deal. Your kind aren't worth shit."

"So, right after you called me," Simmons said, "I fired her. She used to have that job, okay? Had it until this week. But now she doesn't, anymore. That's why the twenty-five. If you take it, you can tell her, it's her severance pay. If you don't, then you can tell her, well, you turned it down.'

"Asshole," Earl said, "you asshole. I am gonna ruin you."

"Right, Earl, right," Simmons said, as the man in the brown suit returned. He took his notepad to the couch and showed a page to Roth. It read: "We have a man in place. Will stay till our men on way get there. In contact by radio." Roth nodded. He lifted his yellow pad and semaphored to Simmons. When Simmons looked up, Roth mimed cutting his own throat. Simmons nodded. "Now look, Earl, I've got to go. I mean, I really have to. And your vocabulary, well, it seems limited. So what is it? Yes or no. You want the cash or not?"

"Go fuck yourself, you asshole," Earl said. He slammed the handset into the cradle and stood trembling in the phone booth, watching the rain slide down the glass. By the time he finished collecting his gear at the motel and stowing it in the car, two of Simmons' security men, both dressed in plainclothes, had a description of the Pontiac Le Mans Earl had parked outside the room. One of them radioed the data back to the Boston office. "Green metallic, 'sixty-seven, boss," he said. "Massachusetts K for *kilo* seven-sixer, three, three, three. And we might speed things up a little— there's a Hertz sticker, the back bumper. Might as well go right to them. Gotcha, gotcha, gotcha."

In the early afternoon the secretary to the northeast regional sales manager of Kimberly Hospital/Surgical Suppliers in White Plains, New York, responding to a visit from a private investigator, confirmed that the company employed Edmund R. Cornell of Suffern, New York, as an institutional sales specialist. "I know he's all right," she said. "He was yesterday, at least, because he was here all day. And I saw him in the parking lot, too, now I think of it. Just before he headed out for Wilmington this morning. He should be back tomorrow." She said he had seemed to be in good spirits, "nothing bothering him except the normal bills and stuff," but declined to divulge further information without a written statement of the nature of the investigation and approval from her superiors. "Company policy."

The private detective was understanding and polite. "Miss," he said, "I know that. But that's not why I'm here. If I wanted to I couldn't tell you what the deuce this is about. All I know is that our firm's affiliated with an outfit that handles security, New England. Mostly Boston, all right? We refer back and forth. And one of their clients has got information that someone by the name of Edmund R. Cornell rented a car up there some time ago, and there's another guy driving it that he doesn't think, well, he don't know, but he thinks he knows this other guy, and his name isn't Edmund Cornell. So that's what he, they, asked me to find out. If you got such a guy, and he works here, and the bills rental cars to this company. And you have told me those things, so now I've done my job and I thank you very much."

"You're welcome," she said primly.

"Now maybe," the detective said, "I can return a favor. If your Mister Cornell does rent cars, and he rented this one up in Boston back the day before Thanksgiving, well then, he didn't give it back, all right? So if he's back, and the car isn't, and Hertz says if it's been stolen, well, they sure don't know about it, maybe if those cars that Mister Cornell rents get billed back here to you, your boss might appreciate it if you let him know all this. Because right now you're telling me that Mister Cornell was in here today, but my people up in Boston there are saying that the car that's rented out to him was driving up around there then, when you say he was in here. Right in your parking lot. Somebody's gonna have to pay for that car—that would be my guess. Mister Hertz is nice people, but when someone keeps one of his cars, he expects to get his money. And he'll most likely come here first."

17

Late in the afternoon of the last Thursday in January, 1968, Penny Slate used the Newbury Street entrance of the Ritz-Carlton in Boston and swept through the lobby into the bar facing Arlington Street, her trotteur mink coat open on her white turtleneck sweater and black pants, her black leather satchel bag swinging from its shoulder strap. She carried a bag logoed "Bonwit Teller," and when the waiter eyed her narrowly as she looked for a table at the window, she recognized him from the old days—his and hers as well—in the bar at the Holiday Inn. She disrupted his efforts to place her by draping the coat open as she sat down, displaying the initials and the Saks label, and saying, "I'm expecting my husband. A dark Dubonnet with a twist on the rocks, please." The waiter frowned and went away, distracted but not giving up.

Allen Simmons arrived at 4:45, rejecting the maître d's suggestion that he check his double-breasted camel-hair overcoat before entering the bar. "I'm meeting a lady," he said. "If she isn't here then I've got the wrong place. Or else the wrong lady. So just let me look around, won't be a minute," and he marched down to the window tables.

He stood over the empty chair opposite her and gazed down. She smiled and opened the palm of her right hand at the chair. "I assume," he said, "that means you've got them."

She inclined her head slightly to the right and looked at him with merry eyes. "So much of life is trust, Allen," she said. "I'm assuming you have something, too."

He pulled the chair out. Then he removed his overcoat and folded it once, dropping it on the window ledge. The maître d' came swiftly down the two steps from his station at the desk and pounced on it. "I'll just have a busboy take this to the checkroom, sir," he said, "and bring the check to you." Simmons, sitting down, raised an eyebrow at his departing back, clasped his hands at his waist, and smiled at Penny. "When I was a little boy," he said, "I hated it when teachers picked me to go to the blackboard. I always got beaten up on the playground after school because I could do the problems. They knew it, and they approved of me getting beaten up, so they did it more. I couldn't fire the teachers, and it never occurred to me to slash their tires or something. So I learned how to make the chalk screech, and after that they stopped calling on me. Parts of me never grew up."

"Good training for business," she said.

"Speaking of which," he said, as the waiter delivered her Dubonnet. The waiter studied her again, and she dismissed him with raised eyebrows. The busboy delivered a claim check for Simmons's coat.

"I have it right here," she said. She patted the small Bonwit's bag.

Simmons smiled. To the waiter he said, "Pernod and water, I think, please." He returned his gaze to meet hers. He patted the left breast of his suit coat. "As good as your word," he said.

"Oh," she said, "it's nothing, really. You know what a fan I've always been of early-morning drives in the winter to New Hampshire. So very stimulating. Up while it's still dark and off into the country for some lovely conversation at a quiet little jail with a lovely bunch of guys. It's really very nice."

"But you didn't encounter any problems," he said.

"Well," she said, "if you mean: After I saw the problem and tried to deal with it, and didn't, and then figured out a way to deal with it and solve it, that I didn't have a problem—right, I didn't have a problem. But before: 'I didn't have a problem'? Well, you could say I had a problem."

"It was the brother, then?" he said.

"I couldn't move him from square one," she said. "I don't know why that was. I mean, I've never met the guy, and I was really startled, I talked to him on the phone, that he sounded just as stupid as Earl always said he was. Which took me by surprise because most of what Earl told you wasn't worth a damn. Maybe that's his secret, Earl's. Maybe he tells just enough truth so you don't always know he's lying. But I was still a little unprepared for the way this guy reacted. I mean, he's known Earl all his life, and anyone who's gone through that, who's known the guy at all, has got to be about as totally fed up with him as anyone could get. And here I am, I come along, another one of Earl's

237

suckers that believed him, and depended, and now look what I have got, and all I'm really asking this guy is to do what, well, what I would certainly want to do, if I'd've been Earl's brother. 'Just call him up, don't have to go there, and tell him you're finished with him. That is all you have to do. So if he wants to get out then he has to deal with me.' And he wouldn't do it. He didn't say he wouldn't do it, and he didn't say he would. He just kept on, oh, I don't know, sort of kept on mumbling. 'I don't know.' 'No, I'm not sure.' 'Well, I'm making up my mind.' 'No, I haven't decided yet.' Very frustrating. Because as long as Earl thought that there still might be another human being he could get a fresh ace from, he was not about to do what I said." She snickered. "I got the definite impression Earl and I are not best friends anymore."

The waiter brought the Pernod in a small carafe and a glass of water. Simmons poured the contents of the carafe into the glass, turning the water milky, stirred it once, and sipped it. He nodded. "So how'd you break the logjam?" he said.

"Wasn't easy," she said. "I know you thought, thought you must think, every time I called and said: 'I haven't got it yet, but I will, a day or so,' after a few of those calls you must've started thinking: 'Well, she can't get it done.' And I was afraid you'd find another way, someone else to do it."

"I considered it," he said. "As a matter of fact I had my people call some other people who do hush-hush private work. Mostly industrial. And they ran a background on Earl and came up with some interesting stuff I could have used."

"Really," she said. "I mean, I don't doubt the bastard's had a really full career, but my impression was that, well, he never really got involved with anyone with clout. I mean, like someone who could get things done that're really hard to do, and wouldn't want it to get out he was involved with Earl."

"Reasonable supposition," he said. "Just not, as it turns out, a fully accurate one. You knew about his prison record, naturally, I guess?"

"Uh huh," she said. "If you've ever known someone that's done some heavy time, well, it seems like it does something to them that lasts after they get out. A few days in the sun and some decent food and stuff, and a couple good rolls in the hay and they lose that pasty look. But what's inside their head stays pasty, like their minds've been bleached. I had a brother that went bad, and he did a couple hitches in a couple county jails. Houses of correction. He was not corrected but he certainly did change. They're like, they get like really hungry dogs with bones. Nobody's really bothering with them, or wants the goddamned bone, but every time they get a bone, by God they act like that. Like someone's going to march right up and take it away from them. Earl was like that. He had this thing about his beer. I don't even like beer. If I have a beer today it'll probably be my last one until a year from now, and it'll be my first one since about a year ago. But Earl, when he was living with me? Fanatic about his beer. Always hadda have two six-packs cold in the icebox. He drank one, part of the other, he got home tonight, tomorrow when he came home he'd have another case. And I figured out why that was. I don't think that Earl, you know, ever liked beer all that much. But when he was

239

in prison he couldn't get a beer, and now he's out he still worries they might shut him off again."

"Yes," Simmons said. "Well, another thing that happens to them, they usually get in prison, is a prison record. One that follows them. A little trail of paper that goes everywhere they roam, just like Mary's little lamb."

"Yeah," she said.

"Well," Simmons said, "I found it interesting, or I should say, Larry Badger did, that when he ran Earl through his files and probably someone else's, he didn't find Earl's name among those having prison records. Not at first, that is. Someone with a fair amount of heavy pull did something, so that unless you're really wired in, Earl looks white as snow. Of course that kind of trick can backfire pretty badly—as soon as you use the right password and you find out he has got one, you know not only that he did time but that he knew some guy who looks clean well enough to wipe it out."

"Blackmail," she said.

"Could be," Simmons said. "Except for the fact that he did such a clumsy job on me—hard to believe anyone who'd pulled it off before, and got his record scrubbed, could've learned so little about shaking down a man. More likely, I think: family. Some family connection. Someone that Earl's father knew, or maybe this dumb brother. Collected on a favor from a friend of one of theirs. Earl probably takes the credit, brags it shows how smart he is, how well he's connected. But chances are it wasn't that, since it worked so well. Things that work well, this is my guess, don't have Earl's prints on them. If it's petty, and it's stupid, and it doesn't work, well then, if Earl takes the credit, I'd

240

accept his claim. But anything sub rosa that worked out and worked out well, if Earl got some benefit I'd say he was innocent of any real work that produced it."

"But I didn't pursue it," Simmons said. "I held it in reserve. There really wasn't any hurry to my interest in this. No urgency, I mean. As long as Earl was safely locked up he could not do much to me. And as events had proven, even when Earl's on the loose, he still can't do much to me. He isn't good enough. There just wasn't any major gain foreseeable from making trouble for some obliging friend of family who'd done the shit a favor once because he liked Earl's father. Or his brother, or his mother, or the family dog. Things got nasty? Might be different. But until they did? Sit tight. Rely on Penny's loyalty. I had confidence in you."

"Oh, Allen," she said, "you're such a gentleman."

"I know it," he said. "It's my one claim to fame. May I see the merchandise?"

"Certainly," she said. She picked up the Bonwit's bag and handed it across the table to him. He looked inside at the end of the shoe box. "Bostonian?" he said. "Twelve double D?"

"He was a basketball player," she said. "Big men have big feet."

"And?" he said. "Do we now have the missing link, the one thing that explains his otherwise perplexing powers of attraction for fine ladies of good taste?"

"No," she said, "we don't. That part's like socks, especially in what I sell. One size fits all. I hooked up with Earl because he fascinated me. I used to know a guy who kept pirhanas in a tank. At the oddest times—he was a real baseball lunatic who'd call me up and have me over, and then forget the reason if there

241

was a big game on and it went extra innings. But he'd get up with the bases loaded, two outs, and the score tied, and feed raw hamburger to his fish. He liked to see them eat. Didn't matter to me—time's what I sell. The price is the same, clothes on or clothes off. But I really liked that nut. He was different. He had imagination.

"And Earl," she said. "Well, he's got weaknesses. But see I grew up on a place that was a working farm before we got it. Outside Portland there. It wasn't a working farm after we got it because nobody in my family really liked to work. At farming or anything else. So the place got pretty run-down. But it was still, you know, fairly big, and we had these dogs. I got used to having dogs around. Real nothing-special dogs. Just dogs. The ones that stayed outside all the time? They stayed outside all the time. The ones that lived in the house? They lived in the house all the time. They all did the same kinds of things. The ones that lived outdoors, they shit outdoors, and the ones that lived inside shit inside. They were nice, friendly dogs. Always coming up to you, scratch their ears and play with them, and that's sort of what Earl's like. Except he lets himself in and he lets himself out, and he knows how to feed himself, but you got him around, and it's sort of homey, you know? You know he really likes you. He might go off someplace and not come back a few days, but generally he does come back. And if someone, you know, attacks you, well, you can say: 'Sic 'em, Earl.' And I think he probably would. Growl, at least. Earl would at least growl. And that was the real reason, I guess. I liked him and he kept me entertained.

"See, what I do," she said, "I keep *men* entertained.

242

I entertained you. I see a man, he whips it out, I spread, he pays me money. He has a good time, I do a job. Nobody entertains me. But I see Earl, he drives me nuts, he's got all these big ideas? I know half of them're off the wall, and the rest he'll never finish, but he's thinking about *me*. Not about Penny's crotch; about Penny. We did it, sure, but sex with Earl was an afterthought. With Earl I could relax. So work is work, and play is play. I kept Earl around for fun."

"Some fun," Simmons said.

"Well, it was," she said. "Don't kid yourself, Allen. I'm the only one in my family that ever amounted to anything. I'm the only one with any money. And they know how I got it, what I did to become something. And they don't like it. They pretend that they don't like it because I'm disgracing them, but I know very well that it's because they're just plain jealous. My two sisters. If they looked like I do and they had my balls, which they don't, and they don't, they would do the same thing in a flash. My brothers did the best they could, but they kept getting caught. My father hasn't drawn a sober breath in all the years I've known him, and if you saw my mother you would say: 'Mammy Yokum.' All that's missing is the pipe. I'm telling you, Allen, it's Dogpatch. And I'm out of it, and I'm damned glad of it, and they hate my guts for that. Which they admit, they hate me, but they say it's something else.

"Earl was sort of like going home for me, you know? I know I can't do that anymore, and I'd never want to stay there, even if I could. But you need, I need, at least, some kind of base where I can go and just be

243

there, you know? Comfortable. And Earl was comfortable."

"Huh," Simmons said. He took the box out of the bag and dropped the bag on the floor. He removed the cover from the box and selected one of the envelopes at random. It contained negatives. He riffled through them, noted the dates on the front, and put them back in the box. He took out another envelope. It contained pictures. He sorted through them. He held one up. "Coming back from Saint Croix?" he said.

"I think so," she said. "That was that white angora jumpsuit that I had. That I liked so much. That I spilled the wine on when we got the turbulence when we flew to Honolulu. Never got it out. 'Red wine and tattoos,' the lady at the cleaners said. 'Nothing we can do.'"

"Umm," he said. He put the pictures back in the envelope and put it in the box. He put the cover back on the box and dropped it into the bag on the floor. He sat back. "I can assume that they're all there?" he said. "Without going through them all now?"

"Not as long as what you've got in that pocket's still in that pocket," she said. "Until what you've got in that pocket moves into my pocket, you can assume I went through that box, and as far's I know, all the pictures that he took, and the negatives, were in it. And that some of the negatives, now, aren't."

"And where might they be?" he said.

"I hired them a limo," she said. "They're having a glass of wine and driving around the block until I give them the signal. Then they'll fly right out of that car, and jump right in the window, and land right in your lap. And they will never go see Phyllis, or let her see them."

"And we used to be such friends," he said. "We had such good times."

"Right, Allen," she said. "Was that my job description, in payroll accounts? 'Friend, for good times'? Gimme the money, old friend."

He took a number-ten manila envelope from his right inside pocket and placed it on the table. She picked it up and opened it. There were fifteen strapped packets of hundred-dollar bills in it. "You're short," she said, "ten short. Earl said twenty-five."

He laughed. "Well, we both know Earl lies," he said. "But this time, for once, he chose to tell the truth. It was twenty-five for Earl. That day. He turned it down. You called me and asked me if the deal was still open. I said it was, I did not say it was still twenty-five."

"Okay," she said, putting the envelope in her shoulder bag. "I guess you got me there. But now I've got you. Here. As Jesus said to Saint Michael: 'We gonna fuck around, man? Or are we gonna play golf?' "

"I don't follow you," he said.

"Damned right you don't," she said. "I'm on my own from now on, and I know it. But a girl on her own needs money, and when what she's got is all gone, she needs a way to get more. So I've got some now, that'll hold me awhile, and I've still got a way to get more."

"I gave you that coat," he said. "That's a nice coat."

"It is," she said, "and I love it. But it was a gift, and what we're doing now, love, is business."

"That was my impression," he said. "Did I miss something?"

"Oh," she said, "it's probably my fault. I didn't

245

mention overhead. All those long-distance calls I had to make to New York, and to Vermont, New Hampshire. The reason this's taken so long is that the guy Earl got the car from can't afford to pay the bill, and the company, his company, said that it won't pay it for him. So he hasn't got the money, but the only way he beats the bill is by going to New Hampshire and telling everybody how Earl got the car from him."

"He doesn't want to do that?" Simmons said. "That doesn't look good either?"

"Hey," she said, "I can understand it. Respectable gentleman, nice and refined, pretty wife and three lovely children. Responsible job, well liked in his field—does he really want to get up there in court and admit he gave Earl the car because Earl let him suck on his cock? He doesn't. I understand that. But the guy's not decisive. He's a fatalist. Maybe God kills him tomorrow, and all of his problems go with him. So finally I lose my patience with him. I say: 'Look, you are being an asshole. It's four hundred bucks, give or take thirty-five, for your reputation and life. Now if you had the brains of a squash, you would pay it and keep your mouth shut. Maybe should've done that sooner and stayed out of this whole mess, but then, nobody's perfect. Now, be sensible, all right?' And still he won't make up his mind. And still Earl's brother won't call him.

"I get pissed off. I got one jerk in Vermont that can't make up his mind, and another one down in New York that won't make up his. But I can't do anything to move the Vermont jerk, and I think I can do something, get the New York guy going. So I call up the cocksucker and say: 'Okay, I'm tired of this. You wore

246

me down. I want him out. You go to Western Union down there, four thirty this after, and you give your name and you will get four hundred fifty dollars. The extra's for a beer, and a sandwich, you missed lunch. Pay for the fuckin' car. For this, blow-boy, you owe me something. You call up that DA in the morning and you tell him you're not coming. You don't do that, I call your wife, and I tell her what's going on.'

"He got the message, finally, the dumb little shit. He called the DA and he bagged it. I was at the jail. 'Okay,' I say to our friend Earl, 'now what's it going to be? I got the fairy, take a hike, so when your case comes up, six weeks or so, he won't show up, and you'll be free to leave. Unless you don't give me the pictures. In which case I sign a charge that you stole some stuff from me. And I will tell them what it is, and just where they can find it. And while they're getting you your clothes, they'll look and they will find it. And then they'll come and take your clothes back, and you'll go right back in the cell. What was the play you liked so much? The good old give-and-go? That's the play I'm calling now. You give and you go.'

"And he did. But it cost me, to do that, plus the five hundred bucks I give him so he can get out of town. And I want that money back. It's not coming out of me."

"You gave him money to get out of town?" Simmons said. "Have you gone soft or something? I'm surprised at you, give a guy a present that's just fucked up your life."

"I was buying something?" she said. "The way I looked at it, I was buying *me* a present. Out of town is where I want him. Far away from me. Earl's gone

247

rancid, like my turkey. Earl isn't fun anymore. You're a tough son of a bitch to do business with, Allen, but you always treated me square, and you never hurt me. Earl's fucking great idea ends up screwing me out of my best client, best I ever had. And I don't think my chances are so good of finding someone else I can make the same arrangement with. So now I've got to scramble, and I don't want him monkeying around, making things harder'n they are. I got to have my head clear now. Him I do not need."

"Where's he go?" Simmons said. "You know?"

She shrugged. " 'South' was what he said. Said he was heading south, he's always hated cold. Could be, I suppose. Cold weather bothered him. But he's got something up his sleeve down there, if that's really where he's going. Earl's a binge drinker. He can get by for two, three weeks, on a hundred bucks or so, it doesn't look like he needs all that much money. And he doesn't think he does. But then he goes off a bat, or decides he can beat the point spread, and it all disappears. So then he needs some more. He thinks in thousand-dollar terms. That's why I never told him what our actual deal was. And I'm damned glad you didn't, either, until the deal was over. If he'd've known I had it coming in, regular basis, he'd've spent it all, and more, the exact same way—on a regular basis. He thinks if he can just get himself a grand, he will be all right for the rest his life on earth. Doesn't think that far ahead. So, I can't imagine what he thinks he can steal down south, or where down south he thinks it is, or who down there has got it. But something like that's on his mind. That's the way it works."

Simmons looked at his watch. "Speaking of the

time," he said, "I really ought to go." He finished his drink. "So, can we wrap this whole thing up now? Or do we part at impasse?"

"Up to you," she said. "You can pay me now, or you can hope my luck is good and I never need to come back for those other ten large ones. But every day you'll wake up knowing this could be the one you get a call from me, see if you're in the picture market."

"I'll give you half of it for the rest of the negatives," he said.

"I'll give you half of the negatives for half of the money," she said. "I'm not bending on this, Allen. I'm a tough son of a bitch to do business with, too, and you oughta know that by now. You and Earl set the price, or he asked and then you did. None of this was my idea, not from the beginning. By the time I find out what he's doing, he'd already done it enough times to stick it to you. He just wanted more. And then when he ducked out on me, and put the boots to you, well, that wasn't my idea either. I'd been stalling him for months, just hoping that something'd happen so he'd drop the whole idea. Well, the shit got in the fan. I'm trying, tidy up here, cut my losses and get myself a little breathing room. You gave me some. I want the rest. Pay now or save for later."

"I'll give you the ten for the rest of the negatives and next weekend in New York," he said.

"On the house?" she said.

"Sort of our last fling," he said. "Just for old times' sake."

She shook her head. "I already sang that song. Sang it New Year's Eve. Except where we're concerned, well, that's one old acquaintance that I'd just as soon forget. Well, I'd better, anyways."

"Seventy-five hundred," he said.

"Ten grand," she said, "and a quickie before dinner. I'm not saying I don't like you, you know, but I'm still a working girl and I don't work for you these days."

He sighed and produced a second envelope from his pocket. He put it on the table. She reached into the shoulder bag and took out a white envelope. She put it on the table and picked up the one he'd placed there, putting it in her bag.

"Huh," he said, leafing through the negatives that she had given him. "You're not counting it?"

"Don't need to, Allen," she said. "I've always trusted you."

On the way out she saw the waiter with his small tray on the counter of the service bar, studying her under a frown. She went over to him, and patted him on the left forearm. "Nice to see you again, too," she said. "Eric, I think—wasn't it?" He nodded. "We've both moved up in the world," she said. "I hope you're not still tipping off house cops, now that you're high class and all." The waiter looked alarmed. "Now, now," she said, "it's all right, Eric. The house cops tipped us off, too."

18

Midway through the morning of the last Friday in January, a northeast wind came down Rhode Island Sound at twenty knots and blew along the rocky beach into Lafayette, Rhode Island. The parking lot of the shopping center was nearly deserted. There were no customers at Chuckie's Discount Liquors. The woman in the black wig with the ringlets leaned her buttocks against the shelf at her checkout station and smoked a Salem, taking deep drags. Between them she held the cigarette aloft in her left hand, her left elbow cupped in her right hand, and stared out the window. She saw a khaki Ford sedan come into the lot from the north and park in the first row opposite the store. There was white lettering that she could not make out on the front doors, and there was more on the lower part of the rear deck. It had no license plate. The driver and his passenger both wore military dress hats. They talked for a few moments and then the passenger got out. He wore a long, dark green overcoat and his green trousers had a black stripe. The skirt of his overcoat flapped in the wind. He was careful to step around the

251

small puddles of melted snow that remained on the macadam as he made his way to Chuckie's. He showed no interest in the stocked aisles when he entered but came directly to her register. He was in his midtwenties, and had blond hair.

"Whaddaya looking for, Lieutenant?" she said.

He grinned at her. "I was going to buy a pack of cigarettes before I asked you," he said.

"No need to be polite," she said. "You should save your money, get them at the PX, right? For what, five cents a pack? No one this business expects military guys to buy what we got for sale in here. Hell, last time my kid was home, I ordered all my booze and smokes from him. Bought in all down at Groton for a tenth of what I'd have to pay here, even with my discount."

"He's in the navy?" the lieutenant said. "Down at the sub base?"

"Nah," she said. "The army. Down Fort Gordon, Georgia."

"Well," he said, "at least that's something. Least you know he's safe."

"Well," she said, "I wouldn't say that, exactly. I mean, he jumps out of airplanes, right? He says it's helicopters, which I say: 'So what? If it flies then it's a plane.' And he jumps out of it. I heard that can be dangerous, matter where you do it. But yeah, I do know what you mean—he's not in Vietnam. So whatcha looking for?"

"The Beachmont Motel?" he said.

"Jeez," she said, "what goes on here? MPs change their uniforms?"

"I'm not an MP," he said. "What made you think that?"

"I know that joint," she said, "the type of guys that go there. Only reason I can think of why the army'd want to go there is because somebody tipped you there's an AWOL staying there. Which'd fit right in—place's perfect for deserters; they'd give it some class."

"No," he said. "Nothing that exciting. Or that pleasant for that matter. Just trying, trace somebody that's supposed to work at it."

She nodded. "Oh, now I get it," she said. "You're with Intelligence. Well, lemme tell you something, Lieutenant: You already found out everything you need to know without ever going there. Nobody ever stayed the Beachmont should get any kind of clearance. They don't draw the kind of people we should tell our secrets to. But if you got to, then you got to. Carry out those orders. You just keep right on heading south, it's right there down the road. Kind of a waste of a good spot—a cheap flophouse like that across the street from a really gorgeous view. It's two stories, faded green, run-down at the heels. Which sort of describes the owner, too, except for the green part."

"He's there most of the time, is he?" the lieutenant said.

"Put it this way, kid," she said. "When he isn't somewhere else, that is where he is. Where somewhere else is, that depends on what scam he's got working, and those change from week to week. But he's usually there, making life hard for people. Drives a big gray Lincoln and acts like he can afford it. Watch him when you talk to him—don't believe too much you hear. He's a shifty bastard and you can't trust him at all."

The lieutenant nodded and winked. "Gotcha," he

said, tipping his hat, "you've been very helpful and your country thanks you, ma'am."

She grinned at him. "Pleasure talking to you," she said. "You're probably the nicest guy I'm gonna see all day."

The sign on the orange trailer remained in the Beachmont parking lot but a line advertising "LOW OFF-SEASON RATES" had been added to the legend above "34 AIR-COND RMS." The listed prices remained "$10.00s. $14 DBL." The sign vibrated in the wind. There were two cars in the parking lot, a rusted brown Dodge Dart coupe and a new blue Ford Fairmont sedan. "No luck," the lieutenant said to the driver, who wore sergeant's insignia. "Hasn't come in here yet."

"Think maybe we oughta check?" the sergeant said. He pulled into the lot.

"Can't do any harm, I guess," the lieutenant said. "But she said if he is here, then his car is here, and it isn't. She seemed to know the guy pretty good. But yeah, it can't hurt to check. You get the wind this time, and I sit in the car. Flag me if he's here."

The sergeant put the Ford in Park. "Suits me," he said. "I sure don't mind. Past ten or fifteen minutes I've needed to take a leak. This goddamned detail anyway. If I didn't hate it anyway, doing what we're doing, I'd hate it just because a man can't take a leak." He shut off the ignition.

The lieutenant said, "No, leave it running. One thing to sit here on my ass; I don't need it getting cold."

The sergeant restarted the car and got out, the wind grabbing the door. He closed it after some effort and walked toward the office. One green metal lawn chair

254

had been turned and tipped against the wall. The other had blown over and rested on its side. The spindly white metal table remained upright, but its glass top was missing. The sergeant saw a sign hanging inside the glass storm door. It read: "Back in Ten Minutes." He opened the storm door. He tried the inside door. It was locked. He shut the storm door and surveyed the first floor. There was a cleaning cart parked four doors down. He looked toward the army car and then pointed toward the cart. He saw the lieutenant nod. He went down to the cart and knocked on the door closest to it. It opened. A small woman in her late fifties with an angry expression glared out at him over the chain lock on the door. "Yeah?" she said. "I ain't got the key to the office and I don't know where he is. So I can't rent you no room and I probably can't help you."

"Well, one of the things," he said, "I was hoping to use the men's room."

"We ain't got one of those, soldier-boy," she said. "Only the can inna room. What's the matter with you, anyway? Never heard gas stations? That's where the men's rooms are."

"Well," he said, "could I use the can in here?"

"I'm not supposed, let anybody in here when I'm working," she said. "You wouldn't think so, look at it, but the owner's very particular. Says he don't want anybody seeing any room that's not made up." She snickered. " 'Gives the wrong impression, people see rooms not made up.' Beat that? Anybody comes to this crummy-looking joint, if the bed's not made up, I didn't put in towels, well, I don't think it's gonna get them all upset so they go off somewhere else. Only people we get here's cheap bums anyway."

"I won't tell anybody," he said. "Please just let me go to the latrine."

She laughed at him. "I dunno," she said. "The bed's not made up or anything, but that might not bother you. You one of those raper guys? That why you really wanna come in? You gonna rape me, is that it? Might have to call the cops."

He laughed. "Look," he said, "I promise I won't rape you, at least not until I've used the bathroom there. Then, we like each other? Well, let's see how things work out."

The lieutenant saw the door close and reopen, and the sergeant enter the room. After a few minutes the door opened again and the sergeant came out. He paused at the threshold and leaned down. He kissed the cleaning lady on the cheek. "Thank you very much, ma'am," he said. "Today you've served your country well."

She blushed. "Ahh," she said, "it was nothin'. You're actually kind of cute. I think I'll tell people that you did come in and rape me. My friends'll all be jealous."

The sergeant returned to the car. He said, "He's not here. She doesn't know when he'll be here. If he's not here, in the morning, it usually means he's home. But not always. She can't call him up because he keeps the only key to the office, and the phones in the rooms don't call out unless someone's in the office and throws a switch."

"Hmm," the lieutenant said. "You find out where his house is? How to get to that?"

"More or less," the sergeant said. "It's about five miles south of here, off back in the woods."

"Or we could have an early lunch," the lieutenant said.

The gray Lincoln came into the parking lot from the south, moving fast. The driver swerved it to park next to the mobile sign but spotted the khaki Ford as he started the turn and racked the steering wheel over so that the tires howled and threw gravel, and the car hunkered down on its port side. It did not fully stabilize until he brought it to a halt next to the Ford. "My guess is, that's him," the sergeant said. "Time to do our full routine. Get your patter ready."

"Crazy fuckin' bastard, isn't he?" the lieutenant said reflectively. "Roll that son-bitch, doing that, someday his luck runs out." The cleaning lady opened the motel room door and stood on the threshold in the wind.

Battaglia left the door open when he got out of the Lincoln. He wore a trench coat, open, and a red velour collared sweatshirt over blue jeans. His hair was standing up, and his face was mottled. He came up to the driver's side of the Ford and slammed his left hand down on the door. "Rollah window down," he said, making a cranking motion with his right hand. The sergeant obeyed the order. "What the fuck're you guys doing here?" Battaglia said. "You just wanna tell me that? What the fuck you're doin' here?"

The sergeant glanced at the lieutenant. The lieutenant shrugged. The sergeant looked back at Battaglia. "We're trying to locate a man named James Battaglia," he said. "Battaglia or Battles. Understand he goes by both."

"Well, you fuckin' did it," Battaglia said. "But I

have to say you got a fuckin' funny way of doing it, the way you fuckin' did it."

"Sir?" the sergeant said.

"You ever been married, asshole?" Battaglia said. "Either one of you two assholes, either one of you been married?" Both of them shook their heads. "No," Battaglia said, "I didn't fuckin' think so. And I knew, I fuckin' *knew*, that if one of you was, you would not've pulled the fuckin' stunt that you just pulled on me."

The sergeant looked at the lieutenant. The lieutenant shrugged. The sergeant looked back at Battaglia. "Sir?" he said.

Battaglia slapped his right hand on the door of the Ford. He took his left hand off the door and put both hands on his hips. He took a deep breath. He looked at the sky. He turned and kicked a small stone along the macadam. He turned back and put his hands on the door of the Ford. He bent down. *"Listen,* all right?" he said. "Just fuckin' *listen* to me. You come down here from God knows where, to do what God knows what, and the minute that you get here, the first fuckin' thing you do's get things in a fuckin' uproar. And, *why'd* you fuckin' do that? Because you don't know anything. There's two of you, for Christ sake, and the two of you between you haven't got enough brains to come in the fuckin' rain."

The lieutenant coughed. He leaned forward and bent down so that he could see Battaglia's face. "Mister James Battaglia?" he said.

"Yeah," Battaglia said, "I'm James Battaglia. And after all the shit you raised, you should be damned glad of that."

The lieutenant nodded. He opened the passenger

door of the Ford and got out, shutting it behind him. He looked at Battaglia over the roof of the car. "Mister Battaglia," he said in the wind, "if you'd permit Sergeant Fulling there to leave the vehicle . . ." Battaglia stepped back from the Ford. The sergeant opened the driver's side door and got out. The wind nearly snatched the lieutenant's hat, and he clamped it back on his head with his right hand. "It's pretty windy here, sir," he said. "Could we use your office?"

Battaglia looked resentful. "I suppose we can," he said, "but I don't see why we fuckin' need to, or the fuck you're doing here."

"Please," the lieutenant said, starting toward the motel. The cleaning woman retreated back into the room and closed the door behind her.

Inside the office Battaglia moved at a half trot behind the counter and seized the stool behind it. He clasped his hands on the counter and stared at the two soldiers. "Aw right," he said, "what is it?"

"This is Sergeant Walter Fulling," the lieutenant said, opening his coat. "United States Army. My name is Oliver McKissick. Lieutenant. Also U.S. Army. It is our sad duty to locate the next of kin of Specialist First Class Keith P. Battaglia, and deliver to said next of kin a telegram from the secretary. Of the army." He took an envelope from the inside pocket of his overcoat.

Battaglia stared at him. "Keithie's down in Georgia, there. Keithie's down in Georgia. Nobody dies in Georgia, asshole. Nobody dies down there. Everybody lives forever."

The sergeant frowned and looked at the lieutenant. The lieutenant cleared his throat. "Sir," he said.

"No," Battaglia said, unclasping his hands and slapping the counter with the palm of his right, "I don't want that shit from you. Keith is down, Fort Gordon, Georgia, with his fuckin' wife and kid. I got a Christmas card from him. Got it what, a month ago? He's down in fuckin' Georgia and I know he's all right there. There's been some kind of a mistake here like you guys're famous for. Like going to the wrong house, in the wrong town, and getting everyone fucked up until it's fuckin' straightened out. Just like you did this morning, in the fuckin' liquor store. Get my fuckin' ex-wife all fucked up so she fucks *me*, the fucking woman. I knew she was fuckin' nuts, but I never heard her like this. Like you guys got her this morning. 'I got a premonition,' she says. The cunt calls me at home. I'm fucking my wife, all right? I got a right, I think. And then the goddamned phone rings, so I have to answer that, and who the fuck is it that's interrupting us? It's my fuckin' ex-wife's who, and why's she doing this? Because you fucking assholes stopped and asked fucking directions, and she's got a fucking 'feeling.' That she knows what you're here for. Well, I told that fucking woman. I said: 'Look, you're fucking nuts. Whatever these assholes want, it's not what you think it is. It's not for fucking Keith, all right? It's not for fucking Keith. He's down in fucking Georgia, I made fucking sure of that. And I made sure he fucking stays there, when I called up a fucking guy that made a call for me. And *you* know that's where he was, because I came in and told you. Which I didn't have to do and I did so you wouldn't worry. So you know that's where he is. And now after I did that, well, I wish you wouldn't fuck with me while I'm fucking Maria.' And she says

260

that's the way I always was, all the things she hates. All I can ever think about is myself and my cock. Well, goddamnit, not *this* morning. Not this morning, I'm not. Because you two assholes riled her up, you got her having visions. And *she* called *me* at home."

"Mister Battaglia," the lieutenant said, opening the envelope and unfolding the document inside, "the secretary regrets to inform you that Specialist Keith P. Battaglia was killed in action while on a routine reconnaissance mission in Quang Tri Province in the service of his country in the Republic of Viet Nam on Sunday, January fourteenth, nineteen sixty-eight, and wishes you to be informed that as his next of kin you may choose whether you wish his remains to be interred there, or to be sent home for burial at a military cemetery or one of your own choosing." He put the document and the envelope on the countertop in front of Battaglia. "On behalf of the secretary," he said, "and on behalf of the army and the commander in chief, the president of the United States, we present the deep sympathy and sorrow we all feel on this sad occasion, and hope that your knowledge of our awareness of his bravery and valor, and our gratitude for it, may sustain you and his family in this hour of your grief."

Battaglia did not read the document. He stared at the lieutenant. "You don't know what this means," he said. "She'll come back here now. I know that's what she'll do. She'll come back here with that damned kid, and I'll have to support them. The little bastard. He did this. He did this on purpose. I wonder how the fuck he did it. How did he get out there without me knowing it?"

"Sir?" the lieutenant said.

"It doesn't fucking matter," Battaglia said. "Just get your fucking asses out of fucking here. You done enough goddamned damage, last you one fucking day. Fucking Ed Cobb. So I know him. What the fuck good did that do? Not a fucking goddamned bit."

In the car after the wind, the sergeant said, "I still hate these things, matter what they do. I think I'd rather be back there. And at least it was warm there."

"I wouldn't rather," the lieutenant said, "matter how cold it gets. And I doubt that you would, either."

19

Late in the morning of the first Sunday in February, Neil Cooke in his blue Mercedes 190SL emerged from the underground garage in the building that housed the duplex cooperative apartment that he shared with his wife, Caroline, at Park Avenue and Seventy-third Street, and headed north toward Bruckner Boulevard and the New England Thruway. The day was warm. He was parked in the commuter pickup lot at the railroad station in Greenwich, Connecticut, when Nora Langley's New Haven Line train pulled in from Grand Central shortly before 12:30. She was wearing sunglasses and a floppy, red picture hat with a black silk ribbon that trailed off the back brim and set off her long blond hair. Her suit was dark blue silk, and she carried a large red shoulder bag made of soft, bloused leather. She wore matching red leather gloves. Her skirt stopped two inches above her knees. He got out of the car and started toward the platform. They embraced and air-kissed, their cheeks barely grazing, and he escorted her back to the car. She stood back and removed the sunglasses. She had brown eyes. "It's very nice, Neil," she said. "It's lovely. And the top's not even down."

"Well," he said, "I could put it down, if you like. But I thought it might be a little too cold. A little too chilly, I thought." He opened the passenger door.

"Oh, no," she said, leaning into the car, taking off her left glove and smoothing the leather seat with her left hand. "No, that isn't what I meant. I was worried about my hat. And if I take it off, I don't have a scarf for my hair." She looked at him. "Aren't I silly?"

He smiled. "No," he said. "Not silly."

"I wish," she said, "I wish I could persuade Barry to get something like this."

Cooke opened the passenger door and she got in, presenting a brief view of the tops of her stockings and the straps of her black garter belt. He shut the door and went around to the driver's side. "So, buy him one," he said, starting the engine. "Find something you like, and when it's Christmas or his birthday, just make that his present." He backed the Mercedes out of the spot. "That's what Caroline did to me."

"Didn't you *want* this?" she said. "I think it's beautiful."

"Oh," he said, "sure I did. I've been looking around, not really very hard, you know, but always on the lookout, for something just like this. Always liked this car. But whenever I thought I was close, close to getting one, well, it always turned out the clown who owned it'd modified it, put in a Corvette engine or something. Or else it was all shot to hell. One guy I met over in Ridgefield one night said he had one, and I got all excited, and the next day I went over to see it, had it in his barn there, and the thing was up on the blocks.

264

Well, that didn't bother me. Showed he was taking care of it, he wasn't going to drive it. And then I opened the hood. No engine. That was why he wasn't driving it, and I must say I couldn't imagine a better reason. Gave me some cock-and-bull story about how he's having it rebuilt. And that was typical. But Caroline saw this one up there in Vermont, and so she snapped it up."

Nora sighed. "Well," she said, "I thought I did that. I had this little white 'fifty-six Thunderbird, with red leather seats and a hardtop. Just a lovely, lovely car. And we were going, this was just before we were leaving for Europe in May. I'd finally persuaded him to take a vacation. And the car was supposed to be ready when we got back. Well, I made a mistake. I left the house one day to do some shopping for the kids, because when his mother comes to stay with them, I like them to be well dressed. She's such a picky woman. And while I was out, the man called, and the maid said that I wasn't there. So he called Barry at his office, something about getting a signature on something or other before we left, insurance or something, and of course that let the cat right out of the bag. Barry came home in an absolute fit. Said he didn't care if we could afford it, he didn't want the damned thing. Well, *I* didn't want it. I like my Jaguar a lot, and it does have room for the kids, when I have to take them with me, or Barry and I take them somewhere. So that was the end of that notion."

"How was the trip?" he said. "It's really been a long time since I've seen you. Much too long, in fact." The Mercedes moved quietly in the travel lane of the Connecticut Turnpike, north through Stamford and Norwalk, traveling at a steady fifty miles per hour, being overtaken and passed by every driver who cared to.

She exhaled loudly. "Oh," she said, "it was all right, I guess."

"Meaning that it wasn't?" he said.

"I don't know," she said. "Maybe I was putting too much on the line. Expecting too much of it. I went to a lot of work, planning it. Drove the travel agent *crazy*. The dinner reservations at Tour d'Argent, and I made sure they'd light the Tower. The suite at the Georges Cinq, right on the Seine. The week at the Beaulieu Sur Mer, at this lovely hotel."

"La Réserve," he said.

"That's the place," she said. "I should've taken you. Then down to Florence. It was all just so perfect. And all Barry could think about was what was going on back home. He was on the phone, three, four times a day. Getting up at six or seven, allowing for the time change. Working himself into absolute rages when the operators didn't speak Texan. Yelling at people in his office for forgetting to tell him things that he asked them about yesterday. What a romantic way to greet the morning. Sunlight streaming through your windows off the Mediterranean, fresh coffee and croissants on a tray outside your door, with fresh orange juice and the morning paper, and your husband screaming like a banshee on the phone because some poor filing clerk in the office back home didn't remember to do something he asked the day before. He doesn't know how to relax. I guess he never did. I just never noticed it till now. Or else I did, and I was so busy, doing other things, it didn't bother me."

"Now it does, though," Cooke said.

"Now, it does," she said. She looked directly at him. "You sound like you're familiar with it," she said. "Same thing with Caroline?"

He shrugged. "Same only different," he said. "We've been married almost twelve years now. Known each other, thirteen. She's a very impatient lady. Always has been, always will be. Craves action, all the time. It's like her ego's on the line, every single day. If something happens, and she didn't make it happen, she feels left out of things. Where I'm just the opposite. Probably about seven, eight years ago, I woke up one morning, it was during the week, and I thought: 'Well hell, I don't feel like going in today. And I don't think I will.' So I called in and said I wouldn't be there. And my secretary naturally assumed I was sick, said: 'Hope you feel better tomorrow.' And I didn't correct her, just thanked her. I spent the first part of the morning in my study, first with the papers and then with some new charts I'd bought, probably a month before, and never even unwrapped, of the Intracoastal Waterway. Just going over again in my mind the route we'd be taking down, jotting down notes here and there, and that's what I was doing when Caroline finally figured out I hadn't gone to work. She sleeps until about ten, ten thirty—she's a night bird and she doesn't really start to function until close to noon. So she came in and found me sitting there in my robe, and she assumed I was sick, too, and I said no, I was just having a day to myself. 'My clients have *all* their days to themselves,' I said. 'They have lunch at Côte Basque and they have lunch at La Grenouille. They have lunch at Sparks' Steak House and they have lunch at Périgord. The ladies go out shopping and the gentlemen retire

267

to their usual positions at the Athletic Club. Then when the cocktail hour comes, they go home and have a drink. Freshen up and go to dinner and then go hear Bobby Short. Well, how can they do all these wonderful things? Why don't they lose all their money? Because their obedient servant, me, is watching over their lives. Coast Guard Cooke: "Semper paratus, numquam dormio." Well, knock out the "numquam," 'cause today is "dormio," least as far's the job's concerned. You wanna screw?"

"Did she?" Nora said.

"More or less," he said. "I'll give Caroline that: she's never turned me down. If she's around, and I get horny, her pants hit the deck. But she's like everybody else. Sometimes she feels like it herself, and sometimes she does it purely to oblige me. This was one of those kind of times. She looked at her watch when I asked her, and said it'd have to be quick, because she was meeting Frieda down at Christ Cella for lunch. Well, that was all right, so I banged her, and she went flying out the door in a rush, and I finished what I'd been doing, took a shower, had a shave, got myself dressed, and went over to the Yacht Club for a sandwich and a drink or three. Another thing I never do. Father and my uncle went through all kinds of hell to make sure I'd get in there, and so naturally, as a result, I almost never use it. 'Bout the only contact I have with the place, one end of the year to the other, 's when the bills for the dues come in, and I tell Maurice to pay them. So nobody paid any attention to me, and I browsed in the library after lunch and some coffee, started walking back home around six, and that night Caroline and I did the same thing we always do, which is go out to some dinner we promptly forget, with people we see all the time, then come home and get into bed. And the next day I went to the office, told everyone who asked me—which was not that many; it's a big shop, and everyone's very busy, and one guy being out doesn't make a big stir—that I felt much better, thanks.

"And you know what'd happened as a result of my being out? Nothing. Absolutely nothing. The same brokers who'd called me the day before to try to talk me into churning my clients' trust assets into some hot new issue, called me again the day I was back, most likely with some newer, hotter issue. And I told them the same thing I would've told them the day before, if I'd been there: 'Thanks very much, Joe,' or Harry, or Tom, or Dick, or whoever, 'but I think everyone's pretty content right now. I think it's time to stand pat.'

"Well," he said, "that day taught me something. First, a little humility. I'm as full of myself as the next man, but it sort of brings you up short when you play hooky and nobody notices. Just how important are you, if they don't know when you're not there? How do you tell when a trust management lawyer isn't at his desk? He doesn't make any noise when he is. He doesn't take his phone calls? What are secretaries for, if not to screen the phone calls that their busy bosses get while they're studying the markets, clipping coupons for their clients, and weighing proxy statements with care and thoughtful judgment. But the second thing was pleasanter, and the third was quite exciting. The second thing was that if they didn't notice I was out, every now and then, then every now and then I could stay out with no one caring and do anything I liked. So long as it didn't involve one of the three or four clubs or restaurants where my partners invariably go for the same lunch and the same iced tea every damned day of the year, and nobody actually saw me, I wouldn't have to explain anything to anybody. Chances are if they *had* seen me, I still wouldn't've had to, either— they just would've assumed whatever I was doing must have something to do with firm business. We trust lawyers, you know, we're very secretive. No point in asking us lots of sharp questions; we most likely can't answer anyway. 'Ethics, you know. Sorry, old boy. Client's trust is inviolable.' They get embarrassed they asked.

"See, Nora," he said, "I know what I am. I guess that I always have. What I am is vanilla. Just plain vanilla. My mother called it 'old-headed.' I never broke a bone when I was a kid. I was never in a fight. I was never on academic probation in school, nor was I in college, and if you searched the dean's list or the honors list, whatever, you'd find I wasn't on them, either. While the big, muscular lads were out on the practice field, preparing to show Yale a few things, I was marching with the band, playing clarinet. Second clarinet. When the scholarship kids with the glittering eyes were up all night at the *Crimson*, I was attending coming-out parties, eating buffets at the Ritz. The first girl that I asked to be my wife said: 'No thanks,' and you know the reason she gave me? She said that her parents said I was 'steady,' and really liked me a lot, and she knew that that meant if she married me, I'd drive her nuts in a month."

Nora Langley squeezed his right bicep. "I don't know," she said, "you seem pretty exciting to me."

"Well, thank you," he said, "but that's because after

that first day, I discovered the third thing I mentioned. When you get to be thirty-six, thirty-seven, and you've been dull all your life, people expect nothing else. Every time they see you again, you can watch them placing your name, sorting the cards through their memory banks: 'Category: Boring. Subclass: Very Boring. Occupation, Line of Work: Something Extremely Boring. Now what the hell's his name?' You know the one thing that most of my college classmates remember about me? In the summer between our junior and senior years, my roommate and I shipped out for the Orient. He signed on as able seaman, on a tramp freighter from New York. I went aboard in San Francisco, the *Princess of Asia*. He spent the summer wearing jeans and getting sunburned, scraping rust all the way through the Panama Canal, then across the wide Pacific. I spent my nights in a white dinner jacket, in the first-class lounge, playing clarinet for people who thought wild abandon was when they began the beguine, and my days playing canasta with old ladies in the sun. Ron got VD in Singapore, and beaten up in Brisbane. One old, addled gentleman was going to cane me for my attentions to his wife, who was over seventy—the bandleader smoothed it over and the barman watered both their drinks till they got off in Hong Kong. My father paid my airfare on Pan Am out of Manila so I'd have a couple weeks to rest before the school year started. Ron got in a fight in a bar in Subic Bay—when classes reconvened in September, Ronald was in jail. In the Philippines. My souvenir of the summer was a locket that a shy girl gave to me with a lock of her hair in it, sort of a mousy brown. That was in lieu of screwing me—she thought her aunt would mind. Ronnie's was a blue panther, tattooed on his left arm, and a real, fire-breathing dragon, green and gold, tattooed on his right.

"Nobody was surprised," he said, "when I graduated, or when Ronnie didn't. Nobody was surprised, either, when I joined the Coast Guard Reserve, and Ronnie got drafted right off. For me it meant two weekends a month, and two weeks more every summer, but with all but ironclad assurance that my orderly progression first through the UVA Law School, and then through the ranks of Arnold, Cooke, would not be interrupted by some inconvenient war. And no one was surprised at all when things worked out that way, without the slightest hitch. The second girl that I proposed to, on a moonlit Vineyard beach—she had long gold hair, like yours—thought about it for a minute and said: 'What the hell, I guess so.' I went around to pick her up for lunch and a sail the next day, and her mother told me that Pamela'd left on the earliest ferry that morning: 'Her best friend from Chapel Hill called her up at three. She tried to kill herself last night. Pam simply had to go.' I never saw her again. And that surprised no one, either."

He laughed. "The only thing I ever did," he said, "the only time in my whole life that people were surprised, was when I brought Caroline up to New York for the weekend, and introduced her around. When Eddie Fisher brought Elizabeth Taylor down the aisle at the Academy Awards—this was right after he left Debbie Reynolds for her—one of the other partners saw it. Said his wife always insisted on watching the damned thing, of course, lest we think it was his vulgar taste—you're not supposed to enjoy anything, and only approve of good taste—and came in the next day laughing like hell. 'I tell you,' he said, 'when I saw that Fisher boy with that high-stepper, all I could think of was some fifteen-year-old kid, just found the keys to Dad's Ferrari. "Okay, now I got this thing—what the hell do I do now?" ' Well, that's exactly the same train of thought that was going through the minds of the people she met, that weekend. They looked at her, and then looked at me, made sure it really was me, with this magical creature on my arm. And then back at her, in complete disbelief. Breathing like goldfishes do. If they hadn't had country-club lockjaw, plus good manners of the finest whalebone, they would've said: 'God, you've got to be daffy, miss, this man's the dullest around. He'll make you wear glasses, hair in a bun, corsets and sensible shoes. Neil Cooke thinks that oatmeal's exciting, especially if it's getting cold. You should be here with a sultan, a pirate or maybe a Bogart'd do.' I tell you, Nora, whatever little disappointments Caroline may have brought me since then, I've enjoyed very few weekends as much as I relished that one. And I'll thank her for the rest of my life."

Nora shifted away from him to lean against the door. The Mercedes hummed on through Connecticut. "So why me, then?" she said. "Why are we doing this, then?"

"Why," he said, "precisely because of those little disappointments. It only occurred to me recently, well, right after I found out that a man with a secure reputation for dullness can get away with quite a lot, if he's careful, and discreet, but when it did occur to me, I was rather shocked. There've been quite a number of those little disappointments, when you sit down and

273

add them up. A rather large number indeed. I don't mean that she's ceased to keep her end of the bargain. Not at all. But unfortunately she's discovered, or thinks she has, at least, that she can keep me in a state that she perceives as contentment, with her left hand, as it were. Leaving her right hand free for more, shall we say, *interesting* matters."

"You think she's having affairs," Nora said. "I know she used to do that. Had quite a few of them."

"Did Barry tell you that?" he said. "That son of a bitch. What is it about being a Democrat that nullifies every gentlemanly instinct in a man?" She laughed. "I mean it," he said. "I say what happened before two people met is just that: it's the past. If they want to reveal it to each other, then that should be their business. It should not be the commerce of their earlier lovers to trade in their mistakes."

She put her left hand on his right forearm. "Neil," she said, "calm down. Barry didn't have any choice. I insisted, when we got serious, we had to be frank with each other. I've had friends who concealed things from their husbands, and whose husbands concealed things from them. And it's like a smoking time bomb in the marriage. The most innocent gathering, it can be, and all of a sudden one of them, it can be husband, can be wife, it dawns on them quite suddenly that this charming person that they've just met used to be the other one's lover. These great jealous rages. Drinks thrown in faces. Fistfights. Hair pulled and scratching. It's awful. I've seen those explosions—I know. So I said to Barry, when we got together: 'We've got to start with the truth, and we mustn't leave anything out.' So I told him my 'mistakes,' as you call them, and he told

274

me all of his. No surprises in store, later on." She paused. "Unless he finds out about us now, of course." She returned to the center of the passenger seat and settled herself again. "So," she said, "I'm only asking, but your reasoning's kind of confusing. Do you think that Caroline's fooling around? Up there all alone in Vermont?"

He shook his head. "No," he said. "I'd stake my life that she is not. Although she could, with impunity, at least as far as biological consequences are concerned."

"Because she can't get pregnant?" Nora said. "I often wondered that, before Barry clued me in. How a woman that attractive, why she never did have children. I'm sure they'd be lovely babies."

"And then, of course, blabbermouth told you," he said.

"He said she had two abortions, he knew of," she said. "One of them his fault."

Cooke slammed the rim of the wheel with the heel of his right hand. *"Bastard,"* he said. "He ought to be horsewhipped for that."

"Neil, Neil," she said, "a lot of women had to go, to Puerto Rico, you know. It's not that unusual. Those were the pre-Pill days and, of course, abortion was illegal. But sex is always part of the merry-go-round. Part of the big carousel. Power affects people that way, you know, power and money, then power. You shouldn't resent her for that."

"Resent her?" he said. "I don't 'resent her' for that. My beef is with Barry, goddamn the man. For telling his tales out of school. Well, it's too late now, I suppose. No, she can't have children. We tried. But apparently one of those pregnancies had partially blocked

275

her tubes. So an ectopic pregnancy resulted, and surgery was required. And the surgeon said there was such scarring, the only sensible procedure would be to litigate those damaged tubes. Another episode like that and she might bleed to death. So that was the end of my hopes for an heir."

"And hers as well, I should think," Nora said.

"Oh, I doubt she really had any," Cooke said. "By the time we got married, at least. I think that she might've liked to, but you women are different from men. You know, or you seem to, what's going on, going on inside of your bodies. I think she knew, when she married me, that she could never have children. And figured as well, knowing me as she did, I'd stick with her nonetheless." He laughed. "She was, of course, right. Caroline's always right. I'm a very predictable man."

"And a very bitter one, as well," Nora said. "I never saw this in you before."

"Bitter?" he said. "I'm not bitter. I just harbor few illusions. As the years've gone by—and it does take me awhile—it's gradually dawned on me why I got that invitation. My friend, Porter Cass, whom I hardly knew, called my hotel when I was in town. In Washington, I mean, of course—my father'd sent me down there with some menial task to handle with the Treasury Department, and my 'friend,' Porter, had been one of Douglas Dillon's protégés at Dillon, Read, New York. 'I heard you were in the building, Neil. Join me for a drink?' And it turned out to be a 'function.' One of those damned things. And the first thing Porter did, after we had gotten drinks, was introduce me to this woman, who just happened to be there." He snorted.

"I was being set up. I knew it—I like to think I knew it, at least—when it was happening. But I didn't care. I was dazzled. She was so beautiful. She had to be damaged goods—she was interested in *me*. And I didn't care, do you understand? I really didn't care." He paused. "Shows you what ego can do."

"But you're not bitter," Nora said.

"No," he said, "I'm not."

"She might not think so," Nora said softly, "if she saw the two of us now."

"Well," he said, "I wasn't. Maybe I am bitter now. A little, perhaps. Aren't you a little, yourself?"

"Quite honestly? No," she said, leaning back. "I think I've done pretty well. Not quite as well as I'd like to've, no, but still, all in all, pretty good. The children are gorgeous, all four of them, and children are what I most wanted. Barry's considerate, generous, too. I don't see him much, but he is. He does have this idea, I will stay happy, as long as I've got charge accounts. Well, maybe he's right. Maybe that's what I want. What he calls 'Parity: Social.' "

"What does that mean?" Cooke said.

"That means," she said, "that you live at your level. Whatever it happens to be. If you have inherited fifty-three million, you live like other rich people. If you don't inherit, you make it yourself, and you make a million a year, then you live just like all the other folks do, that're making a million a year. His theory is that if you don't do that, if you don't keep up the standards, well then, pretty soon, you start slipping down, and not just in social things either. If you look like you're making half a million a year, that's the way people will treat you. And that is the way they will look at your bills.

277

They'll think you're trying to cheat them. 'If they get a bill for two hundred K from a millionaire lawyer? It's fine. But if they get a bill for one hundred K, from a lawyer who looks like five hundred, they think to themselves: "Hey, this guy's moving up in grade here, or trying, at least, on my money." They'll pay that damned bill, and they'll pay it right off, and you'll never see them again.' I don't know if he's right about that, but I live just as though I was sure. It isn't a bad way to live."

"So then," Cooke said, "reversing your question, what is it you're doing here? If you're so contented, I mean."

"Probably about the same thing you are," she said. "I craved a little excitement. And one day I was out, shopping in Georgetown, and I saw one of my friends. Having lunch with a man in the 'Seventy-six House. I almost went up and said hi. And it hit me, just like a punch, that man was Catherine's lover. Her husband's name's Jerry, and he works like Barry, and this is how Catherine gets by. She wasn't, of course, the first one that I knew about, just the first one who made me think. And all the way home I was thinking about things, all the things Barry had said. That I should have everything, every last thing, that all of his colleagues' wives have. Well, it seemed to me I was missing one thing. So I started looking around. And now my whole life's nice and round." She squeezed his arm again. "You're right, I'm contented. You're part of the reason. A very big part, I might add."

The view from the table at the window of the Prospect of Stonington restaurant looked southeasterly out over the harbor and the steeples of the town rising on the hill behind it. The waitress cleared away the remains of their greenhouse blueberries and cream, leaving them with their coffee and the remains of their Moulin-a-Vent in the big balloon glasses. "So," she said, "I've got the nine fifty back to the city. What'll you do, follow me?"

"No," he said. "I'll stay at the house. I left word I wouldn't be back. Not tonight. I'll go to the boatyard tomorrow, instead of this afternoon, like I said, and then around noon I'll go back to the city. After the traffic's thinned out."

"And she'll believe this," Nora said.

He laughed shortly. "I doubt it'll cross her mind, whether it's true. I don't think she'll think about it. She'll pretend to believe it did take me more time, to make sure the house is all right. What she's thinking about is Benjamin Chapman. That's all she's got on her mind."

"Who the hell is Benjamin Chapman?" Nora said. "Some guy she's fooling around with?"

"You could say that," he said. "Benjamin Chapman's the name Richard Nixon used when he signed into the motel in Nashua the morning before Groundhog Day." He sighed. "She hates him. Hates him with a passion. I wish she gave as much thought to me as she does to Richard M. Nixon.

"She's a very strange and beautiful woman," he said. "I don't know whether she's become amused at me, in the past few years, and is trying to conceal it, or if she's always been amused, and has stopped trying to hide it. Either way, I know she is, and either way, I dislike it. I resent amusing people. *Damn,* I always have, always without meaning to. You know that's the reason, the principal reason, why I've taken to Washington so? I always enjoyed the state politics, they've given me great satisfaction. But when I started taking those random off days, and spending them down there with Ferdie, well, all of a sudden, I was a *player,* you know? Just by getting on the Metroliner, I became one of the boys. You can say what you want about Richard M. Nixon, and I'm sure that Barry's said plenty. But there's a lot of us out there that know why Dick wants it, and by God, we'll see that he gets it. No matter what Caroline thinks. Or wise guys like Barry think either. We'll get it for him, and we'll get it good. Because we want it ourselves."

Shortly before 7:00 P.M., Neil Cooke drove his car into the northerly abutment of the bridge at the tidal river next to the boatyard. He suffered head cuts. His companion declined medical treatment. Local police investigated.

20

There was little hard news to report on the evening of February 6. The powerful VHF television stations in Boston gleaned the Associated Press and the United Press International printers for every item of potential regional interest. All three of them gratefully made lavish use of tapes and film from their libraries to expand Russ Stanley's stories into long reports of Henry Briggs's planned transition from baseball to politics, running them during their news programs at 6:00 and 11:00. Channel 9 showed more enterprise than its competitors, calling Ed Cobb and Briggs at their homes in Vermont for fresh quotes.

The master of the jail in Manchester allowed the inmates to watch television after they finished the evening meal, served at 4:30 P.M. Earl Beale sat in the recreation room with a morose middle-aged man who had been charged with beating up his estranged wife and limited his conversation to sullen declarations of his intent "to really beat her up this time, soon's I get out, for telling all those lies." Earl told him to be quiet when he saw Channel 9's file tapes of Briggs pitching for the Red Sox. "Shut up," he said. "I know this guy." The other man said, "Bullshit. Everybody did. I seen him pitch a hundred times. Never trusted him. Men on base? He always fucked up."

Channel 9 showed a picture of Ed Cobb while the announcer quoted him expressing confidence that Briggs would beat Wainwright. "I know him, too," Earl said.

"More bullshit," the other man said. "These fucking ball players and movie actors—who the fuck do they think they are, they should run the country?"

"You know," Earl said, "when I get out of here I'm gonna look up your wife and call her and say: 'If they ever let that asshole husband of yours out, call me up and I will come and kick his slats out for him.' Now shut the fuck up, all right?"

"I could take you," the other man said.

"You could in here with the guards," Earl said. "I said: 'After we get out.' When I'm out I can do things. I'm gonna do things, too."

Ed Cobb parked the maroon Chrysler in the Beale dealership lot early in the evening of February 7 and went directly upstairs. Donald Beale was in his office. Cobb went in and sat down. "I had two calls," he said.

"Only two," Beale said. "That surprises me."

"Two is enough," Cobb said.

"I'm sure," Beale said.

"The first guy wants me to give him a good reason why he shouldn't call somebody else," Cobb said. "He said the guy that got that car that Earl swiped cracked it up in Connecticut, and now the cops're after the guy that wanted it stolen."

"I know," Beale said.

"You know," Cobb said.

"The FBI was in here this afternoon," Beale said. "Interstate transportation, stolen motor vehicle. They did not seem impressed that I had all the papers."

"Ah," Cobb said.

"Who was the second guy?" Beale said.

"The first guy," Cobb said. "He's gonna have him killed, you know. He's gonna make a call. The minute Earl's first foot hits the pavement outside that jail down in Manchester, he's living on borrowed time. And he also heard about the other fella."

"About Henry Briggs," Beale said.

"Uh huh," Cobb said.

"He saw it on television," Beale said.

"I guess so," Cobb said.

"And what's he gonna do about Henry?" Beale said.

"Well," Cobb said, "I don't know. I don't think he really does either. He's about beside himself. His kid did get to Vietnam."

"Uh huh," Beale said.

"And his kid did get killed," Cobb said. "What he is is wild. He doesn't think a whole lot of me about now. I wouldn't predict what he'll do. About Henry, I mean. About me, for that matter. Probably nothing. But I don't know."

"We don't ever learn, do we?" Beale said.

"Well," Cobb said, "we pick up a few things. Here and there."

"Leave him make the call," Beale said. "Earl's getting out in the morning. His girlfriend called me up and gave me a ration of shit. I've reached my quota. I've picked up enough things to suit me."

"Whatever doesn't kill us, makes us strong," Cobb said.

"Fuck Nietzsche," Beale said. "He's never around when you need him"